"Sarah?"

At first, Reece couldn't believe his eyes. He was seeing things, the way he sometimes saw Sarah when he looked at Drew. Or the way he sometimes remembered her in his dreams.

She took a step into the office. "Hello, Reece."

Her voice snapped him out of it. This was real. His ex-wife stood in his office. The woman who'd walked out on him and their infant son over eleven years ago. A long-familiar anger grew in his heart.

"What do you want, Sarah?"

"I've come about Drew," she said stiffly. "I know he needs help."

A slow roll of anger built inside him. What right did she have to come here now, claiming she could help the boy she'd deserted as an infant? "If you go anywhere near him, I'll slap a restraining order on you."

Sarah closed her eyes and nodded. She turned and headed for the door—and nearly collided with Drew, who came to a screeching halt just inside the room.

ABOUT THE AUTHOR

Patricia Keelyn's love of writing began in the ninth grade. Her first book was a Western about a character named Johnny Boy Brown, who was a cross between Jesse James and Cat Ballou. It wasn't until years later, after a computer science degree and a successful computer programming career, that Patricia discovered romance—reading it *and* writing it. And she's been doing both ever since.

Patricia loves to hear from her readers. You can write to her at: P.O. Box 72753 Marietta, GA 30007

Books by Patricia Keelyn

HARLEQUIN SUPERROMANCE
590—KEEPING KATIE
631—WHERE THE HEART IS

Patricia Keelyn

ONCE A WIFE

Harlequin Books

TORONTO • NEW YORK • LONDON
AMSTERDAM • PARIS • SYDNEY • HAMBURG
STOCKHOLM • ATHENS • TOKYO • MILAN
MADRID • WARSAW • BUDAPEST • AUCKLAND

ISBN 0-373-70682-0

ONCE A WIFE

Copyright © 1996 by Patricia Van Wie.

For Debbie St. Amand,
who taught me how to write a sentence
and then made me do it.

&

For Pam Mantovani,
who taught me that the story
is more important than the sentence.

I never would have done it without the two of you.

Thanks.

PROLOGUE

EVEN THE WEATHER had betrayed her.

The day should have been dim, with gray wintry skies. Instead, cold clear Wyoming sunshine streamed through the dingy second-floor window where Sarah Colby stood watching the parking lot below. Leaning forward, she pressed her forehead against the icy glass, letting it soothe her fevered skin. She closed her eyes, welcoming the momentary relief, wishing she could as easily ease the ache in her heart.

She thought of her son, Drew, sleeping soundly in his crib behind her. How could she leave him? Or face the future knowing she would never again take him in her arms, never feed him, never care for him? But that was the problem, wasn't it. She couldn't care for him. Not the way he needed.

Now there was another baby to consider. The unborn child she'd kept secret. What kind of life could she give either of her children if she stayed?

Sarah turned from the window and moved to her son's crib. Soundlessly she reached down and brushed her fingers across his silky dark hair. He looked so perfect. You couldn't even tell he was sick.

But she'd learned that looks could be deceiving.

Juvenile diabetes, the doctors had said. A disease that would affect him for the rest of his life. She'd never even heard of it until a couple of months ago.

Nor had she had any idea about the expensive medicine he would need, or the constant care. She would have given her life for her son, but she hadn't the means to guarantee his health. Without her, though, Drew would get everything he needed. He'd have a chance.

She pulled away, resting her hands on the wooden rail. The feel of the polished surface beneath her fingers made her think of her husband Reece and the hours he'd spent restoring this old crib. It seemed so long ago, much longer than ten months. They'd been happy then and so much in love as they'd awaited the birth of their son.

They'd been so young.

Sarah no longer felt young. She felt old. Decades older than her eighteen years.

With one last look at Drew, she returned to the window.

Reece should be home soon. That is, if he didn't stop at Belle's first, where no one seemed to care that he was still two years shy of the legal drinking age. More and more lately, he'd taken to stopping at the bar with the other men from the construction crew. And no matter how many times she told herself not to nag him, they'd end up fighting afterward about his drinking.

Today she'd called the construction office where he worked and left a message that she was sick. That much was true. But it wasn't her real reason for the call. What she had to do was going to be difficult enough. If she waited until Drew awoke, she'd never be able to go through with it. So Reece needed to come home. Now. If he'd gotten the message.

He'd be here soon, she told herself. He had to be.

Then she would leave this apartment, this town, and try to forget she'd ever been in Laramie, Wyoming. She'd already packed, two suitcases and a box of mementos, and loaded them in the trunk of her car. There was nothing left to do but wait. And think.

You're doing the right thing, Sarah.

The words came back to her, floating through her thoughts, reassuring her. Words her mother-in-law had spoken in this very room not four hours earlier. Words Sarah needed desperately to believe.

Outside, Reece pulled up in his sleek black Corvette, jarring her back to the present. He'd wanted to sell the car months ago—and God knows they needed the money—but she wouldn't let him. The car was the only thing he had left of the life he'd known before marrying her, the life she was giving back to him today.

As he climbed out of his car, Sarah caught her breath. It amazed her that after all they'd been through, he still had the power to take her breath away. He'd been his hometown's fair-haired son with his tall athlete's build and his blond good looks. She'd never understand why he'd chosen her when he could have had anyone. But he had. And look where it had gotten him.

By the time Reece stepped through the door, she sat waiting for him on the couch, her coat over one arm, her purse clutched tightly in her lap.

"Sarah?" Reece looked at her, concern darkening his blue eyes. "Are you okay?" Without bothering to remove his coat, he crossed the room and laid his hand on her forehead. "God, you're burning up."

His concern nearly crumbled her resolve. For a few seconds she considered throwing herself into his arms and telling him everything—about his mother's visit. And about the new baby. She wanted to lay her problems at his feet and let him sort through them. Just as she'd done more than a year ago when she'd told him about Drew.

Instead, she stood and took a step away from him.

She couldn't lean on Reece anymore. He was too young to be saddled with a wife and a sick child—his mother's words, but no less true because of their source. Reece deserved more. He should be in school, not working a minimum-wage construction job and frequenting bars with men twice his age. And for once, Sarah was going to do the right thing. With her gone, his family would step in and take care of both him and Drew.

"I've got a touch of the flu," she said, putting some more distance between them. "But that's not why I wanted you to come home."

"You need to see a doctor."

"We can't afford a doctor, Reece."

She saw the frustration cross his features, those perfect all-American features that set him apart from her own half-breed heritage. "I'll give Doc a call—"

"No. I'll see someone on my own."

His expression clouded, and then, for the first time, he seemed to notice the coat she was holding. "Where are you going?"

She gripped her purse tighter. "I'm leaving you."

"What?"

She lifted her chin and toughened her expression. But it was hard. So hard. "I've had enough."

"Enough? What are you talking about?" He closed the space between them and grabbed her arm. "You can't leave."

"Watch me." She shook off his hand. "This marriage business hasn't turned out the way I expected." She moved toward the door and set her purse down to slip on her coat. "I thought your family would come around eventually. But it's not going to happen. They're going to let us rot in this hellhole of an apartment until we're old and used up."

"What about Drew?" Reece's confusion had turned to anger, and the accusation in his words sliced through her heart. "Are you just going to walk out on your son?"

It's for his own good, she wanted to scream. *And for yours.* Instead, she shrugged and forced a disinterested tone into her voice. "He's your son, too. *You* take care of him."

For a heartbeat Reece remained silent, the anger in his too-bright eyes washing over her. Then he said, "Tell me this is some kind of joke, Sarah."

She wished she could, but she shook her head. "I'm tired of being poor. And," she forced the lie, praying he'd believe it, "I've found someone else."

He flinched as if she'd struck him. He took a step backward, his face a mask of disbelief while his eyes filled instantly with pain. "I don't believe you," he said, his voice a ragged whisper.

It took all her willpower to continue to meet the anguish in his gaze without begging for his forgiveness, all her strength to continue the lie. "Believe it."

"Don't do this, Sarah." He moved toward her, but she took another step back. She couldn't let him touch her again. If she did, she wasn't sure she'd be able to go through with this. "Whatever's wrong, we can work it out."

"I *am* working it out, Reece. My way."

"I love you." This time he succeeded in grabbing her arm. "I thought you loved me."

She braced herself for the biggest lie of her life. "Well, you thought wrong."

CHAPTER ONE

DREW COLBY was bored.

He'd planned on sneaking off as soon as the music started and the grown-ups began dancing. Instead, he'd been stuck with Jeb Rawlins and his sister, Rachel. Jeb was bad enough, being only ten and all, but his sister wasn't much more than a baby.

"Come on," he said, letting his annoyance show in his voice. "Let's go down to the barn." At least there he wouldn't be constantly getting the evil eye from his grandmother. He set out across the yard with Jeb and Rachel close behind.

Tod Beaumont, the ranch foreman, greeted them as they stepped inside the barn. "Hey, Drew, I thought you went on a hayride."

"Nah," Drew answered. "That's kid stuff."

"And your friends here..."

"This is Jeb and Rachel from the Double R." Drew shoved his hands into the back pockets of his jeans. "They didn't want to go, either."

Tod nodded. "Abe Rawlins's kids. So, what are the three of you up to?"

"Just checking out the horses," Drew answered. "I thought I'd show 'em the new breedin' stock."

"Bored, huh?" Tod smiled, and Drew had to smile back a little.

Tod was cool. He seemed to understand things the other grown-ups didn't. Like what a drag it was to be twelve and forced to hang around all day for a stupid cookout, while being on your best behavior so you didn't embarrass your dad. And then getting stuck with a couple of babies like Jeb and Rachel.

"Well, I guess it's all right," Tod said. "The mare's bedded down for the night. But I left the Appaloosa out in the corral for a bit."

"Thanks." Drew motioned for the other two kids to follow him. "Come on."

"Drew," Tod said, stopping them before they could go farther. "I'm heading on up to the shindig. You keep your distance from that Appaloosa. You hear?"

Drew nodded. "Sure."

"So, what's with the Appaloosa?" Jeb asked after Tod left.

"He's the new stallion. And he's meaner than a cornered rattler."

"So let's go see him."

"Jeb," Rachel said, "we aren't supposed to go near him."

"Don't be a baby, Rachel. We're just gonna look. Ain't that right, Drew?"

Drew hesitated a moment and then said, "Sure. Why not?"

A few minutes later, Jeb and Rachel stood hanging on to the corral fence while Drew sat on top. Across the way, the big Appaloosa stallion pranced nervously.

"Wow, he's really something," Jeb said.

"My dad says he's the best breedin' stud in these parts."

"Can you ride him?" Rachel piped up.

Drew shrugged. "Sure. If I wanted."

Jeb rolled his eyes skyward. "Right."

"He ain't no cow pony, but he's saddle broke."

"But *you* can't ride him," Jeb insisted.

"Who says I can't?" Drew glared at the younger boy.

"I say." Jeb backed off the fence and stared right back. "'Cause you ain't normal, Drew Colby. You got a *disease.* Come on, Rachel, let's get out of here. We might catch something."

Drew leapt down and grabbed the younger boy by the arm. No way he was gonna take this from a crummy fourth grader. "I ain't got no disease."

Jeb shook off Drew's hold. "Then how come you're in the principal's office every day before lunch?"

"None of your business."

"I heard you gotta get a shot."

"You don't know nothin', Jeb Rawlins." Drew took a step forward, towering over the other boy. "And I say I can ride that horse if I want."

"Well then, go ahead, big shot." Jeb held his ground. "Prove it."

REECE COLBY stifled a yawn.

The cookout was certainly a success. Just about everybody in the entire county had shown up. Their cook, Millie, had certainly outdone herself. She'd made more food than even all these folks could finish in one evening. Too bad he was just too darned tired to enjoy himself.

He'd decided months ago that he hated the whole campaign process—the weeks of traveling, seeking endorsements from various quarters, the endless receptions, luncheons and speeches. He wasn't a man

made for public display. He'd rather be back on his
own land, on the Crooked C, riding herd on a few
thousand head of cattle. Fortunately or unfortunately, depending on how you looked at it, his being
a rancher first was part of his appeal. It was going to
win him the district seat as a Wyoming state representative.

But after being on the road for two months, he
needed a break. He'd planned on settling back into life
on the Crooked C for a short while. His reprieve had
only lasted three days. That was all the time it had
taken for his mother and Millie to throw together this
cookout for the local folks—a huge barbecue, the likes
of which the town of Devils Corner hadn't seen in
years—to gain support for his campaign.

"Reece, there you are, boy." A big hand clapped his
shoulder, snapping Reece out of his musings.

Smiling, Reece turned and extended his hand to the
older man. "Senator Hawthorne. Glad to see you
could make it."

"Wouldn't miss it for the world. And what's this
'Senator' bull?" Hawthorne draped his beefy arm
around Reece's shoulders. "You and I've known each
other too long for that nonsense. It's Bob to you. And
besides—" he nodded toward a tall blonde across the
yard "—it'll be Dad soon."

Reece chuckled. "Well, I guess it will be at that."

The two men watched Michelle Hawthorne charm
the small group of people surrounding her. The word
elegant fit her perfectly. It didn't matter whether she
wore a five-thousand-dollar designer gown or a pair of
jeans. She graced a room full of Wyoming's upper
crust as easily as she sat a horse or charmed a bunch
of wizened old ranchers. A beautiful woman, Reece

thought, with more brains than any half-dozen men he knew put together.

"She's really something," Hawthorne said, voicing Reece's thoughts aloud. "You're a lucky man."

Reece nodded. Hawthorne was right of course. He should consider himself fortunate to be engaged to the lovely Michelle Hawthorne. So what was wrong with him? Oh, Michelle and he were friends, but that was about as far as their relationship went. There was no spark, no chemistry.

"She's your ticket to the governor's mansion, Reece. And maybe further."

Reece chuckled. "First things first, Senator. I don't think we need to worry about a gubernatorial campaign just yet. Let's concentrate on the state-representative seat for now."

"Just thinking ahead." Hawthorne paused to down the last half of the beer he held in his hand. Then, nodding toward Michelle again, he added, "She can work a crowd better than any woman I've ever seen. Even better than her mother—God rest her soul. Yes, sir, you and Michelle are gonna make one fine team."

Reece took a sip of his own beer and thought about Hawthorne's words. On the surface, Reece and Michelle were the perfect couple. The Hawthorne ranch butted up against Colby land, and they'd known each other all their lives. They'd ridden the same bus to school, traveled the same social circles. Their engagement came as no surprise to anyone—except maybe Reece and Michelle themselves. Because underneath it all, they were just friends. A team, as Hawthorne had said, but nothing more.

They'd been honest with each other, if not with anyone else. Neither of them believed in love, but they

wanted the same things. They were friends with a
common goal, as Michelle often said; both wanted to
put the state of Wyoming on the map. They'd agreed
it was as good a foundation for marriage as any other.
And better than most.

Suddenly Michelle noticed the men watching her,
and she smiled. It struck Reece at that moment that
maybe they were cheating themselves. Then he quickly
dismissed the errant thought. He'd married once for
love, and he wasn't a man to make the same mistake
twice. He needed a partner, not a lover.

After a few final comments to the group she'd been
speaking with, Michelle headed toward her father and
Reece. She dropped a kiss on Reece's cheek and then
slipped her arm through her father's. "Did I hear my
name mentioned over here?"

"You just mind your own business, young lady."
Hawthorne, his daughter on his arm, went all blus-
tery, puffing up like a peacock. "We're having a man-
to-man talk here."

"Young lady, is it?" Michelle grinned and winked
at Reece. "That's how he used to admonish me when
I was seventeen. He hasn't quite got it through his
head that I'm a grown woman. Not to mention an at-
torney."

Hawthorne ignored her teasing. "We were just
heading inside for a shot of that eighteen-year-old
scotch Reece's daddy used to hoard away."

"Dad, you can't spirit Reece off. This is his party,
and winning this election depends on the support of
these people."

"Don't be ridiculous, Shelly-girl." Hawthorne once
again clapped a hand on Reece's shoulder. "Reece
here is a shoo-in."

"Shelly-girl?" She rolled her eyes.

"Now don't go giving us a hard time," Hawthorne said, nodding toward the house. "We'll just be a bit."

Reece smiled at the interchange between Michelle and her father. They adored each other, and Reece experienced a moment of envy. He'd never been close to his father. Their relationship had more resembled that of two bulls forced to live in the same paddock, rather than that of father and son. And then there was Drew, who seemed more like a stranger than Reece's own flesh and blood. Of course it didn't help that every time he looked at the boy, Reece thought of Drew's mother, Sarah.

"Mr. Colby, come quick!"

Reece turned toward the high-pitched voice and the small hand tugging on his sleeve. "Rachel, what is it?"

"It's Drew. He's gonna ride that devil horse!"

"Devil horse? What devil? You mean the Appaloosa?"

Rachel nodded, and fear knotted Reece's stomach. He scanned the crowd looking for Tod and then took off toward the barn, calling to the foreman as he went.

Drew had just untied the lead rope from the fence and was getting ready to step into the stirrup, when Reece came to a stop at the corral fence.

"Don't do it," he said, though he knew Drew couldn't hear. Reece wanted to yell, but didn't dare for fear of startling the already skittish horse.

"Damn," Tod said, coming up beside Reece. "If he ain't got that big boy saddled."

"Yeah, and Drew's gonna end up on his ass in the dust in about two minutes."

"Won't be the first boy to take a spill."

"Circle around and see if you can get hold of that horse."

But it was too late.

Drew swung into the saddle and all hell broke loose. The stallion flattened his ears and pranced sideways before bolting and taking off across the corral, bucking, his eyes wild. Drew's hold lasted for a couple of seconds, then he flew from the saddle, landing hard. Reece vaulted the fence and headed for his son, pulling him from under the flailing hooves, just as Tod grabbed the half-crazed horse.

Drew tried to stand, and Reece slipped an arm around him, half carrying him toward the gate. A group of people had followed Reece and Tod down from the house, and someone opened the gate, allowing them to slip out.

"You okay?" Reece asked as they both collapsed against the fence.

Drew nodded, coughed and took a swipe at a trickle of blood on his top lip.

"You sure?"

"Yeah." Drew pushed himself upright as if to prove it, wobbled slightly but steadied when Reece grabbed his arm. "I'm fine."

A smattering of nervous laughter erupted from the group standing nearby. Everyone there had taken their share of spills. Happened all the time. Usually the results were nothing more than a bruised ego and a sore backside. But they'd all seen someone seriously hurt by a bronc, and with a stallion like the Appaloosa, this could have been one of those times.

"Come on, folks." It was Michelle's voice. "We better get on back before those musicians decide the party's over."

"Way to go, Drew," one of the ranchers said as he turned and headed back toward the house.

"Yeah. You're a real cowboy now," said another. "Just like your old man."

There was a general round of laughter as the group moved off, leaving Reece alone with his son. A hush fell over the empty yard. The distant music, Tod's voice soothing the stallion and the pawing of hooves on the hard ground were the only sounds.

"That was a damn fool thing to do, boy." Fear had given way to anger, and Reece's words were like a low roll of thunder.

"I thought I could ride him."

"You were wrong."

"Yeah." Drew kept his gaze locked on the ground in front of him. "I guess."

"You guess!" Reece pushed away from the fence and turned to face his son. "Look at me when I'm talking to you."

With obvious hesitation, Drew looked up, his liquid brown eyes meeting his father's gaze. "I've been thrown before."

"What about that horse, Drew?" Emotion—shame, regret, pain maybe—broke across the boy's face. A niggling voice urged Reece to let it go, but his anger had grown to full force now. It had been a stupid stunt. Drew could have been hurt. "That's one expensive piece of horseflesh you were fooling with. What the hell were you thinking?"

"I…" Drew looked away, but not before Reece saw the sheen of moisture. Drew wiped furiously at his eyes and then said, "Sorry."

Reece took a step back, silenced by the boy's tears, his anger evaporating. He realized that he'd responded just like his old man—blowing up and going on about a damn horse when it had been Drew he'd been worried about. His anger had been the aftermath of fear, exploding with relief when Drew sported nothing more than a cut lip. And here the boy had already suffered the humiliation of being thrown in front of a dozen old cowboys.

But Reece didn't know how to say any of that to his son. Damned if he knew how to talk to the boy at all.

"Head back up to the house," Reece said. "Get Millie to tend to that cut and give you something to eat. Then go on to bed. We'll talk more in the morning."

"Yes, sir."

Reece watched Drew walk toward the house, hands in his pockets, shoulders straight. He reminded Reece of Sarah more than ever, with his large brown eyes brimming with tears, even as he held himself prouder than that damn Appaloosa. The last time Reece had seen Sarah, she'd looked just like that, strong and hurting, proud and unrelenting.

"You were pretty hard on him, don't you think?"

Reece turned toward Tod, his foreman and the closest thing to a best friend Reece had ever known. "Maybe. But he could have been hurt."

"Drew's a good rider. He's going to be a fine horseman someday."

Reece felt a twinge of guilt. Tod knew more about his son than *he* did. When you grew up on a ranch, learning to ride was a given, but who'd put Drew on his first pony? And when? It hadn't been Reece, and the realization resurrected some of his earlier anger.

"Am I just supposed to forget that he knew better than to mess with that stallion? That he could have been seriously hurt or ruined an expensive animal?"

Tod shook his head. "I ain't suggestin' any such thing."

"Then what *are* you saying?"

"Don't know, Reece. I just think you were a little hard on him, that's all." Shaking his head, Tod turned and headed back toward the corral.

"Damn," Reece said, and sank back against the fence.

As SHE DROVE into the yard of her grandmother's ramshackle old house, Sarah Hanson Colby had other things on her mind besides dinner and her ten-year-old daughter's impatience.

"Hurry up, Mom. Grandmother's waiting." Lyssa bounded out of the car almost before it stopped.

"Wait, Lyssa. Take these." Sarah reached into the back seat and grabbed the two blankets she'd brought along. "Put one on Grandmother's lap."

Lyssa grabbed the blankets and took off toward the yard, where the old woman sat in a dilapidated lawn chair.

They *were* later than usual, Sarah admitted as she climbed out of her car. She just hadn't been able to get herself moving this morning. The letter she'd received yesterday weighed heavily on her mind, and she'd lain in bed until late, unable to sleep but unable to get up, either.

Circling to the back of the car, she unlocked the trunk and pulled out a small cooler. She needed to put the letter and its contents out of her mind—at least for the next couple of hours. It wouldn't be fair to ruin

Lyssa's evening, and if Lyssa's great-grandmother, Tuwa, picked up on Sarah's mood, she'd want an explanation. Sarah didn't want to burden the old woman with her problems.

By the time Sarah reached her grandmother and daughter, Lyssa had spread one blanket on the ground and tucked the other securely around Tuwa's legs. Moving to her side, Sarah kissed the old woman's weathered cheek.

"How are you feeling, Grandmother?"

"It's going to storm."

Sarah followed Tuwa's gaze toward the western horizon, where dark clouds had accumulated about the mountains. "Probably." She brushed a wisp of wiry hair away from her grandmother's cheek, tucking it into one of her long gray braids. "We brought you Kentucky Fried Chicken."

Tuwa nodded, but for a few more moments she kept her gaze locked on the far-off drama. Then she turned and smiled, her eyes like two bright pinpoints of light in her ancient face. "Good. I am hungry."

Sarah smiled and moved to put together their meal.

Ever since she and Lyssa had moved into town six years ago, they'd come back to the reservation on Sundays to spend the afternoon and early evening with Tuwa. At first, Sarah had cooked. She'd bring the ingredients and make dinner for the three of them. Her grandmother soon let them know, however, that she didn't want home-cooked meals on Sunday. She ate her own home cooking every day of the week. She wanted restaurant food. Which to her meant any of the variety of fast-food places surrounding the nearby town of Oaksburg.

Sarah still couldn't quite get over the fact that her eighty-year-old full-blooded Shoshone grandmother was a junk-food addict.

But to Sarah it made no difference what they ate. Her grandmother had done so much for her in the past ten years. Sarah figured she owed the old woman much more than a weekly meal of fast food. So in good weather, the three of them ate outside while watching the sun set behind the Wind River Mountains. Other times, Sarah would build up the fire in the house, and they'd make a picnic on the floor or gather around Tuwa's wobbly mica table.

This afternoon, they managed to finish their meal, with Lyssa chattering nonstop, before the ominous clouds forced them inside. With Lyssa's help, Sarah moved everything into the house, grabbing an armload of wood on the way. It was still early in the season, and the temperature could easily drop twenty to thirty degrees in a matter of hours.

Sarah built a fire, and they settled in to wait out the storm, which turned out to be more lightning and thunder than rain. She sat on the floor next to her grandmother's rocking chair, her daughter stretched out on the rug next to them. Then, as the night deepened, Lyssa fell asleep, lulled by the fire and the soft voices of Sarah and her grandmother. Yet Sarah found no peace in the serene setting. Her thoughts had once again returned to the upsetting news she'd received the day before.

"It's the boy, isn't it?"

Sarah winced at her grandmother's question but kept her eyes focused on the fire. The old woman's uncanny insight made Sarah uncomfortable. She considered letting on she didn't understand, but Tuwa would know better. In the end, she'd have the answer to her question.

"I received a letter yesterday," Sarah said.

"From the woman? The cook at the Crooked C?"

"Yes. Millie Danton." Sarah kept her eyes on the fire, losing herself in the pop and crackle of the flames and the patter of rain on the roof. "It's the second letter I've received from her in less than six months."

Still Tuwa remained silent, her rocker squeaking against the rough-hewn floor. But Sarah knew the old woman listened, pulling the information from Sarah with silence more surely than with a dozen questions.

"For eleven years I've received exactly two letters a year from Millie," Sarah continued. "Every December and June." She glanced at her daughter, afraid she'd overhear.

"Don't worry about the child, Sarah. She's asleep."

Sarah nodded, not doubting her grandmother. "Millie has been my only source of information about my son."

"And now?"

"She says that Drew . . ." Sarah hesitated, taking a deep breath before continuing. "He's having problems. At home, in school, with other kids. And he's ignoring his medical needs. Almost like he's trying to make himself sick." Sarah closed her eyes and, pulling her knees up, wrapped her arms around them. "I don't know what to do, Grandmother."

Again the silence engulfed them. Sarah rested her head on her raised knees, and her grandmother continued her steady rocking, back and forth, like the ticking of a clock.

Finally Tuwa spoke. "It's time."

"Time?" Sarah shifted to look at her grandmother.

"Go to him."

Sarah shook her head and turned away. "No."

"The boy needs you."

"He may need *something,* but it certainly isn't me." Sarah let out a short self-deprecating laugh. "He probably hates me."

"You are his mother."

"I gave up my rights as his mother more than eleven years ago. I can't claim him now."

"You gave him life."

Yes, she'd given birth to Drew, but what else had she ever given him? A chance, a voice inside her whispered, but she shoved the thought aside. She'd stopped being certain that she'd done the right thing a long time ago. *If* she'd ever been certain to begin with.

She remembered when she'd first come here after leaving Reece. She'd run home to her grandmother, to the woman who'd raised her since her parents' death when she'd been five. As she'd done before, Tuwa had taken Sarah in without question, giving her a roof over her head and a place to wait for the birth of her second child.

Then later, after Lyssa's birth, her grandmother had watched the baby while Sarah used Elizabeth Colby's money to return to school. Four years later, with her teaching credentials in hand, Sarah moved into Oaksburg to take a job at the small, local high school. She'd begged Tuwa to come live with her and Lyssa, but the old woman had refused to leave the reservation.

In all that time they'd never discussed Sarah's leaving her husband and son. She'd often been tempted to speak to her grandmother about it, but never had.

"Grandmother, did I do the right thing?" she asked, finally voicing the question that had burned in her heart for so long.

For several minutes her grandmother didn't answer, and Sarah thought maybe she wouldn't. Then Tuwa said, "You have to decide that for yourself."

"I can't."

"Go to him. That's all I can tell you." She scooted forward in her chair and pushed herself to her feet. "Now, take the little one home." She nodded toward Lyssa still asleep on the floor. "We have spoken enough of these things."

Sarah closed her eyes and sighed. She'd been dismissed.

On the way back to town, her grandmother's words echoed in her head. *The boy needs you. You are his mother.* Yet how could she go to Drew now? What would she say? Would Reece even let her near him? And even if he did, what could she possibly do to help this child she hadn't seen in eleven years?

And what of Lyssa? If Sarah went to Reece, what were the chances he'd find out about the daughter she'd kept from him? And what would he do about it?

She couldn't count the number of letters she'd written him after getting settled here, telling him about his daughter. Dozens, at least. Yet she'd never mailed them. Not even one. She should have. Reece had a right to know he had another child. But she'd always been afraid his family would swoop down and take Lyssa away from her. Or that Lyssa might prefer to live on that big ranch in eastern Wyoming with her father and brother. Sarah had lost so much. She didn't think she could survive losing her daughter, as well.

Later, as she lay in bed, the questions continued to whirl in her head. Sleep eluded her, and she knew she must find some answers, come to some decision. Yet fear and guilt continued to cloud her thoughts, and only one thing remained clear.

Her son needed her.

CHAPTER TWO

"DAD?"

Reece looked up from the ledger on his desk.

Drew stood in the doorway, his hands buried in his pockets. "Millie said you wanted to see me."

"Yes." Reece set down his pen and leaned back in his chair. "I do."

Drew took a few tentative steps into the office, as if gathering his courage to face a firing squad. Reece couldn't blame him. After the stunt Drew had pulled last night, he was probably expecting a severe reprimand and punishment.

"Sit down."

Drew nodded and slid into one of the big leather wing chairs facing the desk. He looked so small in that chair, Reece thought. And brave. Ready to face whatever his father dished out.

"I've thought a lot about what happened last night," Reece said. "I think you understand why I'm upset, so I'm not going to waste time discussing it further."

"Yes, sir." Drew sat a little straighter, and just like last night, a jolt of recognition jarred Reece.

Damn, if the boy didn't look like Sarah.

Her Shoshone blood ran strong in him. He had her hair and eyes, both a shade lighter perhaps, but still hers, and the high cheekbones of her ancestors. Reece shook off the unsettling thought. This wasn't the time to be thinking of Sarah.

"For the rest of the summer," he said to Drew, "you're going to be working for Tod."

"Tod?"

Reece leaned forward, resting his arms on his desk. "You want to ride a horse like the Appaloosa? Well then, I think it's time you started learning what you need to know. From the bottom up."

Drew still looked confused.

"You're to do whatever chores Tod gives you. That means mucking out stalls, loading hay, grooming or helping with the breeding." Understanding flickered in Drew's eyes. "Tod will expect you down at the barn by six, and you'll work until dark. Just like the rest of the hands." Reece paused, letting his words sink in. Then he added, "And you're going to have to manage your insulin shots and make sure you eat on time. Millie will help you work up a schedule. Understood?"

Drew nodded, obviously fighting a grin. "Yes, sir."

Reece leaned back in his chair again. "Then maybe you'll know a little something about horses. Enough not to let last night's events repeat themselves."

"Gee, thanks, Dad. I mean, I'll—"

Reece lifted a hand, cutting him off. "This isn't going to be a picnic, Drew. Caring for the horses is hard work."

The boy immediately sobered, though his eyes still danced with anticipation. "Yes, sir."

"Okay. Go on now. Tod's expecting you."

Drew slid from the chair and headed toward the door, then stopped and turned to his father. "I can do it, Dad. Just wait and see."

"I know you can."

Drew grinned and raced out of the house.

Reece leaned back in his chair with a sigh. He'd had a long sleepless night, wrestling with his thoughts and his guilt. He'd always been busy, and as a result, hardly knew his own son. That had been made pretty clear last night. Although he'd always seen Sarah in the boy, he now realized there was some of himself in Drew, as well. A stubborn streak. Climbing onto that Appaloosa last night, just because someone had told him he couldn't do it, well, that was something Reece himself might have done.

He'd also spent time considering whether he and his mother had been overprotective of Drew because of his diabetes. He'd never been asked to perform the chores most boys his age took for granted on a ranch. Maybe it was time to let him be normal.

"What was that all about?"

Looking up at the sound of his mother's voice, Reece frowned. "Come in, Mother."

Elizabeth Colby glided into the room and lowered herself into the chair Drew had just vacated. "Well?"

"I've decided Drew is going to work with Tod this summer," Reece answered. "He wants to be a horseman, so let him learn what that means."

"I see."

"You don't approve?"

She frowned and folded her hands in her lap. "I wish you'd checked with me first."

"I didn't realize that was necessary."

"Drew was suspended from school last week."

Reece leaned forward in his chair. "It's summer. How could he be suspended?"

"Summer school. He failed two subjects this year."

The news came at him from left field, startling him. "Why wasn't I told?"

"You were on the road." She leaned back in her chair, dismissing his question with a flick of her wrist. "I didn't think you needed the distraction."

"Distraction! Mother, Drew is my son. Don't you think I should know what's going on in his life?"

Her eyes flashed angrily, though she didn't so much as move a muscle. "Suddenly you don't trust me to care for him?"

"Of course I trust you."

"Who was it who cared for him when he was an infant?"

"You did, but..." Though he wondered how much of Drew's care actually fell to Millie.

"While you were at school back East, who watched him like a hawk, traveling back and forth with him to the Diabetes Center in Cheyenne? Who watched his blood-sugar count, gave him his insulin shots?"

"Mother, please." Reece held up a hand to stop her tirade. She was right of course. He couldn't blame her for the fact he'd never been around. First there'd been school, and then the ranch to run. "I'm not trying to undermine what you've done for Drew over the years. You've helped us both. Still, I should have been told about his trouble in school."

She glanced away, lifting her chin as if hurt. Reece knew better. It was just one of the dozen little ways she had of keeping everyone around her in line. After a moment, she turned back to him and said, "I was planning to tell you when things settled down. After the get-together yesterday."

"All right." Reece rested his elbow on his desk and ran a hand through his hair. Now was not the time to argue with his mother. "So, let's back up. What exactly is going on?"

"I've already told you. Drew failed two courses."

"What courses, Mother?"

"Math and English."

Reece let out a snort of disgust.

"Summer school was the only option if he didn't want to be held back in the sixth grade. But now..."

"What happened?"

"His teacher said he was a disrupting element in the class."

"What the hell does that mean?"

"It seems he rigged a set of those fake rattlesnake eggs to make her think she had a snake under her desk."

Reece shook his head. "Teacher new?" The rattlesnake-egg trick was an old one. Every boy in Wyoming had probably pulled it on a teacher at one time or another.

"From somewhere in the South." His mother almost smiled. "Scared her half to death."

Reece sighed. "So we make him apologize and then get him back into school. He can still work with Tod before and after class. It won't hurt him to get up early."

Elizabeth pressed her lips together and frowned.

"What?"

"That's not all."

Reece just looked at her. Getting information from his mother required the patience of a saint and the determination of a pit bull. He had both.

"Drew had an insulin reaction at school last week," she finally said.

Again Reece didn't say anything. An insulin reaction wasn't necessarily unusual for a insulin-dependent diabetic like Drew.

"His teacher believes he did it on purpose," Elizabeth continued. "She thinks he purposely missed his midmorning meal."

"That's ridiculous."

His mother just stared at him without blinking an eye.

"Why would he do such a thing?" he asked.

"I don't know, Reece. After all, he's *your* son."

Reece winced at the jab, realizing he probably deserved it. Elizabeth Colby never missed an opportunity to claim the upper hand. "Okay," he said. "What if I call his teacher. Miss . . . ?"

"Adams."

"Miss Adams. I'll call and talk to her. I'm sure we can work something out."

"You can try. But I don't think it will do any good. She was adamant about not letting Drew back into her classroom this summer."

"We'll see."

FIFTEEN MINUTES later, Reece's frustration peaked. He'd thought he'd found the solution to Drew's problem. He would turn the boy over to Tod. A little hard work promised to be the perfect vehicle to straighten him out. But the problem went deeper than Reece had realized. His brief chat with the prim Miss Adams had convinced him of that.

Evidently Drew had been acting up for months—getting into fights, pulling stunts like the one with the rattler eggs, failing to finish or bring in homework. Stuff every kid did on occasion. But according to Miss

Adams, Drew's behavior had become progressively worse since she'd first arrived in Devils Corner six months ago. She'd stated in no uncertain terms that Drew wouldn't be allowed back in her classroom this summer, and Reece believed her.

But Drew's behavior in school was no longer Reece's main concern. Nor did he believe it was Miss Adams's fear. The real danger was the insulin reactions. Drew'd had four in six months, and his teacher believed every one was deliberate.

Reece sighed and leaned his head back against the chair. He was out of his depth. He understood Drew's stunt on the horse last night, but Reece hadn't the faintest idea why Drew would do something as stupid as ignore his medical needs. With proper diet, exercise and insulin, diabetes could be controlled. Drew knew that. But by defiantly ignoring his health, he courted disaster.

SARAH WONDERED if she was well-and-truly crazy.

She couldn't believe she was here, sitting in her car outside the gate that marked the entrance to the Crooked C Ranch. Less than twenty-four hours ago, she'd been at her grandmother's, still certain there was nothing she could do to help Drew. She didn't remember when she'd made the decision to try. Actually she doubted now whether there had ever been a decision to make. Maybe it was just a matter of accepting the inevitable.

She needed to see her son and help him if she could.

Early this morning, she'd packed a couple of bags and taken Lyssa back to the reservation to stay with Tuwa. Then she'd headed northeast. She'd considered trying to contact Reece, or at least Millie, before making the three-hundred-mile drive across Wyoming, but decided against it. Reece would most likely tell her not to come, and that was no longer an option. He would just have to deal with her when she showed up on his doorstep.

Of course, she still had absolutely no idea what she would say to him. What could you say to the husband you deserted eleven years ago? Or to the son?

Before she could change her mind, she started her car and drove through the gate. On either side of her, the land rolled by, wave upon wave of rippling grasses, while above, the sky stretched forever, clear and blue and endless. The panorama was the same as it had been for the last twenty miles. Nothing indicated she was now on Colby land. Yet Sarah felt the difference, and the farther she drove, the more unsettled she became. With each passing mile she grew closer to the man who'd been her husband. And to their son.

Fifteen minutes later she spotted the ranch buildings, and panic seized her. The thought that it wasn't too late to turn around scurried through her head, but she kept on, passing the barn without seeing anyone and then pulling to a stop next to the house.

She couldn't bring herself to get out. Not yet.

She'd only been here once before, but she remembered every detail. Nothing had changed. The sprawling two-story ranch house of wood and stone, with its wide red-tile veranda wrapping around three sides of the house, and the row of cottonwoods running along its west side, shielding it from the late-afternoon sun, stood as testament to the prosperity of the Crooked C. Or more specifically, to the wealth from the oil Reece's grandfather had found on the northwest corner of his land fifty years before. The

Colbys were still ranchers, but unless their wells went dry, they didn't have the worries most ranchers had.

She remembered her awe the first and only time she'd seen this house. Reece had brought her here to meet his parents and announce their marriage. She'd learned a hard lesson that day—one she'd thought she already knew. She'd learned what it truly meant to be a half-white and poor.

She shook off the unpleasant memories and got out of her car. She wasn't seventeen any longer. She'd come to see her son, and she wouldn't let her fears stand in her way.

She walked around to the back and knocked on the kitchen screen door, hoping to talk to Millie first. It was the coward's way, she knew. After all, she could put off the inevitable only so long. But she breathed a sigh of relief when a gruff female voice answered her knock.

"Come on in. I'll be right down."

Sarah opened the door and stepped into the big modern kitchen. She only had a second to look around before Millie appeared on the back staircase.

"Well, I'll be..."

Sarah smiled tentatively. "Hello, Millie."

"Sarah." Millie nodded her greeting and took the last few steps down into the kitchen, but didn't come any closer.

"I hope my being here won't cause a problem for you."

"Nope." Millie settled her hands on her hips. "I figured you'd come."

"I had to see Drew for myself."

Millie nodded again and crossed the kitchen to one of the gleaming white counters. "Coffee?"

"No, thanks. Is he here?"

"Somewhere." Millie proceeded to rinse out the coffeepot and dump out the grounds and filter without looking at Sarah. "He's due back for his shot in about an hour."

The information stung like a reprimand. From Millie's letters, Sarah knew Drew had been careless with his health lately. She wondered if Millie blamed her for Drew's problems. Lord knew, Sarah blamed herself. "And Reece?"

"In his office. Down the front hall, second door on the left."

"Do you think he'll see me?"

"If you go in there, he'll have no choice."

"I don't know." At the thought of confronting Reece, panic once again threatened to overcome her. "Maybe if you told him I was here..."

"You tell him."

Millie was right. She'd already done enough—possibly even jeopardized her job by keeping in touch with Sarah. "Is anyone else in the house?"

"Nope. Mrs. Colby's over at the Hawthorne place."

Sarah took a deep breath. At least she wouldn't have to face both Reece and his mother at the same time. "Okay. I guess the worst he can do is kick me out."

Millie finally turned and met her gaze. "Go on. I'll bring coffee for the two of you in a bit."

A few moments later, Sarah stood silently in the doorway to Reece's office. In truth, she wasn't at all sure she could have spoken if she'd wanted—not once she saw him. She'd told herself on the long drive from Oaksburg that she was only here to see Drew. She'd tried to stop thinking of Reece years ago.

She hadn't succeeded.

He looked wonderful. So much better than the grainy snapshots she'd cut out of the newspaper. Those pictures hadn't done justice to his broad expanse of shoulders or his sun-tipped hair. Or his skin, seasoned by sun and wind and long days on the plains.

He must have sensed her presence, because suddenly he looked up. For a heartbeat, she saw the man she'd loved in his eyes, and a rush of warmth wrapped itself around her.

"Sarah?"

At first Reece couldn't believe his eyes. He was seeing things, the way he sometimes saw Sarah when he looked at Drew. Or the way he sometimes remembered her in his dreams.

She took a step into the office. "Hello, Reece."

Her voice snapped him out of it. This was real. His ex-wife stood in his office, the woman who'd walked out on him and their infant son more than eleven years ago. A long-familiar anger grew in his heart.

"May I come in?" she asked.

"It looks like you already have."

She pressed her lips together and moved farther into the room, motioning toward a chair as if asking permission to sit. When Reece didn't respond, she sat, anyway.

He realized then why he hadn't immediately recognized her. Everything about her had changed. When he'd known her, she'd been a rough-and-tumble cowgirl in jeans, denim shirts and boots. This woman wore a long brightly colored skirt, a plain white top and moccasins. And her dark hair, which had once flowed untamed about her shoulders, hung in a single neat braid over one shoulder.

"What do you want, Sarah?"

She looked away for a moment, before turning back to meet his gaze. "You look well, Reece."

No. Not everything about her had changed. Her eyes were the same, dark and hypnotic, eyes that could make a man forget. But not him. He'd never forget. "You didn't come here to exchange pleasantries."

"I was hoping we could be civil to one another."

"Now why would you think that?"

"We were once—"

"Yes, Sarah." He crossed his arms and stared at her. "What were we? I've asked myself that question a time or two."

"We had a son together."

"An inconvenience it took you little time to correct."

She lowered her gaze and turned away again. "Reece, I didn't come here to discuss what happened between us."

"No, I don't expect you did." He couldn't keep the bitterness out of his voice. Though he would have liked to. He didn't want her to know how badly she'd hurt him all those years ago—when he'd been young and foolish and head over heels in love with her. "So, why don't we get right to the point? What is it you want? Money?"

She looked at him, anger flashing in her dark sorceress eyes. "I've never cared about your money."

"Oh, no? Funny, that's not what you told me the last time we spoke."

A blush darkened her cheeks, but she held his gaze, straightening slightly with a movement so familiar it sent a jolt of recognition and pain through him. He focused on the pain.

"And what about the man you left me for?" All the bitterness Reece had stored inside for the past eleven years rose up, striking out at this woman he'd once loved. "I imagine he's long gone. Or you wouldn't be here."

"I've come about Drew," she said stiffly.

"What about him?"

She paused before saying, "I want to see him."

"No."

"What do you mean, no?"

"It's a simple word, Sarah." He sat forward in his chair and rested his arms on the desk. "One even you should be able to understand."

"Reece, I know he's having trouble..."

"How would you know that?"

"I know he's failing classes and he's been kicked out of summer school. And I know he's neglecting his health."

Her words struck him silent. How could she know this when he'd just found out himself? "I'm a teacher," she continued. "Maybe I can help."

"How did you know about this?" The question was out before he could stop it.

Sarah shrugged. "What difference does it make?"

"Did my mother contact you?"

She laughed, a sharp, almost bitter sound. Then she said, "I want to help."

"The only way you can help Drew is to leave him alone." He stood and leaned across his desk. "Leave *us* both alone."

"But—"

"Go back to where you came from, Sarah." A slow roll of anger had built inside him. Who had contacted her? And what the hell right did she have to come here now claiming she could help the boy she'd deserted as an infant? "If you try to come near him, I'll slap a restraining order on you."

She sat for a moment without moving. Finally she stood. "I'll be staying at the motel in town. I'll be there for a couple of days. If you change your mind..."

He straightened and crossed his arms. "I won't."

"Give me a call. I'm registered under the name Hanson."

"Goodbye, Sarah."

She closed her eyes and nodded. Then she headed for the door and nearly collided with Drew, who came to a screeching halt just inside the room.

CHAPTER THREE

SARAH COULDN'T BREATHE.

Her chest tightened painfully. Her vision blurred and then sharpened to a surrealistic clarity. She watched, as if from outside herself, the meeting of some other woman with the son she hadn't seen in eleven years.

"Sorry," Drew said. "I didn't know my dad had company."

He was nearly grown. Of course, she knew that. She'd seen pictures. Millie had sent them. Still, Sarah had always pictured him like she'd last seen him, a chubby sweet-scented infant. This lanky twelve-year-old, smelling of hay and horses, with a mop of dark hair and dirty hands, wasn't the child she remembered.

"It's okay, Drew." The words came from Reece. She heard them as if from a distance. "Miss Hanson was just leaving."

Suddenly air rushed into her lungs, easing the pain, and Sarah came back to herself with a start. This might be her only chance to speak to Drew. Ignoring Reece, she stepped toward her son and offered him her hand.

"Hello, Drew." Somehow she managed to make her voice sound normal. "It's nice to meet you."

Drew grinned and took her hand. "You're not from around here, are you?"

"No." She smiled, liking his directness. "I live in Oaksburg. It's a small town near the Wind River Reservation." She wanted to hold on to him a little longer, pull him closer. Instead, she let go of his hand and took a step back. "I knew your father years ago, when we were teenagers. Since I was over this way, I thought I'd stop in to say hi."

"Cool." He shoved his hands into the pockets of his jeans. "Did you know my mom, too?"

Sarah's smile froze. She glanced at Reece and saw the warning in his eyes. Taking a deep breath, she turned back to Drew and said, "Yes." She didn't know how she managed to speak. "I did."

"Can you—"

"Drew." Reece moved around the desk and placed an arm around the boy's shoulders. "Miss Hanson was just leaving." Although he was speaking to their son, Reece's words were for Sarah. "Isn't that right?"

She met his gaze and saw more than a warning in his eyes, she saw fear, as well. He wanted her out of here. Now.

"I'm afraid your father's right," she said. If Reece didn't want Drew to know her identity, Sarah wouldn't go against his wishes. Not yet, anyway. Not until she knew more—about Drew himself, and about what Reece and his family had told Drew about her. "I need to get going." It took all her strength to smile. "But it was nice meeting you. Maybe we can talk again sometime."

"Yes, ma'am."

Sarah shifted her attention to Reece and almost faltered as again she caught a brief glimpse of the man she'd once loved. It was an unexpected warmth in his eyes. But as before, it lasted only a moment before fading, chilling her.

"Remember my offer," she said.

"Goodbye, Miss Hanson." His words were stiff and formal, as if they were strangers. And maybe they were.

She hesitated a moment longer and then left, placing one foot in front of the other without looking back. As she'd done eleven years ago, she forced herself to keep going, to keep walking away from her ex-husband and their son. And for some reason she couldn't begin to understand, leaving them was even harder than it had been the first time.

REECE NEEDED to get out.

He waited until Sarah was well away and Drew settled in the kitchen with Millie for his midmorning snack. Then Reece headed down to the barn and saddled his horse. Calling to Tod that he'd be back before dark, Reece turned the animal toward the Black Hills.

For more than an hour he rode without letting any of the morning's events penetrate his thoughts. He was back on a horse, riding across the range. It was almost full summer, and the land was ripe with life, the air fragrant, the sun warm. He belonged here, out in the open, not inside going over the books or on a campaign trail soliciting votes.

As the sun climbed past its zenith and the day grew warmer, he stopped to water his horse at a shallow stream that bisected the prairie. Dismounting, he sat on a small knoll beside the water and finally let his thoughts turn to Sarah.

Why had she shown up now?

It had taken years for him to forget her. Years during which he'd struggled to put the memory of her out of his mind. Less than twenty-four hours ago he'd have sworn he never wanted to see her again. But today she'd waltzed into his office and, in a matter of moments, resurrected their past and made him doubt everything he'd been telling himself for the past eleven years.

She was a woman now, no longer the girl he'd known. But she was more beautiful than ever and just as proud and defiant as he remembered. It shouldn't have surprised him. She'd always been strong.

They'd met in Riverton while competing in the weekend rodeo. She'd been riding the fastest little barrel racer he'd ever seen, handling the mare like a pro. He'd asked around about her, but no one seemed to know her. Finally he'd spotted her one afternoon, eating alone in one of the food tents set up on the rodeo grounds. All around her, other contestants laughed and talked, but not Sarah. She sat straight and proud, as if unaware there was another soul in the place. Reece had walked over, sat down next to her and fallen in love.

Later he'd found out that she lived on the Wind River Reservation with her grandmother. She was competing in weekend rodeos in hopes of winning enough money to pay her first-year college tuition. He couldn't help but admire her determination and courage. Not only was she a newcomer on the circuit, she was half-Indian. She was an outsider from day one and determined despite it.

He'd loved her and married her, ignoring his father's threats and his mother's tears. He'd given up everything. Because the only thing that had mattered to him was Sarah.

Then she'd thrown it all in his face.

"Damn," Reece cursed, and lay down on the soft grass. For a few minutes, he watched the ribbons of white clouds drift across the sky, letting his mind wander over the past. Then he reeled in his thoughts.

He couldn't let Sarah's sudden emergence in his life distract him. Drew was his priority. Reece needed to find answers about how to deal with the boy. Something had to be done—that much was clear. But beyond that, Reece was at a loss. He was no good at this father stuff. The boy climbing on a skittish stallion or even failing subjects in school Reece could understand. He didn't like it, but it wasn't unusual behavior for a twelve-year-old. What he couldn't begin to understand was why Drew would toy with his life by ignoring his diabetes.

A half-dozen ideas skidded through Reece's head— everything from grounding the boy for the next year to taking a leather strap to his backside. All answers Reece's own father might have come up with. But Reece had never cared for his father's heavy-handed methods, and he wasn't about to make the same mistakes.

Standing, he brushed off the back of his jeans. It was time to get back. The sun rested just above the horizon, and he was at least an hour's ride from the ranch. He'd sat here long enough, looking for solutions and wallowing in memories. Mounting his horse, he turned toward home. He still didn't have any answers about Drew, but at least he felt better about the questions. The open range always had that effect on him. It cleared his thoughts, bringing them into perspective and focus.

Smiling to himself, he realized he'd been cooped up too long. No matter what he decided about Drew, he needed to spend more time on the ranch, out in the open.

IT WAS ALMOST DARK by the time Reece arrived home and found Michelle waiting for him. He'd forgotten all about their plans to discuss the campaign this afternoon. Apologizing for being late, he went upstairs to shower. Thirty minutes later, he reentered the spacious living room. Heading directly for the wet bar, he poured himself a stiff shot of scotch.

"Sorry I'm late, Michelle."

"Don't worry about it." She lounged on the couch, sipping a glass of white wine. "Your mother and I had a nice visit."

Reece smiled at her typical response. Nothing ever seemed to bother her. She was about the most easygoing woman he'd ever known. For the hundredth time he wished he felt more for her than friendship.

Moving over to the fireplace, he leaned against the stone mantel. "Where is Mother?"

"She went up to check on Drew. He was pretty tired this evening and fell asleep right after dinner."

"Did she tell you about his problems at school and the insulin reactions?"

"Yes."

Reece sighed and ran a hand through his hair. He was about to shatter Michelle's calm demeanor. "Then you'll understand why I'm considering withdrawing from the campaign."

She didn't look surprised. Still, she took a moment before answering, as if carefully weighing her words. "Of course it's your decision, Reece." She sipped her wine. "But I think you should think about it very carefully."

"That's what I've been doing all day."

"What about hiring a tutor?"

"That won't help Drew's habit of purposely making himself sick."

Michelle shook her head and glanced away. After a few minutes of silence, she said, "Once you withdraw from the race, Reece, there's no turning back."

"There'll always be another election."

"Give yourself some time." She looked back at him, and despite her calm manner, he realized she was more concerned about this than she would have him think. "This is a big decision. Consider all your options."

"And what are my options?" He knew how badly she wanted him to get into politics, and he'd wanted it, too. He'd wanted to make a difference in his home state. It was what had drawn them together. "My son's playing Russian roulette with a disease that could kill him. I can't ignore that."

"Of course not, but have you talked to him?"

Reece shifted uncomfortably. "No, not yet."

"Don't you think that should be your first step?"

Reece let out a short laugh and shook his head. "Always the logical one."

"Well, it only makes sense."

"What do I say to him?"

"Just ask him why, Reece." She leaned forward, resting her arms on her legs. "Give him a chance to tell you what's bothering him."

It seemed so simple. Too simple actually. And for Michelle and her father, maybe it would have worked. But Reece had never been able to talk to his own father. And as for talking to Drew, he didn't know where to begin. In all honesty, his mother *had* raised the boy, while he...

"I see you finally made it home."

Michelle and Reece turned at the sound of Elizabeth's voice. She stood in the doorway, dressed in cream-colored slacks and a silk blouse. Simple but elegant. Too elegant for a working ranch in the middle of Wyoming.

Reece ignored her implied criticism. "How's Drew?"

"Fine." Elizabeth joined Michelle on the couch. "We went ahead and ate dinner without you."

"I'll get something later."

Michelle leaned over and laid a hand on Elizabeth's arm. "We were just talking about Drew."

"Really." Elizabeth looked first at her future daughter-in-law and then shifted her focus to her son. "Did he tell you that Drew's mother was here today?"

"How—" Reece began, but she cut him off.

"Drew told me." She kept her gaze locked on him. "At least he told me there was a Miss Hanson here today. I assumed..."

"Yes, Mother. It was Sarah."

"What did she want?"

Reece took a sip of scotch. "To see Drew."

"And you let her?"

"No," Reece snapped. "I didn't *let* her, Mother. She showed up, and Drew just happened to come inside."

Elizabeth sighed and sank against the couch. "At least you didn't tell him who she was."

Reece glanced at Michelle and saw her confusion. They'd never really discussed Sarah or what Drew knew about her. He supposed it was because of the nature of his and Michelle's relationship. But it couldn't be helped now. He'd have to explain things to her later.

Turning back to his mother, he asked, "Would that have been so bad?"

"Don't be ridiculous, Reece. We decided years ago that the less Drew knew about Sarah the better."

"Well, I'm not so sure that was such a great decision."

He remembered Sarah's expression when Drew had walked into Reece's office this morning. It wasn't the look of a woman who didn't care about her son. "She heard about Drew's problems and came to offer help."

"How did she find out about that?"

"I thought you'd contacted her."

"Me? Why would I? The best thing that girl ever did for you and Drew was leave you. Now she probably wants more money."

Reece stiffened and went perfectly still. "More money?"

Elizabeth flushed. She'd obviously said more than she'd intended. "Well, of course she wants money. What else could she want?"

"*More* money, Mother?" A kernel of suspicion tightened in his gut. "What money are we talking about here?"

"Forget I said anything, Reece." Elizabeth tried to brush his question aside. "It was a long time ago."

He wasn't going to let it go. "No, Mother. I want to know what you're talking about. What money?"

"Really, Reece. It's hardly important now."

"Mother." The kernel had exploded, leaving a sick feeling of dread churning inside him.

Elizabeth looked at him and flinched, then quickly turned away. "Oh, if you insist. I didn't tell you before because I knew you'd never understand."

"Tell me now."

"When Sarah decided to leave you, I gave her some money. That's all there was to it."

"You gave her money?" The sickness within him spread.

"Well, yes. She was such a foolish girl really."

Elizabeth finally met his gaze, and he could see the wariness in her eyes. This was something she'd never intended for him to know.

"Sarah realized she was poison for you and Drew," she continued. "You were so young and stubborn you couldn't see it. But she did. And she was more than happy to take the money I offered her to leave."

Reece didn't move. The sick feeling had turned to anger, a hard dangerous anger, threatening to erupt at any moment. "Let me get this straight, Mother. You bribed my wife to leave me?"

"Now, Reece, 'bribe' is such an awful word."

"Answer me, Mother. You gave Sarah money to leave me?"

"Why, yes. Of course." She folded her hands in her lap and lifted her chin. "But it was for your own good."

SARAH SAT in the small diner attached to Devils Corner's only motel, toying with the food on her plate.

She'd picked the back booth, anxious to avoid the curious stares and questions inherent in a town this small. She needn't have bothered. No one seemed the least interested her. With nothing more than a "What can I get you?" the waitress had taken her order and filled it. It was just as well. Sarah didn't know if she could deal with anyone else today. Talking to Reece, seeing Drew, had taken the last of her strength.

When she'd left the ranch earlier, she'd driven aimlessly for hours, unaware of anything except the dull ache in her heart.

She'd known before coming here that seeing Reece again would be difficult, but she realized now that she'd had no idea just how difficult. She'd looked at him and seen the boy she'd loved grown into a man. A jolt of desire had coursed through her system, surprising her with its intensity. Then the momentary warmth of his eyes had hardened to cold disdain, and she'd wanted to scream at life's injustices. He wasn't her husband and hadn't been for a long time.

And Drew.

She'd looked at her son and realized just how much she'd missed, how much she'd given away. She'd been a fool to leave him all those years ago—a young stupid fool. But knowing that only made things worse.

While driving, she'd considered turning southwest and heading for home. She and Lyssa could stay on the reservation with Tuwa for a few days. It would be good to spend time at her grandmother's house, to take comfort in the old woman and Lyssa. She could be in Oaksburg by midnight and at her grandmother's before one.

Instead, Sarah had headed into town and checked into the motel. She'd made the mistake of running once. She wouldn't do it again.

She wished, however, that she could at least talk to Lyssa. Just hearing her daughter's voice might ease the pain. But Tuwa didn't have a phone. The only way Sarah could get hold of them would be to call one of the neighbors. It would be a long involved expensive process, and everyone on the other end would panic, thinking it an emergency.

Sighing, she shoved the uneaten plate of food away. She'd stay here a day or two in case Reece changed his mind. Then she'd head home.

"May I join you?"

Startled, Sarah looked up as Reece slid his tall frame into the seat across the booth from her. He looked older than he had this morning. And tired.

"It looks like you already have," she said.

A whisper of a smile nipped at his mouth but quickly disappeared. The waitress approached, set a cup in front of him and filled it with coffee. "Anything else, Reece?" she asked.

He shook his head. "This'll be fine."

The waitress moved away, and he turned his attention to the steaming cup in front of him. Sarah watched him sip his coffee, wondering what had brought him here. Had he decided to let her see Drew? Or had he come to run her out of town?

Finally she had to ask, "Why are you here, Reece?"

He didn't look at her but turned, instead, to stare out the window. "I had a talk with my mother this evening."

Sarah's stomach tightened, but she remained silent, waiting for him to continue.

"She told me an interesting story."

Sarah knew where this was headed and couldn't let him go on with it. "Reece, this isn't—"

"She told me about the money, Sarah." He turned back to look at her, his eyes hard and angry. "She told me that she gave you ten thousand dollars."

Sarah bit back a cry of dismay. Elizabeth had promised never to tell Reece about the money. After everything else Sarah had done to him, it seemed like such a little thing. Still, she'd thought at the time that she couldn't bear for him to know about it. Evidently Elizabeth had kept her promise only as long as it served her purpose.

"Say something," he demanded.

She took a deep breath and knit her fingers together in her lap. "What do you want me to say?"

"Tell me she's lying."

Sarah wished she could. Just as she wished she could tell him the entire truth. Why she left. Lyssa. All of it. But she knew now she couldn't. "Reece, no matter what I tell you, you're going to believe what you want." *And if I tell you about your daughter, I'll lose her, too.*

"What about the other man?"

She fought her growing nausea. "The man?"

"The one you left me for. Or was that a lie, too?"

"What do you think?"

He didn't have to answer. The look in his eyes said it all. He thought he knew the truth. His mother and wife had both betrayed him in more ways than one. Sarah had all she could do to keep from reaching out to him, from trying to explain—even though she knew it wouldn't do any good. There was so much anger in him. Even if he listened to her explanation, she doubted the truth would make any difference.

He turned away again, staring out the large plate-glass window as if he could see something beyond the darkness and their reflections.

"You're a teacher," he said finally.

Sarah nodded. "Yes. I teach at Oaksburg High School. Why?"

He didn't answer for several minutes, keeping his eyes focused on the dark world outside the diner. Then he turned and looked at her again, his eyes bleak and haunted.

"My son," he started, and then corrected himself, "*our* son needs a tutor."

It took a moment for Reece's words to register. Even then, Sarah feared she'd misunderstood. "A tutor?"

"Someone qualified to teach sixth-grade math and English."

She held herself back, hoping, yet afraid to jump to any conclusions. "What does that have to do with me?"

"I want to hire you for the summer."

Relief swept through her. She was going to see her son. "Yes. I mean, I'm qualified. And—"

"There are conditions," he said, cutting her off.

"Such as?" She leaned forward, not really caring about his conditions. All that mattered was she would be spending time with Drew, working with him, teaching him.

"First of all, I'm going to check and verify your qualifications."

"That won't be a problem."

"Also, besides tutoring, you'll have to monitor Drew's meals and insulin injections. He's been—"

Reece hesitated as if searching for the right word
"—careless lately."

Sarah nodded, remembering Millie's disturbing letter.

"Mother is going back East for the summer," Reece
continued. "And Millie has enough to worry about
without constantly keeping an eye on Drew."

"Okay." Sarah had come here to help her son, and
Reece was giving her that chance. Then a disturbing
question surfaced in her thoughts. "Wait a minute."
She leaned back and crossed her arms. "Why are you
doing this?" A few minutes ago, she'd have sworn
he'd never let her near Drew again.

Reece shifted, the hard plastic seat crackling beneath him. "I told you. Drew needs a tutor."

"But why me?" She studied his face, looking for
the truth behind his words. "This afternoon you made
it clear you didn't want me anywhere near Drew. And
tonight, after what you found out about..." She
couldn't make herself mention the money. "What
made you change your mind?"

"I didn't."

His features remained impassive, and it struck her
just how different this man was from the boy she'd
loved and married. He was as devastatingly handsome as ever. More so, really. And the chemistry between them still existed. Sitting this close to him,
separated by nothing more than the width of a table,
she felt his presence, like a low pulse of electricity
running through her. But when had he grown so distant, his warm blue eyes turning to glacial ice? When
had he forgotten how to smile? She knew better than
to examine those questions too closely, because she
wasn't at all sure she was ready to face the answers.

Then she wondered if his coolness was for her benefit, or if he was this way with everyone. Including their son.

"The only other qualified teacher within fifty miles is teaching summer school," he continued. "Drew has already been kicked out of her classroom." He paused, and she noticed the slight tightening of his jaw. "If there was anyone else, I wouldn't be sitting here."

She remained silent, her eyes searching his face. She wanted to believe he lied, that he had other reasons for asking her to work with Drew—like the fact she was his mother. But nothing in Reece's expression indicated that he thought of her as anything more than a potential employee, the only available teacher within fifty miles. And it hurt.

"Okay," she said finally. She couldn't possibly give up a chance to spend time with Drew—whatever Reece's motives.

"Good. You'll stay out at the ranch."

It made sense, though the idea disturbed her. Again she didn't want to look too closely at why. She'd be just another hired hand. "When would you like me to start?"

"As soon as possible."

Sarah thought of Lyssa, and the guilt wound itself tighter within her. But she refused to give in to it. She couldn't tell Reece about Lyssa. He'd made his feeling for Sarah all too clear. There was no telling what he'd do if he found out she'd kept his daughter from him.

"I'll need to go back to Oaksburg this weekend to make some arrangements," she said.

Reece nodded. "Okay."

"Other than that, I can start tomorrow."

"Make it after noon. I'll check your credentials in the morning, along with some other arrangements I need to make."

She thought he'd leave then, but he made no move to stand. Instead, his attention shifted back to the darkness outside the window. For several moments he remained silent, yet she could sense the tension building in him, like a wildcat ready to spring.

"There's one other thing," he said.

He turned back to face her, and she barely kept from rubbing her arms to ward off the sudden chill. "Yes?"

"Drew's not to know you're his mother."

His words struck like a fist, and she recoiled from the impact. This time she didn't want to believe she'd heard him correctly as anger quickly replaced her initial surprise.

"You bastard!"

Reece's eyes narrowed and he leaned toward her, his voice sharp and bitter. "I'm not the one who walked out on him eleven years ago."

"And this is your way of punishing me?" She couldn't believe he was doing this, that he could be this vindictive.

"This isn't about you, Sarah. It's about Drew. He needs a tutor, and you're convenient. The last thing he needs right now is his long-lost mother waltzing back into his life."

"Maybe that's exactly what he does need."

"I doubt it." He sat back with a smug smile. "He thinks you're dead."

CHAPTER FOUR

"WHAT DID YOU SAY?"

The pain on Sarah's face nearly leveled him. He hadn't expected it, nor his own reaction to it. He glanced outside, unable to look at her, fighting the urge to move beside her and pull her into his arms. He wanted to apologize and tell her everything would be okay.

Then he reminded himself of what she'd done, how she'd betrayed both him and Drew. He'd only done what he'd had to do for his son. Turning back to meet her gaze, he said, "Drew believes his mother is dead."

"How...?" Her voice trembled.

"How could I? It was very easy, Sarah." Resting his arms on the table, he leaned forward. "The first time my son asked about his mother, I told him she'd died when he was nine months old."

She managed to shut down, to mask the pain he'd seen on her face. But her eyes...damn if her eyes didn't betray her. They'd come alive, betraying the roll of emotions behind her expressionless features. There was more than pain now. There was anger, as well.

"You had no right," she said.

"I had every right. You left. So the way I see things, you gave up any say in the matter. I did what I thought was best for *my* son." He pushed himself out of the booth and stood, towering over her. "If it hurts you to be around him without telling him who you are, well, I can live with that. Can you?''

Sarah lifted her chin to look up at him, and he could almost see her fighting for control.

"So," he said, "do you want the job or not?"

"What's to keep me from telling him, anyway?"

Reece leaned over and placed his hands on the table, inches from hers. "I guarantee you'll never see him again if you do.''

He let that sink in a moment and then turned and walked out of the diner, unwilling to look at her one more time.

He refused to admit the power this woman still had over him, the momentary need he'd felt to pull her into his arms and comfort her. To tell her everything would be all right, for God's sake! She'd nearly destroyed him eleven years ago when she walked away, and he couldn't let that happen again.

And yet he felt nothing but disgust at himself for the way he'd just treated her. He'd purposely struck out at her, wanting to hurt her for what she'd done. For leaving him and Drew. For never really caring about them to begin with. His plan had backfired, leaving a bitter taste in his mouth and the memory of her dark pain-filled eyes in his heart.

"Damn," he said as he climbed into his truck and slammed the door behind him. He sat for a moment, finally able to look back at her, now that he'd put some distance between them. He watched her through the large plate-glass window, still sitting in the booth where he'd left her, stiff and motionless, and as proud as ever.

He could have broken it to her easily. He could have explained, but he hadn't. Instead, he'd let her think he'd told Drew she was dead out of spite, as a way to strike back at her.

"Damn," he said again, slamming his hand against the steering wheel before starting the engine.

REECE HARDLY REMEMBERED the drive back to the ranch. There was nothing but a churn of emotions, feelings that ranged from anger at himself and Sarah to a deep longing for something that had never been. He didn't even try to sort it all out. The emotions were too fresh, the turmoil too recent. He just drove, letting it wash over him.

When he pulled into the yard, it was nearly midnight. The house was dark, but Michelle's car still sat in front. She must have decided to stay the night. Probably Elizabeth had spent most of the evening bending her future daughter-in-law's ear.

He entered through the kitchen and made his way quietly through the house, heading for the stairs. He'd noticed the single light coming from the living room, but he had no intention of stopping.

He didn't want to see or talk to anyone else tonight.

"Reece." Michelle's soft voice caught him just as he put his foot on the first step. Reluctantly he turned to see her silhouetted in the doorway. "I've been waiting for you."

"Can we talk tomorrow, Michelle?" He wanted a hot shower and about ten hours of uninterrupted sleep. "It's been one hell of a long day."

She crossed her arms. "For everyone."

Reece sighed. He knew that look. His shower and bed would have to wait until Michelle had her say. And

to be honest, he owed her that much. "Okay," he said.
"I guess I could use a nightcap."

Michelle nodded and headed back into the living
room.

"Want something?" he asked as he crossed to the
bar.

"No, thanks." Michelle settled onto a chair next to
the only lamp on in the room. Reece noticed the law
books and yellow legal pads on the table and wondered if she ever stopped working.

"You went to see her, didn't you?" Michelle asked
without preamble.

The question surprised him, and Reece looked up
from the glass he'd just filled with scotch. Michelle
watched him with an expression he'd never seen on her
face before. When he'd stormed out of the house after his mother had admitted giving Sarah money, he
hadn't been sure of his intentions. It had taken the
long drive into Devils Corner before he'd known
he was going to ask Sarah to tutor Drew. Yet Michelle had guessed, and she didn't look entirely happy
about it.

He crossed the room and sat on the couch across
from her. "I asked Sarah to tutor Drew this summer."

"Do you think that's a good idea?"

Reece sank further into the couch, closing his eyes
and resting his head against the back. Damn, he was
tired. "Hell, I don't know. I know I needed to do
something."

"Your mother's not going to be happy."

Yeah, Elizabeth would be angry. She was going to
be even angrier when she found out he was going to
send her back East for the summer. She'd planned to

go anyway, but not for a few weeks. At the moment, he didn't give a damn about his mother's anger. Eleven years ago she'd gone behind his back and paid his wife to leave him. He wasn't at all sure he'd ever be able to forgive Elizabeth for that. And he knew he'd never be able to forgive Sarah for taking the money. Then he remembered Michelle and opened his eyes.

"What about you, Michelle?" He sat a little straighter. She was acting strange, and he was suddenly worried about how all this would affect her. "Is it going to bother you having Sarah here?"

She let out a short laugh and abandoned her chair. "Well, it wouldn't be my first choice."

"Michelle—"

She turned back to him and held up a hand to silence him. "Reece, we've always been honest with each other. From the very beginning our plans to marry have been... convenient. For both of us. I'm just worried about you. I'm your friend, and I don't want to see you hurt."

Her concern touched him. "That was a long time ago, Michelle."

"Yes, but—"

"My feelings for Sarah died when she walked out." The words slipped easily from his mouth, but he wondered if there was any truth in them.

"Did they?" Michelle voiced his own question, but before he could reassure either of them, she moved over and sat next to him on the couch. "You've never told Drew anything about her, have you?"

"Not much." Reece sipped at the scotch he'd almost forgotten he held in his hand, not particularly anxious to get into this—though he knew he really had no choice. "Actually we've never told him anything. Except..."

"Except?"

He closed his eyes again for a moment. If he did this right, maybe she'd understand. "I wasn't around much when Drew first started asking about his mother. My father had recently died, and I had my hands full trying to run the ranch." It had been a difficult time for him, but not an unhappy one. He'd been training to take over the ranch from the time he could toddle out to the barn, and his dad had lifted him onto the back of his first cow pony.

"Mother managed to deflect Drew's questions for some time," he said. "But eventually she let me know what was going on, and we had to decide how much to tell him." Reece sighed and ran his free hand through his hair. "I didn't know what to say to him. I mean, how do you tell a five-year-old child that his mother abandoned him?"

"So what did you do?" Michelle's voice sounded strained.

He hesitated again, but silence wouldn't change things. And Michelle would find out sooner or later. "We told Drew his mother had died when he was an infant."

"Oh, my God." He felt Michelle's withdrawal as surely as if she'd physically moved away from him.

"I thought it was kinder than telling him the truth."

She looked stricken. "All the times I've talked to Drew, he's never—"

Reece shook his head. "He doesn't ask about her much anymore." *Except today when he met Sarah.* "And he almost never talks about her."

For several long moments, neither of them spoke. Reece watched Michelle, wishing he knew what she was thinking. He could almost see that fantastically logical brain of hers sorting through all the facts.

Then she asked, "Didn't it ever occur to you that Sarah might come back one day, wanting to meet her son?"

It hadn't. Although in the beginning, he'd dreamed of it. Of her. Coming to him and telling him it had all been a mistake. A terrible mistake. "I didn't think about it that way. At the time, when Sarah left, I was just so..."

"Hurt?"

"I was going to say angry."

Michelle sighed and sank back into the thick cushions. "I don't know what to think about this, Reece. I mean, I understand your reasoning at the time..."

Reece smiled gently and reached over to take her hand. "I don't deserve you."

Michelle returned his smile and gave his hand a squeeze. "And don't you forget it." Then she leaned over and kissed him on the cheek before disentangling her hand from his and rising from the couch.

"We don't have to make a decision about the campaign for a couple of months yet," she said, changing the subject.

She moved to the table, where she'd evidently been working before he came in, and started gathering her things. "Who knows, maybe this will work out for the best. Sarah is Drew's mother. If anyone can get through to him, I suppose she can." She turned back to Reece, her arms loaded with books and legal pads. "It'll be good for the two of them to get to know each other."

"Wait a minute." Reece straightened and set down his scotch. "I haven't changed my mind about Drew and Sarah. I've asked her not to tell him the truth."

"What?"

"It would be too traumatic for him. Especially now."

For a moment, Michelle remained silent. Then she said, "Reece, you can't do this." She took a step toward him. "I understand why you and Elizabeth told him what you did when he was a little boy, but now—"

"The only thing that's changed now is that Sarah is here."

Michelle looked doubtful.

"Think about it." Reece sat forward, resting his elbows on his knees. "What would it do to Drew if we told him the truth now? Now while he's having trouble with school and fighting his diabetes. Do you think he'd respond to her tutoring him?"

"I don't know. But how do you plan to keep this a secret? There must be people around who know her."

Reece rose from the couch and shoved his hands in his pockets. "I brought Sarah out here once. Twelve years ago. None of the hands knew her. Hell, none of them even saw her. And Mother and Father certainly never talked about her. So the only one who ever met her was Millie."

"What about in town?"

Reece paced to the stone fireplace before turning back to face her. "No one. Oh, there might be one or two of my old high-school buddies who may have seen her at one of the rodeos. But Sarah and I kept our relationship pretty quiet. I doubt if they'd even remember her, much less make the connection between her and Drew. Even if they did, the chances of Drew running into any of them are pretty slim.''

"What about her name? Won't Drew notice that his new tutor, who you just happened to know in high school, has the same name as his mother?'' She paused. "He does know his mother's name, doesn't he?''

Reece ran his hand through his hair. "He knows her name, but Sarah is fairly common. It could be just coincidence.''

"You're taking a big chance. If Drew finds out...''

"I have to risk it.''

Shaking her head, she started to turn away and then stopped. "You're just going to let him think she's a stranger.''

"I'm doing this for Drew. For my son.''

Again she seemed to hesitate before saying, "If you believe that, Reece Colby, you're a much bigger fool than I ever thought.'' With that, she turned and left him alone.

WHEN SARAH PULLED into the yard of the Crooked C the next afternoon, she spotted Drew immediately. He stood in the center of the main corral, holding the head of a small but beautifully formed mare, while a tall cowboy groomed her. Stopping the car, she sat for a moment and watched her son handle the skittish animal.

He had a gift. Like Lyssa.

Even from this distance she could see it—his confidence and ease while holding the mare's head, calming her. Though Sarah couldn't hear him, she'd have bet he was making meaningless soothing sounds that let the animal know no harm would come to her.

Pride welled within her, and Sarah wanted to go to him and tell him so. But Reece's ultimatum and her own decision eleven years ago had taken that option from her. Now she'd have to live with the consequences of both.

She drove farther on and, as she'd done yesterday, parked near the back of the house. Except for Drew and the cowboy working in the corral, the ranch seemed deserted. Although she couldn't really say what else she'd expected. Certainly not Reece coming out to greet her.

And a part of her was grateful.

She wasn't sure she was ready to face him. It had taken half the night to get her pain under control. A little extra time to deal with things could only help.

As before, she went around to the kitchen door and knocked. Today Millie opened the door almost immediately.

"Come on in," she said. "I've been expecting you."

Sarah stepped inside. "Glad someone is."

Millie chuckled and took Sarah's small suitcase from her and deposited it on the floor next to the back stairs. "You always did have a way of stirring things up."

"Thanks, Millie." Sarah returned the older woman's grin. "That makes me feel a whole lot better about being here."

Millie's smile broadened. "Reece has been stomping around all morning, arguing with Mrs. Colby and delivering ultimatums to Drew."

"Maybe I should just tiptoe back out the door before anyone else knows I'm here."

"Not on your life." Millie slipped an arm through Sarah's and, grabbing her suitcase, led her up the stairs. "This place needs a little excitement. Things have been awfully dull around here for too long. And that boy of yours..." Millie stopped at the top of the stairs and shook her head.

"Reece doesn't want Drew to know—"

Millie cut her off with the wave of a hand. "I know all about what Reece wants and doesn't want." She leaned toward Sarah as if in confidence, but her voice lost none of its volume. "I never approved of what they told that boy to begin with. But the man never did learn to think before he spoke. Then he was always too damn proud to admit when he was wrong."

Sarah glanced nervously down the hallway, wondering who might be within earshot of Millie's very vocal opinions. Evidently she didn't care who heard her. Sarah wondered why she'd been worried that Millie might endanger her job by sending letters about Drew. Obviously Millie herself had no such fears.

"Come on," she said, leading Sarah into a spacious sun-filled room. "Here we go."

Sarah glanced around at the beautifully appointed room, with its massive four-poster bed and hand-crafted furniture of bleached oak. A white eyelet spread covered the bed, with matching curtains fluttering at the windows. The hardwood floor gleamed to perfection, with only an occasional braided rug hiding its beauty. Sarah had never had a room like this, never even spent the night in one.

"Is this okay?" Millie asked.

Sarah turned and grinned at the older woman. "Are you kidding? It's beautiful."

Millie smiled broadly and moved to smooth an invisible wrinkle from the pristine bedspread. "It's always been one of my favorite rooms. A little feminine for the boys, and not quite fussy enough for Mrs. Colby.''

"It's perfect," Sarah assured her.

"Well," Millie said, "I'll let you get settled. The bathroom's in there." She nodded toward a closed door on the left side of the room. "There's fresh towels and everything you should need, but just holler if you want anything else."

A little overwhelmed, Sarah merely nodded.

Millie moved to leave, but stopped at the door and turned around. "I'm glad you're here, Sarah. That boy needs you."

The unexpected show of support almost broke Sarah's control, and she had to fight back the sudden swell of tears. Forcing a smile, she said, "Thanks, Millie."

Millie pressed her lips together, nodded and headed back down the stairs.

Sarah sat on the edge of the bed, letting her gaze drift around the room, taking a moment to enjoy its charm. She thought of Lyssa, three hundred miles away on the Wind River Reservation. She would love this room. Sarah missed her already.

Her thoughts drifted easily to the next few weeks and what she faced. She knew she could win Drew over. Children responded to her, and this boy was her son. She would get him caught up in schoolwork and figure out what was bothering him. Why he toyed with his health. She wasn't sure she could fix his problems, but she never doubted for a moment that she could determine the source.

It was Reece who worried her.

She couldn't pretend he didn't affect her. His presence would be a constant reminder of what they'd once shared and what she'd thrown away. Avoiding him would be next to impossible, but she knew that was exactly what she would do. *Had* to do, if she wanted to help her son and leave here with her heart still in one piece.

"So, you've finally gotten what you wanted."

Startled, Sarah turned at the sound of her ex-mother-in-law's voice. "Hello, Elizabeth."

"It's Mrs. Colby to you," Elizabeth said as she stepped into the room.

The eighteen-year-old Sarah would never have addressed the older woman as anything else. But Sarah was no longer eighteen. Rising from the bed, she asked, "And what exactly is it that I've always wanted?"

Elizabeth frowned. "To live at the Crooked C of course."

"Is that so?"

"Isn't it?"

"No." Sarah sighed and picked up her small suitcase, setting it on the bed. She'd hoped that she and her son's grandmother could at least have some peace between them. After all, Sarah had only come to help, not take Drew away. Evidently Elizabeth Colby wasn't buying it.

For several minutes neither spoke, and the silence hung heavily between them. Sarah started unpacking, arranging her things in the dresser, trying to ignore the other woman while breathing deeply to remain calm.

Then Elizabeth broke the silence in a venom-filled voice. "We had a deal."

Sarah faced her, keeping the image of Drew firmly in her mind. Her son needed her, and that thought alone gave her the strength to face whatever Elizabeth

Colby threw at her. "And I've kept my end of the deal for eleven years."

"There was no time limit."

Sarah refused to be intimidated. "My son needs me."

"Since when?"

"Since he began failing courses in school and missing meals." Anger replaced her earlier reserve. She'd left her son in this woman's care. "Since he started endangering his own life by ignoring his medical needs." Taking a step forward, she fought Elizabeth on her own terms, with the one weapon Sarah knew she possessed. "Since *you* let him down."

Her words struck home, and Elizabeth took a shaky step backward. "I never let him down. Who do you think you are to come in here and make accusations like that?"

Sarah sighed and turned back to her suitcase, her anger vanishing as quickly as it had surfaced. All she wanted was to be left in peace to work with Drew. "I'm not a threat to you, Elizabeth."

"How dare you!" the older woman said, outraged. "Where have *you* been the past eleven years while I raised your son?"

Sarah sighed. "Obviously not where I should have been."

DREW WATCHED the small white car head toward the house. He'd caught a brief glimpse of the woman inside as she passed the corral and thought she didn't look much like a schoolteacher. Not any he'd had, anyway. She was too young and pretty. Still, he reminded himself, he didn't need any dumb tutor.

"Pay attention here," Tod said.

Drew quickly shifted his attention back to the mare, soothing her with a touch. "Sorry."

"That the tutor your dad hired?"

Drew shrugged. "Guess so."

"I thought you met her yesterday."

"Yeah. Sort of." It had been neat meeting someone who'd known his mom. He'd had a million questions he'd wanted to ask. But that had been yesterday, before he'd known his dad had found out about summer school and all hell had broken loose.

"Seems to me either you met the woman or you didn't," Tod said, giving the mare a few final strokes of the brush.

"She didn't say she was a teacher."

"Oh." Tod dropped the brush and currycomb into the pail he used to carry grooming tools. Then picking up the bucket, he nodded toward the barn. "We're done here. Bring her on in."

Leading the mare, Drew followed Tod inside. "I just don't see why my dad had to go and bring some stranger here."

"Seems to me like you brought it on yourself. From what I hear, you scared that new summer-school teacher half to death."

Drew kicked at a stone. "It was just a couple of those dumb gag rattlesnake eggs."

"Women are funny about things like that."

"I guess."

Tod opened a stall door, and Drew led the mare inside, unhooked the lead rope and then slipped out. "But why do I need a tutor at all?"

"I don't think you need me to answer that," Tod said, closing and bolting the stall door.

"Dad doesn't want me to be held back."

"Do you blame him?" Tod headed for the tack room with Drew right behind him.

"He doesn't want to have a dummy as a son."

"You're no dummy, Drew. But my guess is your dad's worried about you."

"Could've fooled me."

Tod stopped and turned, crossing his arms. "Now what's that supposed to mean?"

"If he's so worried, how come he's never here?"

"The man's got responsibilities."

Drew rolled his eyes skyward. "Right."

Tod stood for a moment and then shook his head and continued on toward the tack room. Tod never went on about stuff. Drew could say whatever he wanted, and even when they disagreed, Tod never lectured or held it against him. Once he'd said his piece, he'd let it go. So the two of them fell into an easy silence as Drew helped put away the grooming tools. Sometimes Drew wished Tod were his dad.

"Her name's Miss Hanson," Drew said suddenly. "And she said she knew my mom."

"That so?" Tod kept on with his work.

"Think she'll tell me about her?"

"Don't know why not."

"My mom's dead, you know."

Tod's hand stilled in the process of returning the lead rope to its proper peg. "Yeah, Drew, I know. And I'm real sorry."

"Yeah, me, too."

REECE HAD MANAGED to stay away from the house for most of the afternoon. Who could blame him, he thought, with the morning he'd had? Things had started out bad and only gotten worse. At least Michelle had left first thing, so she didn't witness his family coming unraveled.

As he expected, his mother had been furious when he told her about Sarah tutoring Drew. She'd wanted to cancel her trip back East, but he wouldn't hear of it. He wanted her out of the house while Sarah worked with Drew. Elizabeth had argued and then cried—always her last resort when she didn't get her way. But in the end, there was no changing Reece's mind. So now he'd earned the silent treatment. Which was just fine with him.

Drew hadn't been much happier. Evidently he'd envisioned getting off scot-free, with no repercussions for failing two subjects and then getting kicked out of summer school. Reece corrected that misconception. Drew was to spend four hours a day on schoolwork. He, at least, had accepted his father's decision faster than his grandmother had. He'd skipped the arguing and crying stages and moved straight to sulking.

Leaving instructions with Millie to get Sarah settled when she arrived, Reece had headed out to check on some fencing that needed repair. Normally Tod would have had one of the hired hands take care of it, but Reece jumped at the chance to get away from the house.

Now he couldn't put it off any longer. Millie served dinner at six, and it was time for Reece to face them all. His indignant mother. His sulking son. And Sarah.

CHAPTER FIVE

BY THE TIME Sarah came downstairs, the other members of the household were already seated at the circular oak table at one end of the kitchen. Reece sat between Drew and Elizabeth, with Millie on the outside where she had easy access to the stove and refrigerator. Sarah hesitated in the doorway, knowing she wasn't exactly welcome. She considered turning around and heading back upstairs. She didn't have much of an appetite, anyway.

Spotting her in the doorway, Millie took that option away. "Don't just stand there, Sarah. Come on in and sit down."

Sarah entered the room, smiling tightly. "Where would you like me to sit?"

"Right here will be fine," Millie answered, motioning toward the empty seat beside her.

"Drew," Reece said, once Sarah had sat down, "you remember Miss Hanson from yesterday, don't you?"

Drew kept his eyes focused on his plate. "Yes, sir."

"And, Mother, you remember Sarah?"

"We talked this afternoon, Reece." Elizabeth smiled at her son, but Sarah could see it wasn't a particularly pleasant expression.

Millie passed Sarah a serving platter filled with fried chicken. "This looks wonderful," she said, grateful for something harmless to comment on. "It's been a long time since I've had home-cooked fried chicken."

"Oh," Elizabeth said. "Don't you cook?"

"Not like this." Sarah plastered a smile on her face. "That's how it is with us working women. By the time I get home in the evening, I seldom have time or energy to make an elaborate dinner."

"That's too bad, dear." Elizabeth managed to look sincerely concerned, but then brightened. "This should be a treat for you then. Staying at the Crooked C, that is. Millie's an excellent cook."

"Yes," Sarah said. "I'm sure she is."

They ate in silence for a few minutes. Still, Sarah felt the tension, thick enough to almost touch. She wondered how she was going to make it through six weeks of this, and hoped it would be better after Elizabeth left.

Reece made an obvious effort to relieve the strained atmosphere. "How did it go with Tod today, Drew?" he asked.

He got the patented twelve-year-old shrug. "Okay."

"I saw you with the mare when I drove in," Sarah said, trying to pull the boy out of himself. She glanced quickly at Reece and then back at Drew. "You handled her very well."

Drew nodded but didn't look up. He obviously wasn't any more thrilled about her being there than his grandmother was.

"My grandmother's people would say you have the gift."

Drew looked at her then, curiosity in his eyes. "Yeah? Are they Indians?"

"Yes. Shoshone. And they value those with the gift to communicate with animals."

This time he smiled, and Sarah lost her heart. He had a beautiful smile, so like his father's. Or at least, the way she remembered Reece's smile.

"Then you're Shoshone, too," Drew said.

"Only half," she answered. "My father was white."

Things would be okay between her and Drew, Sarah thought. Especially once they were alone, away from his father and grandmother.

"My son tells me you teach high school now," Elizabeth said, jumping into the conversation.

Sarah turned back to Elizabeth. "Yes. I teach in Oaksburg."

"Why, isn't that just wonderful. How in the world did you manage? To get your degree, that is?"

"Mother." Reece's voice held a definite warning.

She waved his warning away with a flick of her hand. "Don't be ridiculous, Reece. Sarah knows I didn't mean anything by that. It's just that when we knew her before... Excuse me, Sarah, for being a bit indelicate, but you were a little strapped for money." Elizabeth looked the picture of innocence. Sarah wondered how she managed it while sticking a knife in someone. It must be something you got better at with practice. "I'm just surprised you were able to get a college degree, that's all."

Sarah met her gaze. "It was tight, but with my grandmother's help, I managed."

"Well, that's wonderful. I do admire initiative."

I bet you do. But Sarah kept her thoughts to herself. She'd never quite mastered the art of subtly telling someone off. Either she said exactly what she meant or she kept her mouth shut. In this case, with Drew at the table, she thought it best to do the latter.

"Are you married, Miss Hanson?" Drew asked.

The question startled her, and Sarah glanced at Reece. He, too, looked a bit shaken. She turned back to Drew and tried to smile. "Not anymore," she said. "I was once. A long time ago."

"What happened? Did he die or something?" Again the insatiable curiosity of youth.

"Drew," Reece said, "you're being too personal. It's rude. Apologize."

Drew looked contrite. "I'm sorry."

"That's okay," Sarah said to Reece. Then she smiled softly at her son. "No, Drew. He didn't die." Again she glanced quickly at Reece and caught his mother's frown out of the corner of her eye. "We were very young. And it just didn't work out."

"Do you have any kids?"

"Really, Drew!"

"It's okay, Mrs. Colby. I don't mind." When in fact, she did mind. Even though she'd known that sooner or later this question would come up. That someone would ask if she had any children. She'd decided she couldn't lie. To deny Lyssa's existence would be to deny a piece of herself and create more suspicion if she was ever found out.

"Yes," Sarah said. "I have a daughter. Lyssa."

This time it was Reece's gaze that found hers. Only she couldn't make out the look in his eye. Did he know? Did he even suspect? *Oh, God,* she thought, *he can read my mind. He can see the truth.*

No!

She fought down the panic. There was no way he could know that Lyssa was his.

"Where is she?" Drew asked.

Sarah gratefully shifted her focus back to her son. Still, she felt Reece's eyes boring into her. But she refused to look at him or give in to the fear threatening her. "With my grandmother on the Wind River Reservation."

"Does she see her dad?"

Sarah shook her head. "No. She doesn't."

"Then she's kind of like me. She doesn't have a dad. And I don't have a mom."

REECE SKIRTED the bunkhouse and headed toward the barn to check on the stock. Technically it wasn't his job anymore. Tod always made sure the animals were taken care of. But tonight Reece needed the familiar routine. He missed the smell of hay and horses, the few moments spent with each animal, the doling out of apple pieces. He craved the solitude and the sounds of the horses settling in for the night. It seemed like he became less the rancher and more the politician every day. And he didn't like it.

Now, all these problems with Drew. And Sarah.

Dinner had been a disaster. To give her credit, Sarah had remained pleasant even during Elizabeth's verbal attacks. Then all of Drew's questions about husbands and children. Where that had come from, Reece hadn't a clue.

Then there was the one thing that poked at him like a burr under the saddle. Sarah had another child. A daughter. Who had fathered her, for God's sake? Was it the man Sarah had left him for? Had she run off on him like she had Reece? The whole thing made him want to drive his fist into the nearest wall. Then he realized what was happening. Sarah was getting to him. She'd been back less than twenty-four hours, and here he was ready to pound some man he'd never even met.

Forget it, he told himself forcefully. Forget his ex-wife. Forget her daughter. It was ancient history. What Sarah had done after she'd left him was none of his concern. He had more immediate problems to deal with. And tonight he'd sat there in the house that had been his father's and grandfather's before him and wondered what the hell had gone wrong.

No wonder he sought the company of horses tonight.

As he approached the barn, he saw that the Appaloosa was still out in the corral, so he headed that way. When he got closer, he realized he wasn't alone. Sarah stood on the bottom rail of the fence, her arm extended over the top, trying to coax the big horse over to her.

The Appaloosa hesitated, shaking his head and shying away. She persisted in a soft singsong voice, offering him a bit of apple in her outstretched hand. Finally, curiosity getting the best of him, the stallion approached her cautiously.

"You always did have a way with horses," Reece said quietly, so as not to startle either her or the animal.

Sarah reached up and stroked the Appaloosa's sleek neck. "He's a beauty."

"But temperamental." Reece closed the distance between them and settled one foot on the bottom rail of the fence.

"The best ones always are."

He caught the flash of her smile in the moonlight, and it reminded him of other, happier times. "Yeah, I remember that little mare of yours," he said. "What did you call her?"

"Whiplash. Whip, for short."

"Yeah, Whip." Reece grinned and shoved his hat to the back of his head. "You were the only one who could get near her."

Sarah laughed softly, and the sound trickled down his spine, stirring old memories. "Whip was a bit unpredictable, but worth the trouble. She was a born barrel racer." Sarah swiveled on the fence to look at him, and he caught the full impact of her smile. "Besides, I seem to remember a certain young bronc rider who liked them wild."

Reece winced at the memory. "A very young cowboy..."

"But very stubborn," she teased.

"And look where it got him. On his ass in the dust mostly."

"Oh, I don't know." He thought he could see the amusement in her eyes. Or maybe it, too, was just a memory. "I seem to remember him making it to the whistle a few times."

"Maybe once or twice..."

"And I seem to remember a silver buckle."

"Yeah, he gave it to some buckle chaser."

She laughed fully for the first time, and something akin to longing tightened in Reece's chest. How many years had it been since he'd heard her laugh, that deep wonderful sound that had once stolen his heart?

"Those were good times," he said before he could stop himself.

Sarah's smile faded and she stood there unmoving for a moment. Then she turned back to the Appaloosa, offering him another piece of the apple she'd produced from one of her pockets.

He couldn't let it go.

"Sarah," he said. "We *did* have some good times together."

After several moments of silence, she said, "Yes. There were many good times."

He let out the breath he hadn't known he'd held. He hadn't been crazy. Then or now. They'd been good together. If even for a very brief time. And, as he often had over the past eleven years, he wondered just where and when they'd gone wrong.

"Too bad," he said before he realized he'd spoken his thoughts aloud. Sarah glanced back at him, and he hesitated before probing at something that had always bothered him. Something they'd never had a chance to talk over.

"It's too bad you had to sell Whip. She would've taken you to the finals that year." Unlike Reece, who'd competed at the weekend rodeos strictly for fun, Sarah'd had an agenda. Maybe if things had been different . . .

After a moment of silence, she nodded. "That was my plan."

Her goal had been the year-end finals and enough money to pay her first year of tuition at the University of Wyoming. She'd been good enough. And so had the horse. Then she'd met him. And the next thing they knew, she'd been pregnant with Drew.

"I don't regret selling Whip, Reece," she said at last. "It's true she was a great horse, but . . ."

"But?"

"She was just a horse. She wasn't . . ." She let her voice trail off and turned back to the Appaloosa.

"She wasn't what, Sarah?"

She didn't answer but let his question linger in the darkness between them. He couldn't have said why suddenly he desperately wanted to hear what she hadn't said yet. "Sarah," he prodded.

"Whip, the year-end finals, even college. None of it was as important as the baby. Our baby." She turned back to face him. "I never regretted Drew."

For just a moment he believed her. She was the girl he'd known and loved, the woman he'd wanted her to become. Now here they were together, sharing memories and the warm summer night. She was within reach, her long dark hair catching fragments of moonlight, her eyes shining with emotions that found their way to his heart. One step and she'd be in his arms. He'd pull her from the fence and hold her lithe slender body close to his. And never let go. She had loved him and their son and had never walked out on either of them.

Then reality returned full force, making him wish he'd never pushed her for an answer. He took an involuntary step backward, distancing himself from his momentary aberration. The woman standing on the fence in front of him wasn't his wife, and she'd never really cared for either him or Drew. Otherwise, how could she have left?

No. He wouldn't walk down that road again.

He'd trusted her once, and she'd torn out his heart and thrown it to the wolves. Now, here she was eleven years later telling him how much she'd wanted her baby. Her regret was just too convenient.

Sarah watched the play of emotions on Reece's face, and in the end she saw him once again harden against her. For a few minutes it had been like old times. They'd talked and laughed together, without throwing hurtful accusations at each other. But it had passed quickly. He thought this was another ruse. Another means for her to gain his sympathy.

She could hardly blame him. She'd given him every reason not to trust her.

Without warning, he changed the subject. "Have you had a chance to look over Drew's work?"

She gave the Appaloosa one final pat and climbed down from the fence. Then wished she hadn't. She'd forgotten about Reece's height, how he towered over her. Taking a step away from him, she answered his question. "We spent about an hour together after dinner."

"And?" He, too, took a step back, further distancing himself from her. She tried not to let it bother her. But it did.

"Drew is going to continue working with Tod in the mornings and then spend the afternoons on his schoolwork." She shrugged. "We'll just have to see how it goes."

"What about getting him into seventh grade in the fall?"

"I talked to his summer-school teacher, Miss Adams, before I came out here today. She's willing to give him a test the first week of August." She rubbed her arms. The air had turned chilly. "But I can't promise anything. He's behind. Probably more from lack of interest than ability. And he's not crazy about having a tutor."

Reece frowned, his frustration obvious. "I know. But if he gives you any trouble—"

"Reece, please." She reached out and laid her hand on his arm. "Let me handle it." He glanced down at her hand, and she quickly pulled it away. "Please," she repeated. And then, trying to lighten the mood, she added, "I deal with unruly teenagers all year long. I think I can handle one slightly disgruntled twelve-year-old."

Reece didn't answer immediately, and for a moment his expression gentled. Then the softness disappeared. "Okay," he said curtly. "We'll do it your way."

"Thanks." Giving him a tight smile, she turned toward the house. "Well, I think I'll head on up to bed now. Tomorrow's going to be a long day."

Reece nodded and touched the tip of his hat. "Night, then."

"Good night."

Sarah started to walk away but stopped when he said, "Sarah, wait." She looked back and saw he'd shoved his hands into the pockets of his jeans. "About the way Elizabeth acted tonight—"

"It's okay, Reece," she said, cutting him off. "She has her reasons."

"No, it's not okay." He moved toward her, and again she was uncomfortably aware of his size. She suppressed the urge to back away. "But she's leaving tomorrow for Boston. It should be easier on you here with her gone."

Sarah bit her bottom lip and nodded, oddly touched. "Thank you."

"One other thing." He hesitated for several moments before saying, "I'm sorry about last night. About the things I said."

Caught off guard, she didn't know what to say. It was one thing for Reece to apologize for his mother. Quite another for him to apologize for his own actions.

"Despite everything that happened between us," he continued, "I didn't ask you here to hurt you. Drew needs help, and I..." He yanked off his hat and ran a hand through his thick blond hair before repositioning it on his head. "It's just that... to tell Drew the truth now, about you, well, it might do more harm than good. I just wish... Well, anyway, I'm sorry."

Sarah stood, unable to move or speak. The silence stretched out between them. It occurred to her that there might be a chance for them, a slim possibility that they could at least be friends. After all, they had a son who needed them both.

Just before she turned and hurried toward the house, she almost told him that a certain buckle chaser still had that young cowboy's silver buckle.

LATER, IN THE SILENCE of her dark room, Sarah was glad she'd suppressed the urge to tell Reece about the buckle. He wouldn't have believed her, and she'd already opened herself to enough pain and humiliation.

She'd gone outside after that hour with Drew to get some fresh air and relief from the tension in the house. It had been a long time since she'd been surrounded by so much hostility. She might have thought she'd found Drew's problem, except that she knew that the friction was largely due to *her* presence. Neither Elizabeth nor Drew wanted Sarah here. And Lord knew, Reece didn't want her around. She'd begun to wonder why she just didn't get into her car and head home. To Lyssa and her grandmother.

Outside Sarah had managed to get hold of herself again, to remember why she was here. The peace and solitude in the falling dusk had worked wonders to restore her reason. She wasn't going to run away from this. Elizabeth would be gone the next day, and Drew was Sarah's reason for being here.

Then Reece had joined her.

With his first words, he'd resurrected memories and feelings she'd fought long and hard to forget. Not that she'd ever totally succeeded. But she'd managed to relegate Reece Colby to a place in her heart where she seldom went anymore. Now that he'd reopened that door, she knew her thoughts of him wouldn't be so easily contained again. Especially with him so close by, reminding her every time she saw him of what they'd once been to each other. And what a fool she'd been to walk away.

She stood by the window, looking out at the yard. The waxing moon illuminated the barn and bunkhouse, like dark sentinels against the night sky. Her gaze roamed to the corral, where she could see the Appaloosa still pacing. And Reece was still there, standing near the fence, as restless and distrustful as the stallion.

She watched Reece, who, with his broad shoulders and easy cowboy grace, still had the power to send her heart racing. For a few minutes, he leaned against the top railing, before shoving himself away to walk the length of the corral.

What was he thinking?

Were his thoughts of her? Of other nights like this when they'd been together? Of one night in particular, his eighteenth birthday, when they'd first made love in a barn not unlike the one down there? Something inside her, in the deepest most feminine part of her, tightened at the memory. Then almost as quickly she shoved the thought aside, dismissing it as romantic foolishness. No doubt Reece was thinking of how she'd once betrayed him. *If* he thought of her at all.

Loneliness wrapped itself around her in the dark quiet room. She wished Lyssa was here. Caring for her daughter all these years had managed to hold Sarah's loneliness at bay. Even when she'd first left Reece and Drew, only the thought of her unborn child had kept her sane. Now, her daughter, her lifeline, was three hundred miles away, and Sarah desperately needed to hear her voice.

She turned away from the window to undress. She should try to sleep. Yet the room that had seemed so perfect earlier now loomed large and empty, and she knew it would be hours before sleep found her. And once again, she ended up back at the window, watching.

Reece. The only man she'd ever loved.

No, it wouldn't have done for her to tell him about the buckle. It was a piece of him she still held, hidden away, to remind her of the boy who'd stolen her heart long ago. And the man who would never be hers.

IT SEEMED to Sarah that she had just fallen asleep when the household began to stir, waking her. It was still dark outside, but she knew Reece planned to drive his mother to the Casper airport this morning, and they needed to get an early start. She considered getting up, but decided against it. Most likely she'd be in the way, and besides, she didn't relish the prospect of another confrontation with Elizabeth Colby.

So Sarah stayed in bed, thinking about what Millie had told her about Elizabeth's trip. Evidently she spent every summer in Boston. She'd grown up there and still maintained her family's home. She went to shop, see relatives and friends and get a taste of the civilized East after being stuck on a Wyoming ranch for the rest of the year. At least that was what Millie had said. And if it was true, Sarah wondered why Reece's mother bothered coming back.

Slowly Sarah became aware of the day starting. She could hear Millie in the kitchen. And Reece—it could be no one else—making trips from Elizabeth's room, down the stairs and outside. She imagined him carrying suitcases and loading them in the trunk of his car. Once she thought she heard Drew, but then someone hushed him. But mostly, there was the low hum of voices, both masculine and feminine.

Sarah smiled.

It was a pleasant feeling, waking up to a household of people. Something she'd never experienced before. But, she reminded herself quickly, it wasn't something she needed to get used to. Her time here was short.

Later, after she heard Reece's car pull away, she went downstairs. She found Millie in the kitchen, but Drew had already gone down to the barn. Apparently she'd have to get up early if she planned to see him in the morning.

When she'd finished eating, Sarah offered to help Millie clean up, but was shooed out of the kitchen. So Sarah retreated to the living room, looking for something to read on the bookshelves she'd seen lining one wall. She had three hours before Drew finished his chores. Three hours until she started her first day as her son's tutor.

"EXCUSE ME, Miss Hanson."

Startled, Sarah sat bolt upright in the chair, her heart pounding. "Drew. I didn't hear you come in."

He shoved his hands into his pockets. "Sorry to wake you."

"No, I . . ." she began, and then smiled sheepishly. Evidently she'd been more tired than she'd realized. Yesterday had been a difficult day, followed by a long sleepless night. "I was waiting for you to finish your chores. And I guess I must have nodded off."

"No one around here sleeps during the day."

"Neither do I usually," she said. "But sometimes it takes me a couple of nights to get used to a strange bed."

He shrugged. "Millie said to tell you lunch is ready."

"Good. I'm hungry."

Drew gave her a half smile and started to back toward the door. "I gotta go upstairs and get cleaned up."

"I'll walk up with you."

She followed him upstairs to put her book away, but stopped short just inside her room. A pair of eggs nestled in the middle of her bed, rattling suspiciously.

"Watch out, Miss Hanson," Drew said from behind her. "Those are rattlesnake eggs. And they look ready to hatch."

"Oh my." She inched over to the bed. "I wonder how they got here." Very gently she reached down and scooped the two eggs into her hands. "I just love snakes."

"You do?"

"Didn't you know?" She stroked the eggs as if they were pets, while trying to conceal her smile. "Long ago the Shoshone were known to other tribes as

Snakes or Rattlesnakes." She gave Drew her most sincere expression. "On the reservation, we're taught from the time we're children how to communicate with them. They're considered sacred."

He looked skeptical. "Really?"

She paused for a moment and then smiled sweetly. "What's the matter, Drew? Haven't you ever seen someone trying to hatch rattlesnake eggs before?"

She saw in his eyes the moment he realized she'd turned his trick back on him. "You know rattlesnakes don't lay eggs," he said.

"You're right." She tossed the fake eggs at him one at a time, and he caught them deftly. "And that'll teach you to try and trick me the way you did your summer-school teacher. I was born and raised in Wyoming, and you'll have to do a lot better than fake rattlesnake eggs to scare me."

Drew grinned. "So is any of that true? About the Shoshones, I mean?"

"Only the part about them being known as Snakes or Rattlesnakes to other tribes," she said, dropping her book on the nightstand. "I made the rest up."

Drew rolled his eyes.

"Go on now. Get cleaned up."

He started to leave the room, but stopped at the door. "You're not mad, are you?"

Sarah smiled and shook her head. "No, Drew. I'm not mad."

"Great." He grinned and scurried off down the hall.

Sarah laughed lightly, thinking how boys never changed. They all had to test you. Well, she'd just passed test number one.

Instead of heading downstairs, Sarah lingered, waiting for Drew to return. When he emerged from the bathroom a few minutes later, she had to smile at his halfhearted stab at cleaning up. He was all boy, from the grime under his chin, with an occasional clean streak on his neck where the water had dribbled, to the dirt under his fingernails.

She wanted nothing more than to pull him into her arms. The way she would have done with Lyssa, without giving it a second thought.

Instead, she fell into step beside him. "I've got an idea," she said. "How about if we work outside today?"

"You mean schoolwork?"

She rested her hand on his shoulder and stopped him at the top of the stairs. "Sometimes I think better outside. How about you?"

"Don't know. Never thought about it."

"You must have a favorite spot away from the ranch buildings. Someplace cool. We could ride out and work there."

"Well, there is a place a couple of miles toward the hills. There's trees and a small creek . . ." Shrugging, he let his voice trail off.

"Sounds perfect."

"But what about . . ." He dropped his gaze to his feet, and Sarah ached for him. "I got to eat in the afternoon."

"No problem." She again resisted the urge to put her arms around him. "We'll take something with us. What do you say?"

He still hesitated. "I don't know."

"Come on." She gave his shoulder a quick squeeze before releasing him and starting down the stairs. "I know you're good with horses."

"Yeah."

"So, what's the problem?"

"Are you sure my dad won't mind?"

"I'll take full responsibility."

"What are you two cooking up?" Millie asked as they arrived in the kitchen.

Sarah smiled, knowing she could count on Millie to back her up. "I thought since this is our first day working together, we should do it outside. Drew knows the perfect place."

"Sounds good to me," Millie stated.

And it was settled.

They ate lunch, just the three of them. Drew remained a bit distant, but the atmosphere was much better than it had been the night before. Sarah was confident she'd be able to get through to her son. Afterward, Millie put together an afternoon snack, while Sarah went upstairs to change into jeans and pack up the books they'd need.

Then she followed Drew down to the barn.

No one else was around, and Drew began readying the horses. As she watched his smooth confidence while working with the animals, it struck her again that this nearly grown child was the infant she'd left behind eleven years ago. It was an odd and unsettling sensation.

IT WAS A PERFECT summer day as they left the ranch behind and headed east toward the Black Hills. They rode along in companionable silence for a while, and

Sarah felt good for the first time since she'd arrived here two days earlier.

"Do you ride out here often?" she asked.

"Sometimes."

The land rolled away from them in wave after wave of flowing grasses. The distant Black Hills, carpeted in dark green ponderosa pine, beckoned to them.

"Paha Sapa," Sarah said, using the name the Shoshone's neighbors, the Sioux, had given it. "The hills that are black. I've always heard they were beautiful."

"You've never been here before?"

Sarah glanced at him, thinking of the one time Reece had brought her to his home. She hadn't come to see the surrounding beauty. They'd seen only each other. And then his parents had kicked them off the ranch. "Only once, and never this close to the hills."

"Where did you meet my dad?" Drew asked.

"At a weekend rodeo in Riverton."

"Were you competing?"

"Sure was." Sarah shifted sideways in her saddle to get a better look at her son. "I owned the fastest barrel racer in the state. And your dad, boy, he could ride a bronc like—"

"No way."

Sarah laughed. "Sure. Didn't he ever tell you?"

"Dad riding in a rodeo?" Drew shook his head, obviously not sure whether to believe her. "I'd like to see that."

"Well, you should have. He was good. He competed in both the saddle and bareback events. But calf roping was where he excelled."

"Yeah?"

"I can't believe he never told you. He even won a silver buckle once."

That silenced Drew. Sarah watched as he digested the information, obviously trying to reconcile this new image of his father. It made her wonder just what was going on with Reece and their son. How come this was all such a surprise to Drew?

"I'm sure he'd tell you about it if you asked," she said.

Drew looked doubtful. "How come he quit?"

"It was just weekend rodeo." Sarah shrugged. Reece had never been serious about it. "We had a lot of fun. But I guess other things became more important."

"Like?" Drew sounded as if he couldn't believe anything could be more important than riding in a rodeo.

"Well, like school..."

Drew groaned.

Sarah turned to him and smiled. "And raising a son."

"What about my mom? Did you meet her there, too?"

Sarah's heart skipped a beat, and she had to grab the saddle horn for a moment to keep her seat. She should have seen this coming. She'd known that sooner or later he'd ask about his mother again. After all, it had been one of the first things out of his mouth the day she'd met him.

"Miss Hanson? Are you okay?"

Sarah took a deep breath and nodded. The boy was too observant. "I'm fine." What was she supposed to say? How could she answer him without lying? They'd ridden up under a row of cottonwoods that lined a small creek and halted the horses. "This it?" she asked.

"Yeah. Are you sure you're okay?"

"Yes, I'm fine. But we better get to work." Sarah slid off her horse.

Drew followed suit, taking both horses and hobbling them so they wouldn't run off. "Can you tell me about my mom first?"

Who was she kidding? There was no way she could answer him without lying. Just being here with him without telling him the truth was a lie. "There's not much to tell," she said, her untruthful words lodging in her throat. "I didn't know her that well. Come on, we better get to work now."

To her surprise, Drew let it go. And although she was grateful for the small reprieve, it both hurt and angered her. Evidently Drew's questions about his mother had been put off before, and he'd grown used to it.

After that, the afternoon passed quickly.

Working with Drew turned out to be a pleasure. He had a quick mind and grasped concepts easily—when she could get him to pay attention. Schoolwork wasn't high on his priority list, and she spent a good portion of the time reining him in. There were any number of things he'd rather talk about, and she was kept on her toes all afternoon bringing him back to his studies. But by the time they'd remounted their horses and were headed toward the ranch, she felt they'd made good progress for the first day. It would get better. He'd opened up to her and begun to trust.

That was what she'd wanted.

Yet her stomach churned and her head ached. And all the way back to the ranch, as Drew chattered nonstop, a tiny voice in the back of her head whispered one word, over and over again.

Liar.

CHAPTER SIX

REECE WAS SURE he'd broken several speed records getting back to the Crooked C. He'd driven his mother to the airport in Casper and then headed home as quickly as possible. Not only did he want to check on Sarah and Drew, see how their first day together went, but he didn't want to leave them alone for too long. Yet he couldn't have said exactly why that particular thought bothered him so much.

He blamed it on lack of sleep.

It had been two days since he'd gotten any. Three if he counted the evening Drew had managed to get himself thrown from the Appaloosa. But it had been two long sleepless nights since Sarah had walked back into their lives.

Last night, after Sarah had returned to the house, he'd stayed out for another hour or so, knowing that going straight to bed would be useless. Finally he'd thought himself tired enough to pass out on his feet. He'd been wrong. Once in bed, he'd tossed and turned, only falling into a light restless slumber a couple of hours before dawn. And his unsettled thoughts had continued as he and Elizabeth drove the two hundred silent miles to Casper.

Somehow he needed to come to terms with Sarah's once again being a part of his life. Even if only for a short time.

Last night he'd almost fallen into the trap of old memories. For a while, he'd been carried back to when they'd first met. He'd remembered what it had been like between them. How much they'd loved each other. But it had been a lie, the memories false. Sarah had never really loved him. And he couldn't allow himself to forget that.

Still, he needed her help now. For Drew. Someone had to get through to the boy, and he wanted to believe Sarah could do it. If for no other reasons than she was used to dealing with kids and he was her son.

In the end, Reece fell back on his original plan. He'd hired Sarah to tutor Drew for the summer. And that was exactly how he'd treat her. Like an employee. Like Millie or Tod.

It seemed a good idea until he arrived back at the ranch a little after five, only to find Sarah and Drew weren't there. According to Millie, they'd ridden off right after lunch. A half-dozen possibilities raced through his head. Everything from Sarah's having taken Drew and run, to her spending time trying to win the boy's favor, instead of teaching him sixth-grade math and English. Reece admitted that the latter option was probably closer to the truth, but it didn't lessen his anger.

He'd hired her to tutor his son. Not to become Drew's best friend. Or his mother.

Reece was in the barn helping Tod feed the horses, when Sarah and Drew got back. The sound of her laughter and Drew's chatter stoked Reece's simmering anger. He went outside to meet them.

"Hey, Dad," Drew called as he slid from his horse. "You won't believe what we did today."

Reece checked his temper. This wasn't the boy's fault. "I'm sure Miss Hanson will explain it to me."

"We went down to the creek," Drew continued, oblivious to his father's displeasure. "And Miss Hanson told me all about how you used to compete in the weekend rodeo."

Reece looked up at Sarah, who still sat on her horse, wondering what else she'd told Drew. She'd obviously won him over. "Did she?"

"Yeah." Drew hardly stopped for a breath. "She said you used to be a bronc rider. She said you were real good, too."

"Go on up to the house and get cleaned up, Drew," Reece said, without taking his eyes off Sarah. "Millie will have dinner ready in about an hour."

"But Dad . . ." Drew's plea brought Reece's attention back to him. "I need to take care of my horse."

"Go, on," Reece said. "Tod will take care of the horses. I need to speak to Miss Hanson alone."

Drew hesitated and glanced back at Sarah, who dismounted and nodded her agreement. His looking to her for confirmation infuriated Reece further. Who did she think she was? She couldn't just walk back into his son's life and take over.

But Reece managed to wait until Drew was almost at the house before turning again to Sarah. "What the hell do you think you're doing?" He kept his voice low, although he no longer made any attempt to disguise his anger.

Sarah straightened and met his gaze. "I haven't the faintest idea what you're talking about." Leading her horse, she started to walk past him.

Reece grabbed the bridle, stopping them both. "Don't play coy with me, Sarah."

"Are you sure you want to discuss this here?"

He took a step closer, backing her against the horse's neck. "I want an explanation. Now."

"Drew and I rode out—"

"I know what you did. I want to know why. You're supposed to be tutoring him in math and English. Not the fine points of weekend rodeo."

"Do you want an explanation, Reece?" Crossing her arms, she lifted her chin. "Or do you just want to stand there and throw your weight around?"

He'd forgotten this about her. Her stubbornness when cornered. The way her dark eyes glittered like black diamonds. But he couldn't allow memories to sidetrack him. "I want to know why you weren't inside working with that boy today."

"That boy's name is Drew." She took a step forward, jabbing a finger at his chest. "And we got more accomplished this afternoon than I could have hoped to get done in a week locked away in the house."

"Oh, I'm sure you did."

"I don't have to take this," she said, pushing by him.

"Oh, I think you do." He grabbed her arm and spun her around. "You're just an employee around here, Sarah. I *hired* you to teach *my son* math and English. And don't you forget it."

"Believe me, Reece—" she jerked her arm from his grip "—I wouldn't dream of forgetting my place."

She stormed off, leaving him holding the reins of her horse. He watched her go, carrying herself as straight and proud as ever, and cursed the day he'd met her.

A sound behind him caught his attention, and he turned to see Tod unsaddling Drew's horse. Reece had forgotten all about the other man being there.

"Did you say something?" he snapped at Tod.

"Not me, boss."

Reece glared at his friend's sarcasm and then turned back around just in time to see Sarah disappearing into the house. "Damn," he said, shoving his fists into the pockets of his jeans.

WALKING BACK to the house, Sarah couldn't remember ever having been this angry. She'd proved herself to be a good teacher years ago and wasn't used to being questioned. Some of her methods were rather unorthodox, but she got results. She had a track record for turning difficult students around after other teachers had failed. And it had been a long time since anyone, parent or school administrator, had questioned her.

She slammed into the kitchen and stopped short when she noticed Millie standing there. "Problems?" the cook asked.

"I can't believe the nerve of that man," Sarah answered before she could stop herself. "Just who does he think he is?"

Millie grinned. "I told you this place needed stirring up."

"Please, Millie." Sarah glared at the other woman. "This isn't a joke."

"So who's laughing?" Millie turned back to the stove.

Sarah paced to the far side of the kitchen and then spun on her heel and paced back. "He hasn't the faintest idea how to relate to Drew," she said, keeping her voice low so it couldn't be heard upstairs. "Reece doesn't even talk to Drew. He talks *at* him. Ordering him around like one of the hands."

Millie mumbled something under her breath, and Sarah shot her another murderous glance. Millie was not helping things, but Sarah was on a roll and needed to get it off her chest.

"He doesn't even use Drew's name." The sound of Reece calling their son "the boy" echoed through her head, fueling her anger. "Do you know that Drew had no idea his father used to ride in the rodeo? Can you imagine? The way Drew loves horses!" She shook her head in disgust and continued her pacing. "And Reece has the nerve to question my methods. To imply that I have ulterior motives."

"It seems to me," Millie said, "you've got your work cut out for you."

Sarah stopped in midstride. "What do you mean?"

"Reece needs to learn how to be a father."

"That's for sure." Sarah let out a snort of disgust. "So show him."

"Well, if he hasn't figured it out by now..." She let her voice trail off as she realized what Millie meant. "You don't expect *me* to show him, do you? I'm the last person he'll listen to."

Millie shrugged and again concentrated on cooking dinner. "Maybe not. But you won't know until you try."

As Sarah stood watching the other woman, her anger faded. Maybe Millie had a point. Maybe instead of squaring off with Reece, which had been her first reaction, she should show him what Drew had accomplished today. It was a simple solution, one she would have used with any of her other students' parents. But she'd been so angry, so tied up in her reaction to Reece, to his doubting her and, she had to admit, her own guilt about lying to Drew that she'd let her emotions rule her head.

Reece needed to know what she and Drew were doing. It was that simple. And if her idea worked, he'd begin to understand and relate to their son at the same time.

"Thanks, Millie," she said, as she headed for the stairs. "I think you may be on to something."

REECE HAD THOUGHT he'd learned his lesson about trusting Sarah a long time ago. Obviously he'd been mistaken. Otherwise why would he have brought her to the Crooked C to tutor Drew? He'd been asking for trouble, and as he should have expected, she'd delivered.

He pulled off his hat and ran a tired hand through his hair before entering the dark silent kitchen. Dinner had been over hours ago. Earlier he'd sent word back to the house that he was helping Tod with the stock and would eat with the other men. In truth, he hadn't trusted himself to sit across the table from his ex-wife without throttling her.

As it turned out, the physical labor had been just what he needed. A few hours doing what he'd been born and bred to do. Ranching.

Since his father's death eight years ago, working and eating with the ranch hands had been a way of life for Reece. His mother's rigid schedule didn't allow for the running of a place the size of the Crooked C. So he'd never even tried to make it back to the house for meals. Everything had changed, however, when he'd started his campaign and handed over the operation of the ranch to Tod.

Tonight had not only been a good reminder of what he'd given up, but it had clarified a few things in his mind. Mainly, how to handle Sarah.

He crossed the kitchen, opened the refrigerator and pulled a beer from the cool interior. Then he headed for his office.

There was no getting around it. He'd created this mess, and he was stuck with it. She was here now. Telling her to leave was out of the question. Drew needed a tutor, and whether Reece liked it or not, Sarah was both available and qualified. So until he found someone else, he'd just have to make sure she did the job he'd hired her to do. Which meant he needed to call Michelle and cancel whatever plans they had for the campaign.

Picking up the phone, he dialed her number.

A familiar soft voice answered. "Hello."

"Michelle, it's Reece."

"How did it go?"

He hesitated, unsure what she meant.

"Drew's first day with Sarah," she prompted.

"Oh." He took a deep breath and sank into the chair behind his desk. "Not good."

She said nothing, and it disturbed him. He knew that she wasn't crazy about the arrangement, but her silence hinted at all-out disapproval. It was unlike her. She was a peacekeeper.

"I need out of whatever we've got coming up with the campaign for the next couple of weeks," he said, despite his misgivings.

Again she answered him with silence.

There was more here than he was seeing, more than just her discomfort about having Sarah live in his house. He wondered if Michelle would tell him what was really bothering her if he asked. Did he want to hear the answer? Now, when his entire focus needed to be on Sarah and Drew?

"Michelle?" he prodded.

"I'm here." She paused for a moment and then said, "I'm not sure how you expect me to respond. You can't just drop out of a campaign like this at the beginning and expect to remain in the running."

"I need time with Drew."

"And Sarah?"

The question startled him. But then, everything about this conversation had been awkward: Michelle's voice, what she'd said, what she hadn't said. "This has nothing to do with Sarah, except to make sure she's doing the job I hired her for." But he knew that wasn't entirely true. Sarah had walked back into his life two days ago and invaded his thoughts, his dreams . . .

"I don't understand, Reece," Michelle said, exasperation obvious in her normally sedate voice. "Do you want this office or not?"

Several heartbeats later, he answered, "To be honest, I don't know."

This time the silence hung long and heavy between them, and Reece had no further words to breach it.

Instead, Michelle shattered it. "Well, you call me if and *when* you figure it out."

The line went dead. Stunned, he returned the receiver to the cradle, hesitating for a moment with his hand resting on the smooth plastic. He should call her back. Apologize. Tell her to forget he'd ever called.

Then he remembered Drew's laughter this afternoon and his excitement when he'd asked about the rodeo. Sarah, not Reece, had put that normal childhood enthusiasm in his son's voice. And it bothered Reece. Just as his own response to her did. Even now, his body reacted to the thought of her, to the memory of her flashing dark brown eyes and the stubborn set of her mouth.

Closing his eyes, he leaned back and rested his head against the back of the chair. Sarah still had the power to stir him in ways no other woman ever had. And because of it, he wouldn't call Michelle back. There was too much at stake, too much to resolve. And he needed a little time.

Just then there was a single knock on his study door. He opened his eyes to see the object of his concern standing in the doorway.

"Do you have a moment?" Sarah asked. "I have something to show you."

Reece sat a little straighter. She'd taken a shower and changed into a full calf-length floral skirt and top. It was one of the changes in her he liked best—her tendency to wear soft feminine clothing, rather than the jeans and boots of her youth. "Come in."

She crossed the room and stopped in front of his desk. "Were you sleeping?"

He shook his head, wishing sleep would come that easily. "No."

"I see." She seemed uncomfortable, standing there clutching a couple of books to her chest.

"Would you like to sit down?" he said.

"No. This will only take a minute."

"Okay, then."

"Before leaving town yesterday," she said, "I went to see Rebecca Adams, Drew's summer-school teacher."

Reece nodded, suddenly feeling a bit wary.

"I needed to find out where to start with him," she said while placing two mimeographed sheets of paper before him. "Miss Adams gave me these. They're the County School District Portfolio Checklists for sixth graders. In other words, these are the areas that Drew needs to master before being promoted to seventh grade."

Reece glanced at the sheets. One was the checklist for language arts and the other for mathematics. Both bore Drew's name and then a list of topics, many of which had a checkmark beside them. It didn't mean a thing to him, and he still couldn't guess what she was getting at.

"As you can see," she said, "Miss Adams has checked off about three-quarters of the items on each list. The others are areas where Drew needs work."

He looked up at her. "Sarah, I don't understand what this has to do with me."

"I thought you should know what Drew and I are working on," she replied. "These are the topics I'll be concentrating on with Drew as defined by the county." She took a step back and crossed her arms. He tried to ignore the way the simple motion tightened the thin cotton cloth across her breasts.

Yanking his eyes and thoughts away from such wayward notions, he picked up the papers. "This is all very interesting but unnecessary."

"You were concerned I was wasting my time with Drew, and you have every right to be. You're his father and you want him to get into seventh grade." She smiled, and he couldn't believe she was actually agreeing with him about this. "So I think the best plan is for Drew to keep you up-to-date."

"Drew?" He wasn't sure he'd heard her right.

"It'll be good for both of you." She stepped forward and retrieved the papers he held out. "Every night after he finishes the homework I've given him, he'll come down and show you the work he's done that day. You can even check it for him if you want."

"Check it?"

She nodded. "It will help both of you know where he stands." She started for the door and then stopped, partially turned and gave him a smile. "And it will make it easier for you to keep tabs on us."

Reece settled back in his chair and watched her go.

He wasn't sure what game she was playing, but he knew a hidden agenda when he saw one. This wasn't about keeping him informed about Drew's progress. No, sir. She was up to something. And he was just going to have to keep his eyes on her until he figured out what.

FRIDAY AFTERNOON, Sarah climbed into her car and headed southwest toward the Wind River Reservation. It had been a long trying week, and she was glad it was over. She needed a couple of days to regroup. And she needed to see her daughter.

She missed Lyssa terribly. They'd never been separated for more than a day or two, and Sarah wasn't sure how either of them was going to deal with an entire summer apart. She hadn't realized how much she depended on her daughter. Caring for Lyssa had held Sarah together those first years after she'd left Reece and Drew. Now, eleven years later, Lyssa remained Sarah's lifeline, the one thing she'd done right.

She couldn't say the same for Drew.

She'd hurt him, and he didn't even realize it. Each day spent with him was equal parts ecstasy and anguish as she struggled with the realities of what she'd done to him. He was her son, yet beyond her reach. She wanted to hold him and comfort him. She wanted to tell him that his mother was alive and loved him. That she had always loved him. Yet she couldn't tell him anything, couldn't offer him anything. She would have liked to blame Reece, but in all honesty, she knew that she alone had created their current situation. And it wore at her, chipping away larger and larger pieces of her heart with each passing day.

Then there was Reece himself, who made everything more difficult. He didn't join her again when she made her nightly trips down to visit the Appaloosa, nor were there any more confrontations. But he was always around. He'd show up unannounced while Sarah and Drew worked, sit listening for a few minutes and then leave again without a word. He watched her, she knew, and it was enough to drive her crazy. She consoled herself that at least he'd taken to eating with the other men, so dinner with Millie and Drew each night was somewhat of a reprieve.

But even when he wasn't around, she couldn't ignore his presence. Thoughts of him hovered at the edge of her awareness, disturbing her on more levels than she could count. So it was good for her to put some distance between them—if only for a couple of days.

She didn't stop in Oaksburg. Instead she headed straight for the reservation. Pulling into the yard in front of her grandmother's ramshackle house felt like coming home, and Sarah breathed a sigh of relief. Lyssa wasn't anywhere to be seen, but Tuwa sat in her old porch chair.

Sarah got out of the car, hurried over and gave the old woman a big hug. "It's so good to see you, Grandmother. I've missed you and Lyssa so much."

Tuwa smiled and patted Sarah's hand. "It's good to be missed."

Sarah kissed her on the cheek and then pulled back slightly. "Where's Lyssa?" she asked.

"She's with Joseph Bright Eagle." Tuwa gestured in the direction of the nearest ranch. "Working with the horses."

Sarah couldn't hide her disappointment. "I should have called and let you know I was coming." Releasing her grandmother, she settled on the top porch step.

"She'll be back soon."

"I know." Sarah smiled tightly. "I'm just anxious to see her."

"She misses you, too. But maybe not so much."

Sarah laughed lightly, knowing her grandmother was probably right. Children seldom missed their parents as much as the other way around.

"Tell me about your son," Tuwa said.

Sarah brightened instantly. "He's a wonderful boy, quiet and thoughtful, but with a quick mind. And he's strong, Grandmother, despite his illness."

"That's good."

"Oh, and you should see him work with the horses." With an even broader smile, Sarah pulled up her knees and wrapped her arms around them. "He has a gift. Like Lyssa."

"And his mother."

Sarah grinned at the compliment.

"You like this child," Tuwa said.

It was an odd statement, and Sarah shook her head, not understanding. "He's my son. Of course I love him." Then she realized what Tuwa meant. Sarah had loved her son from the moment she'd first learned of his existence. But now she'd found that she *liked* him, as well. The child she'd known only through pictures and an occasional letter was truly captivating. And Tuwa had sensed these new feelings in Sarah.

"Despite his illness, he's everything I could ask for in a son," she said, thinking how much she enjoyed being with him. "I'm very proud of him." *If only I could be his mother.* The thought caught her unawares, darkening her mood.

"What is it?" Tuwa asked.

Sometimes Sarah wished her grandmother was less observant. Taking a deep breath, she fortified herself for the harsh truth. "He will never *really* be my son."

Tuwa hesitated a moment and then said, "You must give him time to accept you."

Sarah almost let it go. She didn't want to admit why Drew would never accept her—no matter how much time she gave him. But there were already too many lies and half-truths in her life. She needed some honesty, especially with this woman who'd given so much to her and Lyssa.

"He can't accept me if he doesn't know who I am." Sarah looked up at her grandmother, meeting her troubled gaze. "I'm just a tutor to him." Sarah's voice broke, and then she forged ahead. "He thinks his mother is dead."

Surprise flickered across her grandmother's face, and then something else settled there. Sadness. Pity. Love. And it nearly broke Sarah's heart all over again.

She turned away, unable to face Tuwa any longer. She let her gaze drift over the familiar yard, dusty and void of vegetation except for the profusion of bright yellow arrowleaf surrounding the house. Although the place would always feel like home, Sarah was now starkly aware that something was missing, something that would always be missing. Her son.

"I can't blame Reece," she said. "He did what he thought was best. He thought it would be kinder to tell Drew that his mother had died." Again her voice broke, and it took a moment for her to get the last words out. "It was better than telling him I'd deserted him."

Silence stretched between them. Sarah kept her eyes focused on the mountains in the distance. Anywhere but on her grandmother's face, where she knew she'd see pity.

"And now?" Tuwa asked finally.

Sarah sighed. "This isn't the time to tell Drew."

"Will there be a better time in the future?"

Sarah looked at her grandmother and saw the spark of impatience in her ancient eyes. There was no answer to her question, Sarah knew, and her grandmother expected none. There would never be a *good* time to tell Drew the truth.

Before either of them could say anything else, a battered red pickup pulled into the yard. Sarah stood, and Lyssa jumped from the cab, hurling herself across the yard into her mother's arms.

"You're home!" Lyssa yelled with an exuberance that was a balm to Sarah's heart. "Grandmother said you'd be back today."

Sarah laughed, hugging her daughter and throwing a quick smile at her grandmother. "She did?"

Lyssa giggled. "She wants me to think the spirits told her," she said in a loud whisper. "But I know better. Every day she told me the same thing." Then, mimicking her great-grandmother's voice, she said, "Today your mother will come home."

They both laughed and grinned at Tuwa, who sat shaking her head at the two of them. Then, squirming out of her mother's arms, Lyssa turned toward the big man who'd followed her out of the truck. "Joseph has been letting me work the barrel racers."

Sarah smiled at the man she'd known all her life. He'd taught her when she was Lyssa's age, too. "Hello, Joseph. It's good of you to help Lyssa. She loves the horses."

The late-afternoon sun glinted on the inky black of his hair, and his smile transformed his broad plain features, making him almost handsome. "No thanks needed. Lyssa earns her way. I can always use an extra hand around the stables, and she works hard. In exchange, I teach her. It's good for us both."

Sarah smiled, acknowledging his kindness despite his claims to the contrary.

"Got to get back," he said, putting his hat back on his head. "Tomorrow, Lyssa?"

Lyssa glanced at her mother, who nodded, before answering. "Okay."

As soon as Joseph left, Lyssa turned to her mother, obviously eager to talk to her. "Mom, Joseph says I might be ready to compete next year in the middle-school rodeo. He's promised to help me." She glanced at her great-grandmother, as if to gain her support, before turning back to Sarah. "So, can I stay out here on the reservation with Grandmother for the rest of the summer?"

The question took Sarah aback. She'd come home to ask her grandmother and Lyssa just this. "Well, I—"

"Grandmother says it's all right with her," Lyssa interrupted, misinterpreting her mother's hesitation. "If it's okay with you."

Sarah glanced at the old woman.

"She's always welcome here," Tuwa stated.

Sarah sighed and lowered herself once again to the porch step. "As a matter of fact, I was planning on asking you two the same thing." She smiled at Lyssa. "I've been offered a tutoring job for the summer. On a ranch near Devils Corner. I was hoping your great-grandmother would let you stay here."

"All right!" Lyssa yelled.

Sarah looked at her grandmother, who nodded and said, "She's a good girl, Sarah. I enjoy having her."

"Thank you, Grandmother."

The next couple of hours passed in the whirlwind of activity only a ten-year-old can create. With Lyssa's help, Sarah fixed dinner while Lyssa chattered about everything that had been happening since her mother had left—which seemed to be a whole summer's worth of excitement in just five days.

Then, right after helping clear away the dinner dishes, Lyssa curled up on the couch with a book and in minutes was fast asleep. Working with the horses all day had taken its toll, and Joseph would return early in the morning to pick her up for another long day. Sarah gave her daughter a half hour on the couch and then carried her into bed. Afterward she joined her grandmother outside.

They sat on the porch, as they'd often done during the summer months while Sarah was growing up— Tuwa in her beat-up chair and Sarah on the top step, her back propped against the railing support. The night settled around them, and the air cooled as the last slivers of light deserted the sky. Overhead the stars shimmered. Already she felt better. The peace of this place slipped into her soul, soothing her, lulling her with its serenity.

Then Tuwa asked, "So, you will work with your son every day, pretending to be a stranger?"

Sarah pulled her sweater closer around her. "Yes."

"Do you think that is wise?"

Wise? Sarah felt anything but. "I have no other choice, Grandmother."

Tuwa sighed heavily. "There are always choices."

"He's troubled. His grades. His health. He doesn't need another upset."

"You said he was strong."

"Yes, physically. And he's a good boy. But he's..." Sarah hesitated and, closing her eyes, rested her head against the wooden support. "Even if I wanted to tell Drew, Reece wouldn't allow it."

"And you have no say in this?"

Sarah thought for a moment and then answered truthfully. "No."

The silence once again surrounded them, but the peace Sarah had felt earlier had vanished. Her grandmother saw too much and asked too many questions. Questions Sarah couldn't answer.

"What about Lyssa?"

Sarah raised her head. "Lyssa?"

"Doesn't she have a right to know her brother and father? And what have you told them of her?"

For a moment, Sarah couldn't answer. She couldn't remember ever seeing her grandmother this agitated, and everything she'd said was true. Lyssa knew nothing of her brother and very little about her father— only that he and Sarah had been married very young and that it hadn't worked out. Lyssa had seemed content with that. But just because she didn't ask questions about her father didn't mean she didn't wonder. At some time in the future she might resent Sarah for keeping him a secret. Her grandmother was right, Sarah thought. Lyssa had been cheated as much as any of them.

It was just one more facet of the lie that hung over Sarah's head. But she couldn't lose Lyssa. "If I tell Reece about Lyssa, he'll take her away from me."

"You don't know that."

"I can't risk it."

"Sarah." Tuwa softened her voice and, leaning forward, rested a gnarled hand on Sarah's shoulder. "You cannot go on like this. You can't continue living this lie."

"Don't you think I know that?" Sarah pulled away, tears welling up in her eyes as she pushed herself off the porch. "It's tearing me apart. Every hour I spend with Drew, the lie grows larger. Every day I gain a little more of his trust, and the lie winds itself about my heart. Tighter and tighter, until I fear it'll strangle us all."

Tuwa sighed and leaned back in her chair. "And it just might at that."

CHAPTER SEVEN

REECE FIGURED it was well past midnight.

The headlights of Sarah's car swept over him as she pulled into the yard and parked near the side of the house. He sat in an old wicker chair on the porch, his feet propped on the railing, a half-empty tumbler of scotch balanced on one thigh. He'd been waiting for hours.

In the dark he could just make out her silhouette as she got out of the car, grabbed her small overnight bag from the back seat and closed the door behind her. She moved toward the house and up the stairs, the graceful length of her skirt swaying about her legs.

"Pretty late, aren't you?"

She jumped and spun around, one hand pressed to her chest. "Reece, you startled me."

Setting the scotch aside, he dropped his feet to the floor and rose from his chair. "Sorry." But he wasn't. He'd wanted to shake her up a bit.

"What are you doing out here?" she asked.

"Waiting." He moved closer, and she took a step back.

"Waiting?"

"To see if you'd come back."

She lifted her chin in that defiant manner of hers. "Why wouldn't I?"

"Why indeed?" He moved a little closer, backing her up nearly to the door. "Especially since you're so good at running away."

Anger flashed in her eyes, but he was beyond caring. He'd been sitting out here thinking of her for hours, damning her for making him wonder whether she'd return. He should have been hoping she'd stay away for good. They'd all be better off. But as the hours had passed and she didn't show, his anger mounted.

Damn it! Damn *her!* He wanted her here.

He lifted the single ebony braid that fell across her shoulder, rubbing it between his fingers. It felt like silk, and the faint scent of her shampoo assaulted his nostrils. He'd loved her hair, especially when it had spread across his pillow, its sleek darkness a sharp contrast to the white of the sheets.

"Why don't you wear it down anymore?"

She stared at him, her eyes wide, like a deer caught by headlights, and shook her head. "It gets in the way."

"Too bad."

There had been a time when she'd only confined it for the rodeos. He brought the braid closer to his face, inhaling its scent while never taking his eyes off hers. She'd tormented him all week. Hell, the memory of her had tormented him for years. "You're a witch."

"You've been drinking."

"Not enough." *Not nearly enough.* He could still remember. Still want. It would take a hell of a lot more scotch than what he'd consumed to make him forget what it had been like to bury himself in this woman. Lust. If only it was that simple. But with Sarah, sex always got tangled with other things, feelings he no longer trusted. "Seems you bring out the worst in me."

"I don't know what you're talking about." She took another step back, coming up against the door.

He let the braid slide through his fingers, the satiny texture catching against his callused flesh. "Don't you?" He moved in closer, placing a hand against the wooden frame behind her.

She glanced at his arm, then attempted to sidestep him. He stopped her by placing his other hand on the frame, effectively trapping her. "Not so fast."

For the past week she'd been everywhere he'd turned, tempting him, teasing him with her scent and that slender female body of hers. She'd invaded his senses as easily as she'd invaded his home.

He wanted her.

God, how he wanted her. It didn't seem to matter that she'd once walked out on him, or that her reason for being here had nothing to do with him. Just as it hadn't mattered thirteen years ago that he'd been too young and unprepared for his intense sexual attraction to her. He'd given in to it then, too. And he'd paid the price.

"What do you want, Reece?" He recognized the breathless quality of her voice and let his gaze slide down to the pulse at her throat. It beat wildly, as he'd known it would, and he contemplated tasting her skin, feeling her pulse with his lips as he'd done dozens of times in the past.

"I think you know what I want," he drawled, bringing his gaze back to her face, to her soft trembling mouth, then to her eyes—dark, frightened and hungry. "Some things haven't changed, have they, Sarah?"

She turned her head sideways, as though she couldn't stand looking at him. "Everything has changed."

He slid a hand down to capture her face and turn it back toward him. "Liar."

Again anger flashed in her eyes. He smiled slowly and moved closer, pressing her against the wall with his lower body. "If nothing else, we've always had this."

"Reece . . ."

He ignored the plea in her voice and lowered his mouth to hers, but stopped just short of meeting it. "Yes, Sarah, what is it?" He rubbed against her, letting her feel how badly he wanted her, how hard he was for her, until her eyelids fluttered shut and a soft moan escaped her throat.

Only then did he claim her mouth.

For one breathless second Sarah resisted, her hands coming up to push against his chest. But it was too late. She was lost. His mouth on hers was everything she wanted and feared. Pain and joy. Anger and desire. Hunger and heat. She felt it all, and forgot everything but the taste of him, the hot demanding feel of him. She melted against his chest, her tongue meeting his, her arms finding their way around his neck.

He moved his hands to her waist, tugged her blouse free from her skirt and slid them beneath the thin cotton fabric. The sudden intimate contact, his work-roughened fingers against her skin, sent a fresh wave of desire through her. She arched against him, reveling in his touch, so familiar and yet so new.

Too long.

It had been too long since she'd felt this way. This need, this ache. She wanted it to go on forever. His hands, his mouth exploring her body. She wanted it all. Here. Now.

A low angry growl escaped him, and he tore his mouth from hers. "Witch," he whispered against her lips, while his hands moved upward to capture her breasts. "I don't want this. I don't want you."

Sarah wound her fingers into his hair and rose on tiptoe, tracing his bottom lip with the tip of her tongue. "Now who's the liar?"

"Damn you." He slid his hands to her bottom, kneading and then lifting her to cradle his erection between her thighs. She rubbed against him, shifting her legs slightly apart so she could feel him against her.

"Damn you," he repeated, then again claimed her mouth, roughly, his anger as evident as his lust. And Sarah basked in it, in once again having him hold her, want her, love her—

The thought brought her up sharp, instantly stilling the passion that had overridden her judgment. She couldn't let this happen. She couldn't let desire overwhelm her. Reece didn't love her. Not anymore.

She pushed against his chest and broke the kiss. "Reece, stop!"

He let her put a fraction of space between them but didn't release her. "Why?"

"I've changed my mind."

His eyes flashed angrily. "I don't like playing games."

"This isn't a game. Now let me go." She twisted away from his hands.

"What's the matter, Sarah?" Reece took a step back. "Can't decide what you want? Again?"

She ignored the barb, knowing she'd let things go too far. "I don't want this. It's nothing but pure lust, and I won't let you use me to ease the bulge in your jeans."

He glared at her for a moment and then said, "There's nothing *pure* about lust, lady. And if you think I have anything else to offer you, you're sorely mistaken." He spun on his heels and in three quick strides was off the porch and heading for the barn.

Sarah sank against the door, trembling, just barely holding back the tears brimming in her eyes. With an effort, she straightened her clothes, tucking in her blouse and smoothing her skirt. She hadn't asked for this, she told herself. She didn't need it. Not now. Not on top of everything else.

She watched as he led an unsaddled horse from the barn, mounted swiftly and headed toward the hills. Just the sight of Reece, leaning low over the neck of his horse, broke her resolve. Crumbling into a ball on the floor of the porch, she surrendered to her tears.

REECE RODE long and hard, despite the darkness and the late hour. He needed to lose the memory of the past thirty minutes, the feel of Sarah in his arms, the taste of her mouth on his. He'd ride all night if that was what it took, but somehow, he had to forget what had almost happened.

As if he could.

It would be so easy to blame her. She'd bewitched him. Just as she'd done before. But the fact remained he could no more think with her around than he could thirteen years ago. Back then he'd been little more than a loved-starved boy. He had no such excuse now.

He didn't love her. Yet his body had its own thoughts on the matter. He wanted her. Still.

SHE HAD NO RIGHT to be angry.

Yet every time Sarah thought of what had almost happened the night before, she wanted to throw something. Preferably something hard. And preferably at Reece Colby's head. She'd come to the Crooked C to help their son. She'd even foolishly agreed not to reveal her identity to him, and where had it gotten her? Reece had dogged her every step, doubting her at every turn. Then, the first time they were alone, he'd backed her against a door frame and stripped away the last remaining shreds of her dignity.

She could hate him for that.

And for making her want him, for reawakening the passion she'd buried long ago. For making her realize how much she still loved him.

"I owe you an apology."

Startled, Sarah turned from the window where she'd been standing, staring blindly at the yard below, for God only knows how long.

Reece sprawled in the doorway, tall, handsome and far from repentant. Just the sight of him unnerved her, brought vivid memories of the night before. And sparked her simmering anger. Straightening her shoulders, she tucked her hands under her arms to hide their trembling. "Yes, you do."

"Then I apologize." He tipped his head slightly, but his mocking blue eyes held no contrition. It set her off.

"That's not good enough."

"Oh, really?" Sarcasm laced his voice. "And what exactly do you expect? Should I don a hair shirt? Or possibly get down on my knees and beg your forgiveness?''

"I want you to stay away from me."

"Might be a little difficult under the circumstances." The sarcasm had been replaced with a lazy drawl that sent shivers down her spine. She ignored it.

"Find a way," she snapped. "I don't want anything more to do with you."

He stood stock-still for a moment, the mockery in his eyes growing hard and unyielding. "Don't be so self-righteous, Sarah. You weren't a totally unwilling participant last night."

Heat flooded her face. "I'm…I hardly asked to be attacked on the porch."

"Attacked?" He stepped into the room, and she instinctively backed up. Reece stopped short and raised both hands. "I won't come any closer," he said. Then with a sigh, he dropped his hands to his waist. "Look, I didn't come up here to argue with you."

"Then why did you come?"

He frowned and shook his head. "I promise, it won't happen again."

"You're right. It won't."

He shoved a hand through his hair. "Look, Sarah, you're here to work with Drew and that's all. Contrary to my actions last night, I have no interest in you other than as a tutor for my son."

The comment stung, though it wasn't anything she didn't already know. She'd once had Reece's love and thrown it away. More than that, really. She'd flung it in his face. How could she expect anything but contempt from him now?

"If last week is any indication," he continued, "you and Drew are getting along well. I don't want anything to come in the way of that."

"Just stay away from me and nothing will."

She turned back toward the window. As far as she was concerned, they had nothing further to discuss. And she didn't want him to see how the past few minutes had affected her—her trembling hands and the tears brimming in her eyes. Being in his arms last night had been the closest thing to heaven she'd ever known. And the closest thing to hell. Somehow she needed to put it behind her and go on. The only way she could do that was if he kept his distance.

"Hey, Dad."

Drew's voice startled her, but she remained by the window. She hadn't realized that it had grown so late, or that Drew was due in from outside.

"Son," Reece answered. "Done with your chores?"

Sarah closed her eyes, praying Drew would drag his dad off somewhere. She needed a few minutes alone.

"Yeah," Drew answered. "Are you going with us out to the creek today?"

"Well, I..."

Sarah spun around and met Reece's gaze, just barely stopping the adamant no that sprang to her lips. Instead, the steadiness of her voice surprised her as she said, "I'm sure your father has work to do, Drew."

"But he promised," Drew insisted.

"I didn't exactly promise," Reece said. Then to Sarah, he added, "Drew mentioned that the two of you planned to take your schoolwork out by the creek again today. I told him I might come along."

"I hardly think that's necessary." She needed some space, and she definitely did *not* need Reece around all day. "Or a good idea, for that matter."

"Oh? Why not?" He crossed his arms and cocked an eyebrow, as if daring her to voice her reasons.

"Well . . ." She groped for words, though she knew Reece was very aware why she didn't want him along. "We have a lot of work to do," she said finally. "You'll only be bored and end up distracting us."

"But I did all my work over the weekend," Drew said. "Did you check it?"

Sarah glanced at the pile of papers she was supposed to have checked for Drew. She'd told him that if he did his schoolwork while she was gone, they'd have a light day on Monday. She'd been sitting here all morning and still hadn't managed to concentrate long enough to look over Drew's efforts.

She returned her gaze to Reece, hoping he'd beg off. From everything he'd said, he didn't want to spend time with her any more than she with him. But his focus was on Drew.

"Actually," Reece said, "this might be a good chance for me to work with the Appaloosa."

Drew's eyes grew wide. "You're going to take him out?"

"Why not?" He smiled faintly at Sarah, his eyes challenging her to come up with another objection. "He's okay in the corral, but he needs to be worked out in the open. To see how he handles." Then he turned back to Drew. "This way, I won't exactly blow the afternoon off by coming with you."

"All right! Can I ride him?"

Smiling broadly now, Reece rested a hand on Drew's shoulder. "We'll see."

So much for Reece's apology, Sarah thought, as he and Drew headed downstairs without bothering to see if she would follow.

IT WAS AN UNLIKELY family outing, Reece thought, as he set out with Sarah and Drew for the creek. But then, they were an unlikely family. A woman who'd deserted her husband and infant son and then returned eleven years later looking for God only knew what. A man, unable to forgive or forget what she'd done, while still wanting her desperately. And a boy, caught in the middle.

It seemed ironic, the three of them riding out, Drew in the middle, chattering away, totally oblivious to the tension between the adults.

In truth Reece would have preferred to let Sarah and Drew go off by themselves today. Putting a little distance between himself and Sarah would be best for both of them. She'd certainly made her feelings on the subject clear. She wanted him to stay as far away from her as possible. A stance he totally agreed with and would have been happy to oblige, except for his promise to Drew.

Glancing at his son, Reece noticed the ease with which Drew sat his saddle, as if he'd been born to it. Which, in a way, he had. He was the product of generations of ranchers who'd worked their herds on horseback, while in his veins ran the blood of his mother's people, the best horsemen on the plains. It would have been surprising if Drew hadn't taken to the saddle.

Strange that Reece had never thought of Drew in this way before. But then there were any number of things Reece was just beginning to learn about his son.

Like how easy the boy was to be with.

With both Elizabeth and Sarah away from the ranch this weekend, Reece and Drew had ended up spending a lot of time together. Reece had worked alongside his son as he did his chores. The boy never questioned or complained, but did whatever Tod asked. It had struck Reece again how much more Tod knew about his son than he did.

Then in the evening, Drew had asked for help with some math problems that Sarah had left for him. To his surprise, Reece had enjoyed explaining the intricacies of sixth-grade math to Drew. It had been heady stuff, watching his son grapple with and then grasp concepts. The pride he'd felt was unlike anything he'd ever known. That was when he'd agreed to accompany Drew and Sarah today. Reece was just discovering his son and couldn't go back on his word. Especially when he'd looked into Drew's eyes and seen how much it meant to him.

WHEN THEY ARRIVED at their destination, they dismounted and Drew loosely tied his and Sarah's horses well away from where they'd be working, making sure the animals had access to grass and water. Then Sarah and Drew settled under a sprawling tree to begin work.

Reece didn't want to put the Appaloosa with the other animals. The stallion was still too unpredictable. So, holding the Appaloosa's reins loosely, Reece headed toward the creek. It was a beautiful day, and Drew had picked a great spot. The stream descended from rocky hills of pine and aspen to cut through a meadow of lush grass and graceful cottonwoods. The crystalline water danced through rocky shallows and then settled into deeper pools.

He let the horse drink and then moved a little farther downstream. The warm summer day and the sweetness of the place had a soothing effect on him, inviting him to meander, to forget all his problems. After a moment he stopped again, squatting down on the bank to dip his hands in the clear cool water. As he leaned forward, the Appaloosa nudged his back, rubbing the bridle against him.

"Cut it out, fella," Reece said. He pushed at the big stallion's head.

"Better watch out, Dad," Drew called from behind him. "He really hates that bridle."

Reece glanced back to where Drew and Sarah sat under a tree. Obviously Sarah had been right. He *was* a distraction.

"You just go on with your studies, Drew," he said. "I'll take care of the horse."

He turned back to the creek, reaching for a handful of water to splash over his face. But the Appaloosa once again nudged him, harder this time, throwing him off-balance. The next thing he knew, he was sprawled face first in thigh-high water. Sputtering, he struggled to his feet and glared at the stallion standing above him on the bank, the picture of innocence. Behind him Drew and Sarah stared, wide-eyed. Then Drew's hand flew to his mouth, but giggles erupted despite his obvious attempt to stop them. Sarah glanced at Drew, then at Reece, before she, too, grinned.

Reece couldn't stop his own laughter. He must have been a sight. Soaking wet, with the big horse standing over him looking smug.

"You got me, you son of a gun." Reece headed for dry ground, just barely grabbing his hat in time before the stream carried it away.

Still laughing, Drew scurried down the hill with Sarah right behind him. "I told you, Dad."

"You sure did, son." Reece took the reins and brought the horse's head down close to his. "You tricky ol' bastard. Well, just you wait. You'll get yours." The horse snorted and shook his head, and Reece lightened his hold.

"Well, I guess I know how I'm going to spend the rest of the afternoon," Reece said.

"How?" Drew asked, grinning from ear to ear.

"Drying off." Reece plopped his hat on his head, only to be drenched once again with a fresh sluice of water.

Drew nearly collapsed in a fit of hysterical laughter. Reece watched him, shaking his head. How was he to know it was this easy to please his son? A dunk in a chilly mountain stream seemed to be all it took. Hell, if he'd known that, he could have saved himself and Drew a lot of trouble. They could come out here weekly just so Drew could watch his father make a fool of himself.

"You think this is funny, don't you, boy?" Reece asked, trying to conceal his own amusement.

Drew nodded, still laughing, holding on to his stomach as if he'd fly apart if he let loose.

"Well, let's see just how funny it is when you join me." In one swoop, Reece had his squirming son in his arms, carrying him toward the water.

"Dad! No!" Drew struggled against his father's hold.

Drew's strength surprised him, and Reece had all he could do to keep his grip, but he strode back into the water, holding Drew for one tantalizing moment before dropping him. Drew let out a screech that echoed off the nearby hills as he hit the cold springwater. He came up laughing and splashing.

"Teach you to laugh at your old man," Reece said, grinning down at his son.

"Oh, yeah. Just wait." Drew launched himself at his father, and the two of them went down, sputtering and laughing as they both ended up in the water.

"So much for schoolwork," Reece said, refusing to feel even a little bit guilty for distracting his son.

"Yeah." Drew's eyes were so full of life. Then he whispered, "Hey. What about Miss Hanson? Let's throw her in, too."

Reece had forgotten about Sarah. Looking back toward the bank, he saw her holding the Appaloosa, shaking her head at the two of them. "You're both crazy," she shouted.

Drew started toward the bank. "Let's get her!"

Sarah backed away. "No way," she said. "You and your father are plenty wet for all three of us."

"Come on, Dad. Help me."

Reece thought it was the best idea he'd heard all day. Drew had her hand by the time Reece reached their side. "I've got her, Drew. You get the horse." He scooped her up and headed for the water.

"Reece!" she shrieked. "Put me down!" She struggled, even as she wrapped her arms around his neck, but she wasn't nearly as hard to handle as Drew.

"I intend to," he said with a grin.

"This isn't funny!"

"Then how come you're laughing?"

She made an effort to stop but failed miserably. "One of us needs to remain dry."

Ignoring her protest, he reached the water's edge and strode in without breaking stride. Then, looking down into her laughing brown eyes, something tightened within him. All at once he became aware of the distinctly feminine body he held in his arms, of her long slender legs and narrow back, the swell of her soft breasts pressed against his chest and the changes in her. The differences between this body and that of the young woman who'd been his wife. Her body had matured, filled out, and he ached to explore it.

"Come on, Dad. Dump her!"

Reece glanced back at his son, who'd trailed them to the water's edge, and then again at Sarah. She'd stopped struggling and met his gaze. She felt it, too. He could see it in her dark sorceress eyes. Her hunger matched his own, and he grew instantly hard, despite the cold water.

"Reece," she said again, her voice a breathless whisper. "One of us needs to remain rational."

He thought about that for a moment, then decided he disagreed. For now, nothing that had happened before mattered. The day was bright and warm, his son's laughter surrounded him, and Sarah was in his arms. "Why?" he asked. And dropped her into the water.

The splash shattered the moment.

"All right, Dad!" Drew cheered and then rushed in to join them. Sarah grabbed his hand as he got close and pulled him down next to her.

For Reece, the next half hour, while all three of them splashed and laughed in the creek, had a bittersweet quality. At one point he realized they were ruining their boots, but he didn't care. His son's hearty enjoyment mingling with Sarah's musical laughter stirred a longing in Reece for things that couldn't be. Things that went deeper than the physical need he'd felt for her last night.

Finally, worn-out and feeling like a drowned rat, Reece made his way back to the bank. He collapsed on the grass and pulled off his boots.

Sarah and Drew followed, but while she moved off toward the horses, Drew plopped himself on the ground next to his dad. "Sure glad you decided to go swimming," he said.

"I didn't decide to go swimming." Reece cuffed him playfully on the arm. "That darn horse..." His voice trailed off as he glanced around, wondering what had happened to the Appaloosa, then saw that Drew had tethered the horse before joining them in the creek. Reece smiled. "Thanks for taking care of the Ap."

"He would've run off otherwise."

Reece reached out and ruffled Drew's wet hair. "Yeah. He would've." Drew had grown into a great kid, Reece thought. He wished he could take credit for it, but any number of other people had more to do with how the boy had turned out than Reece. Millie. Tod. Even Elizabeth. That was about to change, however. It was, in fact, already changing. From now on, Reece planned to be part of his son's life.

"So what's the verdict on schoolwork today?" Sarah asked as she joined them and handed Drew a package of crackers. "Here, Drew."

"Thanks." Drew took the snack.

The casual exchange between Sarah and Drew momentarily stunned Reece. Neither Sarah nor Drew had broken stride over Drew's need to eat on a regular basis. Sarah had remembered and handed him a snack. Drew had taken it, seemingly without giving it a second thought. It was more the unconscious actions of a woman and child who'd spent their lives together than that of a teacher and her pupil. Sarah and Drew had become mother and son, despite Reece's best efforts to prevent it.

Surprisingly the thought made him smile. Then, glancing at Sarah, he answered her question, "My guess is that studying is pretty much a washout for the day."

Sarah groaned and shook her head at his pun.

Climbing to his feet, he offered her his hand. "Come on. I think it's time we headed back."

"Next time," she said to Drew as she let Reece help her stand, "we leave your father at home." But she was smiling as she started gathering their belongings.

They took it easy going home. Riding in wet jeans wasn't the most comfortable way to travel, but Reece suspected their reasons for going slowly had nothing to do with comfort. The day had turned out better than any of them had thought possible, and he suspected that none of them wanted it to end.

Drew was quieter than he'd been on the way out, probably because he was worn-out. But every now and then he'd pipe up with some remembered moment from the time they'd spent in the water. If nothing else, Drew had enjoyed himself.

As for Sarah, she smiled at Drew and laughed lightly at his comments. Other than that, she remained quiet, obviously lost in her own thoughts. Reece wondered what those thoughts were, but couldn't begin to guess. He could see how easily she and Drew fit together after only a week. Possibly she was thinking the same thing. He couldn't blame her. Each day she spent with them on the Crooked C, things got more complicated, and today had only aggravated the situation.

Still, he couldn't regret the day or the fun they'd had together. It was how it could have been for the three of them if Sarah hadn't run out on them. How it *should* have been. The thought came at him from nowhere, and he waited for the old resentment to surface. When it didn't, he realized that a simpler emotion had taken its place. Disappointment.

When he'd married Sarah, he'd wanted very little from life. His wife. His son. To be a rancher. Evidently it wasn't meant to be. Today he'd had a little piece of that dream, a glimpse of what fate had stolen from him. That glimpse had ripped the anger from him, leaving only a treasured memory that he'd hold close to his heart. That, and the thought that maybe there could be some measure of peace between him and Sarah, after all.

But Reece's serenity lasted only until they rode into the yard of the Crooked C and headed toward the barn. Because next to the corral, talking to Tod, stood Michelle.

CHAPTER EIGHT

No ONE HAD TO TELL Sarah the identity of the tall blond woman talking to Tod. She'd seen Michelle Hawthorne's picture in the paper nearly as often as she'd seen Reece's. Michelle was even lovelier in person—and a sharp reminder to Sarah that the family-like ambience of the past few hours had been nothing more than an illusion.

She, Sarah, was an outsider here.

Michelle came toward them, flashing a flawless smile, and took hold of the Appaloosa's bridle. "Well, it's about time. I'd just about given up on you."

Reece glanced at Sarah, then turned back to Michelle. "Sorry," he said as he dismounted. "I wasn't expecting you."

"It was a surprise," she said, grinning mischievously, "but that's okay." She threw a flirtatious smile at Reece's foreman. "Tod entertained me."

Tod tipped his hat. "Anytime, Miss Hawthorne. Anytime."

Michelle laughed lightly and then turned and kissed Reece lightly on the cheek. Her easy familiarity with him sent an unexpected jolt through Sarah's stomach, but she tamped down the emotion immediately. She already had enough to deal with without adding jealousy to the list.

Meanwhile, Michelle had backed up a little from Reece, evidently just noticing his soggy appearance. "What happened to you? You look like you got caught in a deluge."

"The Appaloosa decided Dad needed a bath," Drew said.

Michelle nodded. "I see." Although it was clear she didn't, especially when she took in Drew's equally wet clothes and then Sarah's.

"Michelle," Reece said as Sarah climbed off her horse, "this is Sarah Hanson. Drew's tutor. Sarah, my fiancée, Michelle Hawthorne."

"I've heard so much about you," Michelle said, moving to take Sarah's hand. "It's good to finally meet you."

Sarah forced a smile past the sick feeling in her stomach. "It's nice to meet you, too, Miss Hawthorne."

"Please, call me Michelle." She smiled, and although Sarah would have preferred to dislike this woman, her genuine openness made it difficult. Releasing Sarah's hand, Michelle turned to Drew. "I haven't seen you in a while, Drew. How are you doing?"

"Okay, I guess." His reply was little more than a mumble—a far cry from the exuberant laughter and shouts of a short while ago. Sarah started to correct him for his rudeness and then stopped herself. It wasn't her place. As Reece kept reminding her, she was only Drew's tutor.

If Michelle noticed anything amiss, she let it slide. Turning back to Reece, she said, "I came over because we have a couple of things we need to discuss."

"Excuse me," Sarah said, thinking they'd probably prefer to talk without an audience. Besides, even though she'd known all along about Reece's engagement, she had no desire to stand here and watch him with another woman. "Come on, Drew, let's get these horses put away."

"Wait, Sarah," Michelle said, turning to Sarah before she could get away. "I didn't mean to chase you off."

"That's okay." Sarah wished this woman wasn't so pleasant. She didn't want to like Michelle Hawthorne. "I need to take care of my horse."

"We all do." Reece looked distinctly uncomfortable, like a boy caught with his hand in the cookie jar, and Sarah wondered why. "Then I'd like to get into some dry clothes," he continued. "Why don't you go on up to the house, Michelle? I'll be there as soon as I'm done here."

"Deal," she said. "That is, *if* you and Drew take care of the horses so Sarah can walk up to the house with me. It'll give us a chance to get acquainted."

"I really should take care of my own animal," Sarah said. The last thing she wanted was to spend time alone with Reece's fiancée.

"It's okay, Miss Hanson," Drew offered. "I'll take care of your horse for you."

For once, Sarah wished Drew was less accommodating.

"Thanks, Drew." Michelle took the reins from Sarah and handed them to Drew. "Now, you can't beat an offer like that, can you, Sarah? Come on."

Sarah shot a glance at Reece, and then followed Michelle toward the house. There was no graceful way out of it. She couldn't very well refuse to accompany the woman.

Once they were away from the barn, Michelle said, "Actually I'm glad we have a few minutes to ourselves. I really wanted to talk to you."

Sarah glanced sideways at Michelle. "About what?"

"Drew, mainly."

Sarah had a hard time believing that Michelle had engineered this time alone so they could talk about Drew. "Really, Miss Hawthorne, I don't see—"

"Michelle, please."

Sarah nodded. "Okay. Michelle."

"How is he doing with his schoolwork?"

Sarah hesitated to say anything. Yet she detected no subterfuge in the other woman. Michelle seemed honestly interested in Drew. Maybe the only one here with a hidden agenda was Sarah herself. But then, why would Michelle Hawthorne need to hide anything? She was Senator Robert Hawthorne's daughter and Reece Colby's fiancée. Michelle certainly had nothing to fear from the likes of her.

"We've only been working together for a week," Sarah said at last. "But he's doing well."

"Is he going to pass?"

"It's too early to say for sure. But if he keeps up the way he has, I think so."

"And his other problem?"

Sarah looked at the other woman, wondering how much Michelle knew. Obviously she knew about Drew's tendency to forget his insulin and his regular mealtimes. But did she know that Sarah and Reece had been married? That Drew was her son? Except for Millie, no one else on the ranch seemed to know.

"I don't think I should discuss this without his father present," Sarah said finally.

Michelle stopped, and Sarah did the same. "I'm going to be his stepmother." She paused, glancing back toward the barn where they'd left Reece and Drew. "And I'm concerned about him. After you're gone, I'll be the one taking care of him." She let the statement stand alone for a moment, letting it sink in.

Sarah felt it deep inside. The truth of it. And it hurt.

Then Michelle added, "I have a right to know how he's doing."

Sarah started back toward the house. The late-afternoon air chilled her through the wet clothing. "Yes, you do." Though it nearly killed her to admit it. "But you'll have to get the information from his father."

Michelle didn't budge. "I don't agree with the way Reece is keeping you a secret, Sarah."

The words stopped Sarah cold. Taking a deep breath, she turned back to face Michelle. "What did you say?"

"I think Drew has a right to know who you really are. I told Reece that before you came here. We argued about it." She took a step closer. "So you see, I'm on your side."

Sarah shook her head and started to back away. "Really, I can't talk about this."

"Won't? Or can't?"

"That really doesn't matter, does it? I won't talk about it." Sarah turned, and without looking back, crossed the remaining few yards to the house. Whatever Michelle Hawthorne wanted from her, whether her intentions were good or bad, Sarah couldn't supply it. Already there were too many secrets, too many lies in her life. She couldn't enter into another with Reece's fiancée.

The moment she walked through the kitchen door, Millie confronted her. "Do the other two look as bad as you?" she asked, taking in Sarah's wet clothes and soggy boots.

Sarah fought the grin and lost. Millie had a talent for lightening any mood. "At least."

"Anybody ever explain that you're supposed to take your clothes off before you go swimming?"

"It's a long story." And not one Sarah wanted to go into right now, especially since Michelle had just followed her into the kitchen. "Ask Drew. I'm sure he'll be glad to explain it in great detail."

"Humph." Then to Michelle, Millie said, "You staying for dinner, Miss Hawthorne?"

Again Michelle smiled that megawatt smile. "If it's no trouble, Millie."

"No trouble at all. Go on, Sarah, get out of those wet clothes."

Sarah made her escape, glad to leave Michelle in Millie's capable hands.

Upstairs, she shed her wet clothes and headed for the shower. The hot water was heaven. Funny how she hadn't felt cold until they'd gotten back to the ranch. She'd been fine out by the creek and all the way home. But for the past few minutes, she hadn't been able to contain her shivers.

She'd been so angry at Reece when he'd decided to go with her and Drew today. Even angrier than she'd been about last night. She'd asked him to leave her alone, and he'd ignored her request. Yet the afternoon had turned magical, giving them all a moment's respite from the pressures of their situation. Of course, that's all it was. A momentary lull. Nothing had really changed between the three of them. She was still only the tutor, Drew her student, and Reece, her employer. The appearance of Michelle Hawthorne had brought all of that home to Sarah with a vengeance.

But Sarah couldn't blame Michelle. Even though she was everything Sarah could never hope to be. Wealthy. Beautiful. White…

Sarah pushed that last thought aside.

She'd never been ashamed of her Shoshone heritage. It had been her mother's people who'd made her feel like she belonged somewhere. Her mother's mother who'd taken her in and raised her after her parents' death. She hardly knew her father's parents; they'd wanted nothing to do with their half-breed granddaughter. No, Sarah was proud of the Shoshone blood that ran through her veins. But she also knew that was one of the reasons she wasn't the right woman for Reece Colby. Michelle Hawthorne suited him in ways that Sarah never had or could. Michelle was the type of woman he should have married twelve years ago.

As Sarah climbed out of the shower and wrapped herself in her robe, she could hear Drew downstairs. He was telling Millie all about the Appaloosa sending Reece for a dunking and the ensuing water fight. His boyish laughter echoed through the house, warming her in a way the hot shower couldn't.

She'd been wrong earlier when she'd thought nothing had changed. Drew had changed. He'd become a child again. If nothing else, she could be proud that she'd given that back to him.

REECE PUT OFF heading back to the house as long as he could. He knew what Michelle wanted to talk about. The campaign. He'd asked her for two weeks with Drew; she'd barely given him one. If he'd been honest with himself, he should have realized she couldn't wait the fourteen days. The word *ambitious* described her perfectly, and the only surprise was that she hadn't stopped by sooner.

What he couldn't have seen coming was her wanting to talk to Sarah alone. The very thought disturbed him, and he'd have loved to be a fly on somebody's shoulder to hear that particular conversation. He couldn't imagine what the two of them had to say to each other. They were worlds apart. If he didn't know Michelle better, he'd have sworn there'd been some jealousy in her display by the corral.

Still, she deserved better treatment than being put on hold while he tried to straighten out his life. It was too much to ask of anyone, especially the woman he intended to marry. So he figured he deserved whatever reprimands she doled out. Although, knowing Michelle, she'd do nothing of the sort.

When he walked into the house, he found her busily setting the dinner table, while Millie fussed over the stove. Neither Sarah nor Drew were anywhere around. Before he could say a word, Millie took over.

"Miss Hawthorne's staying for dinner," she said. "Go on up now, and get out of those wet clothes. Dinner'll be ready in fifteen minutes."

Knowing better than to argue with Millie, Reece headed upstairs.

THE LAST TIME Reece had eaten dinner in the house had been the night before Elizabeth left for the East Coast. He dreaded another meal like that one.

To his surprise, however, things were subdued. For one thing, Michelle was too gracious to pick and prod at Sarah the way his mother had. Although she did ask a polite question or two. Other than that, no one had much to say. Everyone—especially Drew—seemed too worn-out to talk.

"I guess we're all pretty tired," Reece said at one point after a long stretch of silence.

"It has been a busy day," Sarah agreed.

"Especially with all of you getting soaked," Michelle added.

Drew stifled a yawn and sat a little straighter in his chair. "I'm not tired."

"I can see that." Reece smiled at his son and then caught Sarah's eye as she, too, smiled knowingly. Lord, she was beautiful when she smiled. Her entire face lit up, her eyes turning a warmer, softer brown than usual, her lips gently curving upward—

"You should make it an early night, Drew," Millie said, interrupting Reece's thoughts.

"Millie's right," Reece said, realizing that the last thing he needed to be thinking about was Sarah's lips. "Right after dinner, hit the sack, young man."

"Aw, Dad." But it was a token protest at best.

Everyone finished eating shortly after that, and as Millie cleared the table, Sarah ushered Drew off to bed. It was the first chance Reece had to talk to Michelle alone.

He led her into the living room, and as soon as he'd closed the double paneled doors, she said, "Things seem to be going very well between Sarah and Drew."

"They get along." Reece headed for the wet bar and pulled a tumbler and wineglass from the rack. "Glass of wine?"

"No, thanks. But you go ahead."

Reece nodded and poured three fingers of scotch into the tumbler, as Michelle settled onto the couch.

"Actually," she said, "I think they're more than just getting along. It's obvious she's crazy about him."

He didn't answer, but reached into the small refrigerator under the bar and pulled out a few ice cubes. He knew Michelle was leading up to something. Though it wasn't like her to take the long way around things.

"Sarah says that Drew's making progress with his schoolwork," she continued. "Though she wouldn't tell me anything about how he's doing with his eating and medication. Have there been any more incidents?"

"Michelle," he crossed the room and sat in the chair beside her, "it's not like you to ramble."

She hesitated, looking away for a moment, before turning to look at him with troubled blue eyes. "I thought you'd at least call me."

Reece fought the guilt her simple statement aroused. She was right. He should have called. "I've been very busy," he said.

"Yes. I can see that."

Resentment rushed through him, although he couldn't have said exactly why. He deserted his chair and moved to stand by the front windows. "For God's sake, Michelle, aren't I allowed to spend an afternoon with my son?"

"Of course you are."

For once her rational manner and calm voice failed to soothe him. He wanted her to snap at him, yell. Tell him to go to hell.

Instead, she said, "What's wrong with you, Reece? I've never seen you like this."

He sighed and turned to look at her. His irrational anger evaporated as quickly as it had surfaced—as soon as he'd realized where it had come from. Guilt. He'd spent the afternoon with Sarah, as well as Drew, and he'd enjoyed himself immensely. It should have been Michelle, his fiancée, with him and Drew this afternoon. Not his ex-wife. "I'm sorry. You're right. I should have called."

For a moment she remained quiet, then said, "Have you made a decision about the campaign?"

"Yes, I have." Actually he'd hardly thought about it until this afternoon. He crossed the room and sat down again in the chair beside her. "I've decided to withdraw."

"I see." Michelle straightened a little, her hands folded neatly in her lap. "Is this decision final? Or can we talk about it?"

"There's really not much to talk about." He took a sip of his drink, thinking about the best way to handle this. He wanted her to understand. "The last few days with Drew have been ... well, let's just say I've discovered I have a son I hardly know. I want to spend time with him." That wasn't all of it, he admitted to himself. There was the ranch, too. He'd missed running it. But he didn't think Michelle wanted to hear that.

She leaned forward in her chair. "Why can't you do both? Run for office and spend time with Drew?"

"You know why." Unable to sit still, he again deserted his chair and returned to the windows. Outside, the day hovered between darkness and light, as his ranch wound down for the evening.

Facing Michelle again, he said, "We've just begun this campaign, and look how much time I've already spent. It's taken me away from the ranch and from Drew. And it's only going to get worse. You know that." Reece ran a hand through his hair. "He's starting to come around. Did you hear him laughing tonight? I've never known him to laugh like that before."

Michelle remained silent for several minutes. Then she said, "Well, you have to do what's best for you and Drew."

It was a typical Michelle comment. Cool. Pleasant. Undisturbed. Yet he knew this had to be upsetting for her, and he wondered what was really going on in her head. It was something he never knew with Michelle. He could never see beyond her composed exterior.

"What about you?" he asked. "What about us?"

"That's up to you." She rose from her chair. "Is there still an 'us'?"

Reece closed the distance between them and gently gripped her upper arms. "Michelle, come over to the ranch more often. Spend some time with Drew and me. Get to know my son, too."

She shook her head and looked away. "I don't think so, Reece."

"Why not?" He took her chin in his hand and turned her head so that she had to look at him. "After all, we're going to be a family soon."

She shifted from under his hands and stepped back. "Are we?"

"Of course." He moved toward her again but stopped when she raised her hands as if to ward him off.

"A couple of weeks ago," she said, "I would've agreed with you. But now I'm not so sure. I'm not sure we want the same things anymore."

"All because I've dropped out of this campaign to spend time with my son?" His resentment stirred. "That hardly makes sense."

"Doesn't it? You forget why we decided to get married to begin with."

"I haven't forgotten."

"We were going to use our family names and money to change things for Wyoming. To make this a better place for the people who live here."

"I don't see how that's changed. This is only one election, Michelle. There'll be others."

"Will there?"

"Of course. Let me just get through this time with Drew."

For a few moments, she didn't say anything. Then she went to pick up her purse on a nearby table. "I think you have a lot of thinking to do, Reece. You have decisions to make that have nothing to do with whether you're ever going to run for office again." She moved across the room but stopped and turned at the door. "And the biggest of those decisions is whether or not you're still in love with your ex-wife."

Then she turned and left him alone.

Reece didn't move for several minutes. He heard the front door open and close and the purr of the engine as she started her car. He shifted to look out the window. The last of the day's light had given way to darkness. He should go after her, stop her from leaving, but his feet remained anchored to the floor.

She was right.

He no longer knew how he felt about Sarah—not the woman she'd become, anyway. He'd once loved her, the reserved proud girl he'd married. This new Sarah, this woman, was an entirely different matter, however. He looked at her and saw fragments of the girl, but there was so much more. He also perceived sadness and regret, compassion and patience.

In some ways, she'd already captured him again. He wanted her. He'd admitted that days ago. But it was more than that. She stirred feelings in him he'd never expected to experience again. He'd vowed years ago never again to trust someone with his heart, never to be that vulnerable again. Yet here he was, questioning what he felt toward the very woman who'd once torn his heart to shreds.

He didn't love her. He couldn't. Even though this afternoon, while he watched her with Drew, something inside him had come alive. Something other than lust.

He moved away from the window as Michelle's car became two red taillights heading away from the Crooked C. Sinking into one of the armchairs, he picked up the scotch and took a long swallow.

The safest course of action would be to send Sarah away. Before she did more damage, before she totally burrowed her way into his heart as she had thirteen years ago.

Then he remembered Drew's laughter.

That was Sarah's doing. Somehow, in one short week, she'd worked wonders on his son. He didn't know how she'd done it, but he couldn't risk undoing it by sending her away. He couldn't trade Drew's happiness for his own peace of mind. Even if it meant risking his own heart once again.

SARAH WAITED until she heard Michelle's car drive away before heading down the back stairs and out the kitchen door. As she made her way toward the barn, she drank in the fresh night air and the myriad stars overhead. The day had been filled with so many conflicting emotions she needed this time alone with her thoughts.

She stopped first at the corral where the Appaloosa paced. She didn't even have to call to him anymore. He was already at the fence waiting impatiently for her, as she stepped onto the bottom rail to feed him the carrots she'd brought from the kitchen. It had become a ritual with the two of them, and Sarah figured she looked forward to it as much as he did. Then, after patting him on the neck, she walked over to the pen where Tod had left one of the pregnant mares for the night. Sarah climbed up to sit on the top railing, and the little mare pranced shyly over to collect her share of the goodies.

It was a glorious night, clear and cool, scented with the pungent smells of the ranch. She realized she felt good tonight, despite the roller coaster of emotions the day had produced. It was wonderful to see her son happy. She could handle anything if at the end of each day she could hear his laughter.

"May I join you?"

She started at Reece's voice and nearly lost her balance.

"I'm sorry," he said as she turned, ready to chastise him for once again startling her. "I have to learn to walk louder."

Sarah shook her head, unable to stop her slight smile. He sounded sincerely contrite this time. "You could try issuing a warning call from twenty feet or something."

"I'll keep that in mind." He pushed his hat to the back of his head and shoved his hands into the pockets of his jeans. "Do you mind if I join you for a few minutes?"

She hesitated and then said, "It's your place, Reece." She wasn't at all sure she wanted company. Especially his. In one way or another he always managed to disturb her, splintering whatever peace she'd found in this crazy situation.

He acknowledged her comment with a nod and moved to lean against the fence. The mare ambled over, checking to see if he had anything better to offer than Sarah did.

He stroked the horse's muzzle and said, "Whatcha looking for, girl?" She nudged his shoulder. Laughing softly, he reached into his shirt pocket and produced a sugar cube. "Here you go, you big baby. How's that?"

"You're a soft touch," Sarah said.

"Yeah, well, she's expecting." He looked up at Sarah, his expression all but invisible in the dim light. "And I've always had a weakness for pregnant females."

Again Sarah almost lost her seat on the railing. Confused, she looked away. He was doing it again. Finding another way to throw her off-balance. What a strange thing for him to say. All day he'd behaved differently from the man who'd hired her to tutor his son, less angry and more like the boy she'd once loved. He'd actually seemed like a different person. It frightened her. Because this Reece was infinitely more disturbing.

"I can't believe the changes in Drew," Reece said finally. "You've worked wonders on him."

Again his words surprised her. First because he'd said them, and second because he couldn't see what had precipitated the change in Drew.

"It's not me," she said.

"You're being modest."

"No. It's you. The time you're spending with him."

"I don't think so."

"As far as Drew's concerned, I'm just a tutor." She reached out to stroke the mare. "You're his father. He wants to be with you."

Reece looked at her with skepticism.

He didn't get it, she realized. He didn't grasp the truth when it was right in front of him. But *she* saw it. Drew was beginning to open up because of the time Reece spent with him: the evenings Reece checked Drew's work, the hours they spent together with the horses and the days, like today, when Reece rough-housed with Drew in a chilly mountain stream. To her, it had been clear from the beginning what Drew's problem had been: he needed a full-time father.

"Whatever the cause," Reece said after a few moments of silence, "I want you to know I appreciate it. Also, in case you're right about Drew, I think you should know I'm pulling out of the campaign."

They'd never talked about his political aspirations. She'd considered it none of her business. But now she couldn't keep the surprise out of her voice. "But why,

Reece? I thought you wanted that seat. That it was only a first step for you.''

He met her gaze steadily. "It's not worth losing Drew over.''

A rush of warmth filled her, momentarily silencing her. Reece planned to give up his political career for Drew. For his son. Suddenly she thought of Lyssa, and Sarah realized how selfish she'd been. Reece had a right to know he had a daughter, and Lyssa deserved to know she had a father.

But she couldn't tell him. Not yet, anyway. She was still afraid of his reaction, still afraid he might demand custody of Lyssa and send her, Sarah, away. And she needed more time with Drew. But she realized she couldn't wait forever. Eventually she'd have to tell him about his daughter.

"Don't worry," he said, obviously misinterpreting her silence. "I'll be taking back the reins of the ranch, so I'll be keeping busy. I'll stay out of your way while you're working with Drew." He paused. "And other times, as well."

Sarah took a deep breath. Reece was offering to stay away from her for the remainder of her stay at the Crooked C. This time, she realized, he meant it. He'd let her work with Drew without interference, without watching over her shoulder every step of the way. But was that what she really wanted? To have Reece avoid her? As few as ten hours ago she'd have sworn to it. Now she didn't know.

"Thank you," she said finally, as she fought the strong sense of loss that settled over her.

CHAPTER NINE

THE NEXT FEW WEEKS passed quickly for Sarah.

It was a bittersweet time. Caught between missing Lyssa and not wanting to leave Drew, Sarah's moods swung from one extreme to the other. Then there was Reece. Always Reece, in her thoughts, in her dreams. She couldn't escape her feelings for him. She loved him. It seemed as though she'd always loved him and had never stopped. Yet she knew that for years, before she'd come back to the Crooked C to help her son, she'd managed to keep her love locked away, hidden, even from herself.

All it had taken to bring it all back was seeing him again. Fortunately Reece had kept his word. He no longer hovered. In fact, except at dinner, she barely saw him. Millie had adjusted her schedule to accommodate him, and he'd started eating with them in the evening. He'd ask about Drew's progress, but it was a far cry from his earlier interrogations. Sarah often wondered if she'd have been able to tough it out if the situation with Reece had remained as volatile as it had been in that first week. She told herself she was lucky she never had to find out, but sometimes she wondered.

Lyssa's letters helped. She wrote her mother several times a week. They were short notes, filled with news of Tuwa and Joseph Bright Eagle and his sons and grandsons. For Lyssa, staying with Tuwa was like being away at summer camp—the very best kind of vacation—because her days were spent with the horses. Hers was a simple straightforward world, and it made Sarah smile every time she read one of her daughter's accounts of events on the reservation.

As for Drew, he became more and more adept at his studies, mastering concepts as easily as any of her best students. Every now and then, she'd have to remind herself that he'd heard all this stuff before. In a classroom. More than likely he'd absorbed more of it than either he or his teachers had realized.

Over and above his schoolwork, Sarah enjoyed his company. Half the time she almost forgot about the secrets she kept from him. Not that he was a perfect angel—far from it. In fact, she'd worry about any twelve-year-old boy who didn't misbehave now and then. He had his days and his moods.

One afternoon in particular, he'd reminded her he was still very much a child. A child who hurt. He'd wanted to spend the day out by the creek. They'd been working on a particularly difficult set of math concepts, and Sarah thought that, under the circumstances, they needed to stay inside. In typical preteen fashion, he'd punished her by sulking and being irritable throughout the lesson. Then, when she'd reminded him about his afternoon snack, he'd gotten angry.

"You don't have to tell me every time!" he snapped, shoving away from the desk and crossing the room to plop himself on the corner of his bed. "I know when I'm supposed to eat."

"Well, good," she said. "Then you won't forget."

"I never forget."

"Is that so?" She'd been wanting to talk to him about his diabetes for weeks, but this wasn't exactly how she'd planned to broach the subject. Nor was he in the mood she'd have preferred. Well, she'd learned long ago that with kids, you didn't always get to pick your times. You took the opportunity when it arose. "According to Miss Adams—"

"What does *she* know?"

"According to Miss Adams," Sarah started again patiently, "four or five times last month, your sugar level dropped so low you had an insulin reaction. She said she had to give you sugar cubes. And once, you almost passed out."

"So?"

"So why did you do it?"

"You make it sound like I did it on purpose."

Sarah crossed her arms on the desk and stared at her stubborn son. "Didn't you?" Sometimes he reminded her so much of his father. Especially at times like this when he dug his heels in about something.

"Are you trying to cause an insulin reaction today by not eating?" she asked. "Are you checking up on me to see how long it will take before I notice you're sick? Or testing me to see if I'll get something in your system before you pass out? Or maybe you're just trying to make yourself sick enough to get out of doing your math problems. Which is it?"

"You don't know anything about it."

"Then explain it to me." She leaned back in her chair and waited for him to start talking.

At first he didn't say anything. He just sat there, picking at a loose thread on his bedspread. Just when Sarah thought maybe she'd pushed him too far, he said, "I hate it."

She breathed a sigh of relief. "What? The diabetes?"

"Yeah." He looked ill at ease, but evidently his need to talk outweighed his discomfort. "The dumb shots. And checking my blood sugar three or four times a day. Who needs it?"

"You do," she answered softly.

He finally looked at her, his anger and pain evident in every rigid muscle of his body. "It's not fair!"

"You're right." Sarah's heart ached for him. "It's not fair. But—"

"I know what you're going to say. 'Who said life was fair?'" He rolled his eyes, bright with unshed tears. "That's Grandmother's favorite line."

Sarah smiled sadly. For once, she agreed with Elizabeth. "What else does your grandmother say?"

"Oh, you know, dumb stuff like living with the hand you're dealt." He pulled his knees up to his chest and wrapped his arms around them. "Well, I'm sick of it."

"I'm so sorry, Drew."

He went on as if she hadn't spoken. "I've always got to watch what I eat. If someone has a birthday cake or something at school, do you think I get any? No way! The teachers make sure I don't slip up. They're afraid my sugar count might get too high. Maybe I'll go into a coma or something. Like that would happen from one dumb piece of cake." He shook his head, and the tears slipped from his eyes. He wiped at them furiously with the back of his hand. "And forget birthday parties. I never even get invited. What would they do with poor sick little Drew Colby when it came time to serve cake and ice cream?" His cynicism nearly broke her heart. No child, no twelve-year-old, should be forced to see things this clearly. "Other kids get to eat anything they want." Again the anger flashed across his face, before he gave in to the tears. "I want to be like everyone else."

She couldn't fight it any longer, she crossed the room and put her arms around him. He resisted at first, trying to pull away from her, but she held on until he finally gave in—as much as any twelve-year-old boy can—and remained in her arms, his face buried against her shoulder. Sarah held him, absorbing his silent sobs while savoring the feel of him, the small frame that usually seemed so sturdy, the sweaty little-boy smell and the tears no mother wanted to see. She'd needed to hold him for so long. Not like this, though. Not like this.

When he calmed down, Sarah reluctantly released him. "Are you okay?" she asked.

He nodded once and pulled up the collar of his T-shirt, wiping his eyes and face. Sarah winced, but refrained from reminding him what tissues were for.

"Miss Hanson," he said, embarrassment taking over now that he'd gotten past the tears. "You won't tell Dad, will you?"

"This is just between us, Drew." She couldn't stop her hand from reaching out to brush the heavy dark hair away from his forehead.

"I mean, don't tell him . . . you know . . . I got upset or nothing."

Sarah smiled sadly. Little boys and men, and their foolish male pride. "I promise. I won't tell a soul."

He nodded his thanks.

"You know, Drew . . ." She hesitated, not sure whether her own story would help or make things worse. Then she decided that if it didn't help now, he might remember it sometime in the future, and it might help him then. "When I was growing up, I was different from all the other kids, too."

He looked at her doubtfully. "I thought you lived with your grandmother on the reservation?"

Sarah nodded. "I did. And my grandmother was very good to me. But I didn't really belong. I'm only half-Indian."

He didn't look convinced.

"When you look at me," she said, "what do you see?"

Drew shrugged. "I don't know. You're a lady..."

"Do you see an Indian?"

He shrugged. "Yeah, I guess."

"When the other children on the reservation looked at me, they saw a white girl."

"But—"

"My hair and skin are too light, my face too narrow." She noticed him looking at her more closely. "I was different—neither white nor Indian."

"Were they mean?"

Sarah shook her head. "No. Oh, every now and then one of them would take a potshot at me—probably the way they do at you. But children do that to each other no matter what. It was nothing excessive. The thing was, *I* knew I was different. Just as *you* know you're different."

She let him think about that for a moment and then reached over and lifted his chin so he had to look at her. "You've got to do a favor for me, Drew."

He eyed her warily.

Dropping her hand, she smiled and again started to brush at his hair, but stopped herself this time. "It's not a tough favor. All you have to do is listen to me, and think about what I'm saying."

"Okay." He didn't sound sure.

"Your grandmother was right. You have to live with the diabetes." He started to say something, but she held up a hand. "I know it's not fair. But you don't have a choice. The only choice you *do* have is whether to live a long healthy life by taking care of yourself. Or whether to make yourself sick by fighting it, to lose a limb or go blind, or go into kidney failure."

She knew he'd heard all this before, and it nearly broke her heart that she couldn't pull him back into her arms and tell him more lies. She wished she could tell him that she'd make everything better, that this disease he'd been born with would go away. But she couldn't. Of all the lies she'd told her son, that would be the cruelest.

Instead, she said, "But I'll be here for you," though she knew even this wouldn't be true for long. "Anytime you need to rant and rave at this condition you're stuck with, you come to me." She reached out and pushed the hair from his face. "You can be as angry as you want. And it'll be our secret."

AFTERWARD, SARAH THOUGHT about Elizabeth Colby and the advice she'd given her grandson. It seemed out of character for the woman Sarah thought she knew. Of course, how well did she really know Elizabeth? They'd only spoken to each other three times. The first time had been when Reece had brought Sarah home to introduce her as his wife. She'd been seventeen and Reece eighteen. Then there'd been the day Elizabeth had shown up at that miserable apartment in Laramie and offered Sarah ten thousand dollars to desert her husband and son. And finally their unsettling confrontation a few weeks ago.

Certainly she'd seen Elizabeth at her worst.

But then there was Drew. A strong boy, living with an incurable disease, struggling every day of his life to come to terms with the differences between himself and every other child he knew. And it had been Elizabeth who had raised him, taught him to deal with it. Sarah had a feeling her son was an example of the best of Elizabeth Colby.

As THE SUMMER wore on, Reece struggled with his promise to stay out of Sarah's way. Not that he didn't trust her as a teacher. He'd seen for himself how good she was with Drew. It was Sarah, the woman, Reece avoided. Even though he would have liked to join her every now and then—when she headed out with Drew to the creek for the afternoon, or when she sat on the corral fence in the evening spoiling his horses. He wanted to talk to her about Drew somewhere other than at the dinner table with other ears present. Hell, he wanted to press her up against a wall again and kiss her silly.

And that was why he kept his promise.

Because he couldn't trust *himself*. He couldn't guarantee that if he spent more time with her he wouldn't do exactly that—kiss her until they both forgot everything but each other. So he kept his distance, funneling all his spare time and energy into Drew.

Then the first day of August dawned clear, bright and hot. The next day was when Drew was supposed to take his test to see if he'd be starting seventh grade or returning to the sixth grade in the fall. He was a wreck, and Tod had told him to forget his chores for the day and sent him in early to work with Sarah.

Reece had a different idea.

Sarah and Drew had evidently just started working when he interrupted them. Strolling into the room, he settled himself on a corner of Drew's bed. "Well, son, are you ready?"

Drew shrugged.

Sarah sprang to his defense immediately, making Reece smile. "He's going to do fine," she said. "He's been studying hard for the past six weeks."

"That's good," Reece said, though he wondered if it was the mother or the teacher in her who was speaking. Either way, it didn't change his plans for the day. Rising from the bed, he crossed to Drew's desk and shut the book he'd been reading. "I think you both deserve a little time off."

"But I can't, Dad. Tomorrow is—"

"I know what tomorrow is." Reece rested his hand on Drew's shoulder and tried to reassure him. "If you don't know enough to pass that test by now, Drew, you're not going to learn it today." Reece gave the boy's shoulder a squeeze. "Besides, when you've prepared for something as hard as you've prepared for this test, it's best to take the day before off. It gives you a chance to relax, so you'll be at your best." Turning to Sarah, he asked, "What do you think? Does Drew deserve a day off?"

She looked surprised that he'd asked her opinion, and it took her a moment to answer. "I think it's a great idea."

"Good." Reece squeezed Drew's shoulder again. "Because I have something special in mind." And he planned to break his promise to Sarah in the process.

Drew hesitated a moment, obviously still worried, and then he brightened. "Are we going to go to the creek?"

"Nope. I've got a better idea." Reece smiled mysteriously, first for Drew and then for Sarah. He knew just how to tempt her. "How about Devils Tower? I don't believe Miss Hanson has ever been there."

Sarah's eyes lit up, and he knew he'd guessed right. Devils Tower was considered a sacred place to the Indian tribes who'd once roamed these hills. The Shoshone were no exception.

"You're right," she said. "I've never been there, but I've always wanted to go."

"Then it's settled," Reece said, heading for the door.

"Wait," Sarah said. "You and Drew should go alone. Spend the day together."

Reece started to argue, but Drew saved him the trouble. "I've been there plenty," he said. "It's really neat. You gotta see it."

Sarah glanced at Reece, who said, "It's his day." *Come on Sarah,* he thought. *Just this once. One day for Drew.*

She didn't disappoint him. After a moment, she smiled. "Okay."

"All right!" Drew cheered, and Reece knew exactly how he felt.

WITHIN THE HOUR the three of them set out in Reece's truck for Devils Tower, the nation's first national monument.

They caught their first glimpse of it as they headed north on Highway 24. They rounded a bend, and it rose from the horizon, a lone mass of gray rock standing like a sentinel over the surrounding valley. Even from a distance, it took Reece's breath away, reminding him of all the legends he'd heard told around campfires about this place. Then another curve, and it disappeared. The tower played hide-and-seek with them for miles, growing larger each time it emerged, only to vanish again.

Suddenly it dominated its surroundings. They'd reached the boundaries of the national monument. Reece pulled into the parking lot, and Sarah hardly seemed to notice the large number of people milling about. She had eyes only for the tower.

"Mato Tepee," she whispered.

"Bear Lodge," Reece translated for Drew. "It's the Indian name for the tower. The Indians have worshiped it for centuries."

Sarah smiled at him, obviously pleased he remembered.

"Come on," Drew said as he jumped out of the truck and grabbed Sarah's hand. "You gotta see the movie at the Visitors' Center first. It'll tell you all kinds of neat junk. You know, like history and stuff."

Sarah's laughter floated through the air, warming Reece's insides. She cast him one final smile and let Drew drag her toward the Visitors' Center. Neither adult enlightened Drew about her extensive knowledge of Devils Tower.

For most of her life Sarah had heard stories about this holy place. She'd always wanted to visit, but as a child, they'd never had the means. Later she'd just never seemed able to find the time. Or maybe it was more that Devils Tower was too close to the Crooked C, her son and Reece Colby. Either way, she knew

Reece had brought her now because he knew how much seeing Mato Tepee meant to her.

After their brief stop at the center, they spent the rest of the afternoon exploring. And for a few hours, Sarah felt part of a real family. If she closed her eyes, she could almost convince herself that this would last, that it was for more than just one day. She could even stretch it and imagine Lyssa with them, teasing Drew and asking her father dozens of questions.

Once, as Drew ran ahead, Reece took her hand to help her over some rocks, and she caught his gaze. She knew for that instant, they shared the fantasy. They both wished today were real.

Then Drew came running back to them, shattering the moment, and they both returned to reality.

They hiked the mile-and-a-half Tower Trail that circled the base of the tower, taking two side paths: one to see the nearby Missouri Buttes, a set of five dome-shaped buttes northwest of the tower; and the other for a spectacular view of the Belle Fourche River. They looked through the peephole to see the old wooden ladder Will Rogers had used to climb to the top of the tower. And when they came up on Durrance Crack, the most popular modern route to the top, they stood for a while and watched a group of climbers start their ascent up the steep rock walls.

"When I get older," Drew said, "I'm going to climb to the top and spend the night up there."

Sarah looked at Reece, and they both groaned.

"Come on," Reece said, throwing his arm around Drew's shoulders and leading him away. "We'll discuss that in a few years."

"How about twenty?" Sarah added laughingly.

They continued their hike, and Sarah reveled in the beauty and variety of the flora and fauna. Pines and aspens and burr oaks. Queen Anne's lace and wild roses. And scurrying amidst it all were squirrels and chipmunks, raccoons and beavers. It was if the animals knew this valley was sacred, and so chose to make it their home.

As the afternoon wound down, they went to eat at Mato Village, a restaurant at the park entrance. Afterward, Reece found a spot alongside the road, and they settled with blankets in the back of the truck to wait for dusk. Slowly the sun set, transforming the tower to a rich golden red. Tears slipped from Sarah's eyes as she watched, grateful for having shared this day and this sight with Reece and Drew. She only wished that Lyssa could have been here with them.

She glanced at Reece, and apparently sensing her eyes on him, he turned to look at her. The expression on his face told her more than words. He, too, had been shaken by the beauty of this place.

Long after the surrounding hills no longer picked up the shades of rose, the tower still glowed. Then full night fell, and the stark stone tower stood out against the dark sky. Bold. Beautiful. A triumph of nature.

Sarah was the first to notice that Drew had fallen asleep. Reaching over to Reece, she tapped him on the shoulder to get his attention. "Your son's asleep," she whispered.

Reece smiled lovingly at Drew. "So he is."

It took some maneuvering to get the sleeping twelve-year-old out of the back of the truck and into the cab without waking him. Somehow Reece managed. Then they rode in silence back to the ranch, Drew curled up on the seat between them, his head on Sarah's lap.

When they got home, Sarah opened and closed doors as Reece carried Drew into the house. In his room, Sarah pulled back the covers and then reluctantly backed away as Reece laid Drew on the bed. She wanted to stay, to help the father of her child get him ready for the night. Then she wanted to tuck the covers around him and kiss him.

It was one fantasy she couldn't indulge.

The day had ended and it was time to remember her position here. Drew's tutor.

She waited in the hall until Reece came out. When he spotted her, he stopped short and closed Drew's door softly behind him. He searched her face, and she felt the hunger in him as surely as if he'd been pressed against her.

"Let's go outside," he said.

She wanted to say yes, to suggest they finish the day together, as they'd started it. Instead, she took a step back and shook her head. "No. I'm tired and need to go to bed." If she went outside with him, she knew what would happen. They would end up making love, and she'd lose the few remaining pieces of her heart. She couldn't allow that to happen. "I just wanted to tell you how special today was."

He nodded without saying anything.

"Anyway," she said, suddenly feeling awkward, "I'll be leaving soon. The day after tomorrow, after Drew takes and passes his test. And... well, I want to know if I can write to him."

Reece looked surprised, but before he could answer, she hurried on, "I won't tell him who I am." She reached out and laid her hand on his arm. "I just want to keep in touch. An occasional card or note." She hated begging, but she would if that was what it took.

She couldn't leave here knowing she'd never see or talk to her son again.

Reece covered her hand with his. "This has been very hard on you, hasn't it?"

She didn't know how to answer. Of all the things she'd thought he might say to her, she'd never considered this. That he'd notice how difficult it had been. Yet... "Some of it has been wonderful," she said truthfully. "You gave me an opportunity to get to know my son."

"But not all of it has been good."

"No. It's been hard, too." Harder than he'd ever know. Not just because of Drew, but because of Lyssa, too. "Living a lie."

"I'm sorry."

She nodded, holding back the emotions—and the tears—threatening to spill out. Then, taking a deep breath, she asked again, "Can I write to him?"

"Yes."

Relieved, Sarah released her breath. "Thank you."

Then quickly, before she could change her mind about going outside with Reece, she turned and fled into her room, closing and locking the door behind her. Leaning against the solid barrier, she waited for the sound of his retreating footsteps on the hardwood floors. Finally, after what seemed an eternity, she heard him leave and she was finally able to breath normally, knowing she'd barely escaped.

THE NEXT MORNING, Drew asked Sarah if she would take him into town for his test. He said he didn't want to drag his dad away from the ranch. At first, Reece objected. Then Sarah took him aside and explained why Drew didn't want him there. If Drew messed up, he didn't want his father to witness it.

So Sarah and Drew headed into Devils Corner alone to meet with Rebecca Adams. Drew remained quiet during the drive. Sarah hated to see him so worried about this test, but there was nothing more she could do. He'd learned as much as one child could possibly absorb in six weeks. It would have to be enough.

As they entered her classroom, Miss Adams rose from her chair and greeted them. "Miss Hanson, Drew, you're right on time." Then turning to Drew, she said, "Miss Hanson tells me you've been working hard."

Drew shrugged—his standard answer to anything he didn't want to talk about.

Sarah smiled at the other teacher. "He's not going to have any trouble today."

"I'm sure you're right." Picking up some papers, Rebecca motioned toward one of the student desks. "Shall we get started, Drew? Or do you need to eat something first?"

Irritation crossed Drew's features, and Sarah started to say something. Drew beat her to it. "I can start now, Miss Adams. I ate in the car. I'm good until around noon."

Sarah's smile broadened. She knew he hated being given special treatment, even though Rebecca had only meant to be considerate. Maybe he'd realized that, because this time he'd handled it well. Sarah considered taking Rebecca aside later and telling her not to single him out, but decided against it. Drew would learn to deal with her, and with all the other well-meaning people he'd meet in his life, in his own way.

"Well," she said, backing toward the door. "I brought a book. I'll just sit out in the hall and read."

"Oh, I meant to tell you," Rebecca said, "there's no need to wait. I'll bring Drew home when we're done here."

"That's not necessary."

"It's no problem. My place is out that way, and besides, I'd like to meet his father."

Sarah glanced at Drew, who nodded. "It's okay with me, Miss Hanson." He was being brave. She knew it. Every maternal instinct shouted at her to wait for him. Instead, she decided to let him be strong.

"Okay, then. I'll see you back at the ranch."

Sarah made her way out of the school, telling herself she was doing the right thing. When she stepped outside, she saw dark clouds gathered ominously on the western horizon.

Shivering despite the August heat, she hurried to her car.

CHAPTER TEN

REECE HADN'T EXPECTED the storm to move in so quickly.

In the fifteen minutes he'd been in the barn securing windows and putting away equipment, the situation had gone from bad to worse. Heavy clouds darkened the late-morning sky, turning the light an eerie shade of gray-green. A gust of wind rolled over him, and he grabbed his hat and pulled it lower on his forehead.

Cursing under his breath, he headed back toward the corrals. Five horses, including both pregnant mares, still needed to be moved into the barn. Wyoming weather was totally unpredictable. Even in the middle of summer, golf ball-size hail and freak windstorms weren't unheard-of. He needed to get those horses inside. Now.

He'd just taken hold of the first mare when Sarah drove up and parked alongside the fence. Climbing out of her car, she hurried over to him. "Can I help?"

"Where's Drew?"

She brushed at the hair blowing in her face. "It's okay. His teacher's going to bring him home when they're done. What can I do here?"

Reece nodded toward the mare. "Get her inside while I get the other mare." Sarah grabbed the horse's halter, and Reece headed back toward the corral.

"Come on, girl," she crooned to the nervous animal.

Once in the barn, out of the wind, the horse settled somewhat. Sarah got her into her stall and was just closing the door when Reece entered leading the second mare. Sarah hurried to help him by opening another stall door while he led the horse in.

"Two more and then the Appaloosa," Reece said as they headed back outside.

"Where's Tod?" Sarah asked. She'd just realized none of the other hands were around.

"Out with the herd. A storm like this could start a stampede. Come on."

They worked together to get the rest of the horses in. By the time the last was safely in his stall, both Sarah and Reece were soaking wet. Reece closed the stall door, and Sarah collapsed against it.

"Thanks," he said. "I'm not sure I'd have gotten the stallion in on time if you hadn't shown up."

"No problem. I enjoy chasing crazy horses in the rain."

Reece laughed lightly and smiled at the sight of her, her dewy rain-soaked skin, the damp tendrils of hair escaping her braid and sticking to her forehead and cheeks. He automatically reached to brush them aside, and her eyes widened at the touch. His hand froze. Then slowly, he finished what he'd started, clearing her face of the damp strands. Her skin felt like satin against his fingers, smooth and sleek.

"Reece," she whispered, and he heard the unspoken question in her voice, saw it in her eyes.

"Yes," he answered, thinking they'd avoided this too long.

His glaze slid lower, to the slim column of her neck and then to her breasts. Her white sleeveless blouse clung to her, revealing the lace of her bra and the darkness of her nipples, stiff and inviting from the chilly rain. Under his scrutiny, they hardened further. He smiled, for the moment suppressing the desire to lean over and taste them through the thin fabric. Instead, he brought his eyes slowly back to her face, past the wild pulse at her throat, to her dark hungry eyes.

"God, you're beautiful," he said.

He heard her breath catch, saw her lips press together. She captivated him like no other woman he'd ever known, tempting him with her existence, teasing him with her presence. He brought his other hand up to frame her face, holding her head for a moment, before slowly lowering his mouth to hers.

This is crazy, he told himself, even as his lips drank of hers, taking in their moisture, savoring their softness. *Sheer madness,* he thought again. But he couldn't, wouldn't stop. Not unless she asked him to.

"Sweet," he murmured against her mouth. "So sweet." He traced her lips with the tip of his tongue, gently requesting entrance. With a soft sigh, her eyes fluttered shut and she opened to him, pulling his tongue into the honeyed depths of her mouth.

She tasted dark and sultry, bewitching him, but he gave himself over to her willingly. She was both the young girl he'd loved and lost years ago, and the woman who'd sneaked past his defenses. Her arms slipped around his waist, tentatively at first. But as he leaned against her, pressing her against the door, she tightened her hold.

Releasing her mouth, he slid his hands to her bare shoulders and bent to sample the pulse at the base of her neck. He'd wanted to taste her there for weeks, to feel her excitement grow through the accelerating throb at her throat.

She moaned, and he lowered one hand to her breast, kneading the tender flesh through the thin material. It wasn't enough. He wanted to touch her skin, to feel the puckering of her nipples beneath his fingers, to taste them as he did her pulse.

He moved his hand to the row of buttons that ran down the front of her shirt and quickly undid the first two, just enough to push the fabric aside and reveal the soft honey-colored flesh beneath it. He pulled back to look at her, running his fingers over the swell of her breasts and then slipping them under the top edge of her bra.

She let her head fall back against the wooden door, and he shifted his hand to take one nipple between his thumb and index finger, rubbing it until she moaned. He covered her mouth once again, mixing her sounds of pleasure with his own.

Still, he wanted more of her.

Freeing her mouth once again, he shoved her shirt and bra strap off one shoulder, exposing one delectable breast.

"Yes," she whispered, and he couldn't deny either of them. Sliding his hands to her waist, he bent and took her rigid nipple into his mouth.

Sarah thought she'd break apart if he didn't take her soon. Caught between torment and rapture, she wound her fingers into his hair, holding his head against her breast, surrendering to the pure physical pleasure of his mouth on her, pulling, sucking, making her want more.

And she *did* want so much more.

She ached. Inside, at the core of her femininity, she needed him, his hands, his mouth, every part of him. She longed to spread her thighs for him, for herself, and feel him hard inside her. She didn't care about their past or even their future at the moment. What she hungered for was elemental and fierce. She was a woman who desired this man, the only man she'd ever known, ever loved.

"Reece," she said, hardly recognizing the harsh plea as her own voice. "Please. Love me."

He released her breast, and she moaned in protest, but he scooped her into his arms, kissing her to silence as he carried her to the ladder that led to the loft. Pulling away, he asked, "Are you sure, Sarah?"

In answer, she found his mouth, showing him how much this meant to her, how much she longed for it, for him. He let her feet slide to the floor and pushed her against the ladder. She laughed lightly, taking one step back and up onto a rung, bringing her exposed breast in line with his mouth.

He groaned and accepted the invitation, catching her nipple between his teeth and tugging gently until her moans matched his own. Then he released her, only to apply his tongue to the swollen tip. Again she moved her hands to his head, twisting her fingers through his hair. His hands moved under her skirt, sliding up her thighs to the edge of her panties, running his fingers along the outside edges, teasing her, tormenting her until she thought she'd shatter.

Then he slipped his thumb beneath the elastic and moved it with tantalizing slowness to her most sensitive spot. She arched against him, and he shifted his other hand to her hip to steady her as he massaged the feminine nub.

"No," she whispered, even as her body began to undulate against his hand. "I want you inside me."

He turned his head sideways, resting it between her breasts, holding her against the ladder. "I plan to be inside you, Sarah. So deep you'll never forget me, never forget what it means to be mine. But first—" he slid two more fingers beneath her panties, into the damp crevice between her legs "—I want to feel you come undone. I want to hear how much you want me."

"Oh, God," she moaned, feeling the last of her control fall away. "I want..."

"That's it, baby, let go. I want to feel you shatter against my hand."

And she did. Like a million shards of glass, splintering and catching in the light, exploding and falling to the ground in pieces. She couldn't think—she could only feel, the sensation of his hand and his mouth against her breasts. And then she cried out in ecstasy.

Reece held her as the last of her cries echoed through the barn. He smiled, hearing the pawing of the stallion and the nervous pacing of the mares and Sarah's gasps for breath.

"Are you okay?" he asked. She lifted her head, and he saw the tears in her eyes. "Sarah..." he said, suddenly afraid he'd hurt her.

"I'm fine." She leaned over and kissed him gently. "But I want what you promised me." Then she twisted in his arms to turn around, and took three steps up the ladder before looking back at him over her shoulder. "Coming?" she asked, and then continued upward.

He watched as her luscious bottom disappeared over the top of the ladder, and then he followed her. She was waiting for him, standing well back from the edge, a picture of dark exotic beauty, with one shoulder and breast bared, the rest of her demurely covered.

For a moment, he couldn't move. He just drank in the sight of her, mesmerized as she undid the last of the buttons on her shirt, then dropped it in the hay beside her. She paused for a moment, her hand poised at the front clasp of her bra. Finally she unfastened it, but didn't remove the offending garment.

A deep growl escaped him, and he started toward her, but stopped when she held up her hand, letting the bra drop to her feet.

Where had she learned to torment a man like this?

He wanted to throw her to the floor, shove her skirt to her waist and drive into her. Instead, he waited as her clever hands moved to the back of her skirt and unfastened it. After a torturous moment, it, too, slid to the floor along with her other clothes, and she kicked it aside.

It was too much.

The sight of her in nothing but a pair of bikini panties destroyed the last of his control. He closed the distance between them in two quick strides and pulled her nearly naked body into his arms. She responded instantly, her arms winding their way around his neck, her legs parting and wrapping around his waist as he lowered them both to the floor.

He kissed her hard, devouring her mouth as he pressed his erection between her thighs. But he'd waited too long, put off his own pleasure too long. He pulled away, grabbing at his belt buckle and then his zipper. She came halfway up with him, tearing at his shirt, snapping buttons and yanking the cloth from his jeans. He couldn't wait to undress. He reached for her panties, ripping them at their narrowest point on her hip and tossing them aside. Then he thrust into her. And found heaven.

She was perfect. Hot. Tight. Wet. God, he didn't remember it being this good, this sweet. He tried to hold still for a moment, to let her adjust to his size, but she shifted beneath him, destroying his hold on reality. He spun out of control, lost in this woman, lost in the feel of her tight wet body and the echo of her sweet moans, as the world around him exploded with light.

Sarah came back to earth slowly. The sweet smell of wood and hay and the horses shifting restlessly in their stalls below surfaced in her conscious mind. She'd been here before, with this man, in a loft much like this one. A very long time ago.

"It was your birthday," she said before she realized she'd spoken out loud. "And we created Drew."

Maybe he'd been thinking similar thoughts, because he didn't miss a beat. "My eighteenth. And you gave me the best present of all."

Sarah laughed softly, remembering. "We were so young."

"So foolish." He kissed the top of her head.

"So much in love."

He stiffened slightly and then relaxed again. "Yes. We were."

For a while neither of them spoke, but lay there in each other's arms, listening to the drum of the rain on the roof. Sarah wished they could stay here like this forever. But she knew from experience that fantasies always ended. Rolling away, she sat up and started gathering her clothes.

"Going somewhere?" he asked. He tried to make light of it, but she could hear the edge in his voice.

"Drew and Miss Adams could be here anytime." She pulled on her skirt and bra, and then worked at the buttons of her shirt with fingers that weren't quite steady. "Or one of the men could come back."

Reece brushed her hands aside. "Here, let me."

She tried not to look at him while he fastened her buttons, but it was difficult with him right in front of her. He'd zipped his jeans without buttoning them, and his shirt hung open, revealing a broad chest, wonderfully bronzed by the summer sun. She just barely resisted touching him, running her hands along the strong muscled contours of him. Everything had happened so fast between them, she hadn't gotten a chance to—

"There you go," he said.

She nodded her thanks, feeling the flush of her thoughts on her cheeks and afraid to trust her voice just yet. Moving away from him, she picked up her torn panties from the floor.

"I'm sorry about those," he said.

She shoved them into the pocket of her skirt. "It's nothing." *God, what have I done?*

"What now?" he asked. "Where do we go from here?"

Sarah shook her head and sat down on one of the bales of hay. "I don't know." She wished with all her heart that she had an answer for him, that this was just the beginning for them. She knew better. The real world had intruded, and it was impossible to ignore. There were no more beginnings for the two of them. "Has anything really changed between us?"

He scowled and stood up, adjusting his jeans and starting to rebutton his shirt. "Funny. I could've sworn we just made love."

"Yes." She glanced away. "But that doesn't change who we are." *Or all the lies between us—past and present.* "You're still Reece Colby. Possibly the next new state representative of Wyoming. And I'm still half-Indian."

He frowned but didn't deny it.

For some reason that hurt. She wanted him to say their differences didn't matter, even though she knew he couldn't. "And besides, you're... Oh, God," she moaned, remembering, realizing that she'd just hurt someone else. Michelle Hawthorne. "You're engaged to another woman."

"Damn." He turned away, running a hand through his hair as if he, too, had just remembered Michelle.

Sarah couldn't believe she'd let this happen. There were so many obstacles between them. Even if they could get past all the social and economic differences between them, even if he could forgive her for deserting him and Drew, there was Lyssa. He'd never forgive her for that, for keeping his daughter secret all these years. And she couldn't blame him.

"Reece, this was just sex." What was one more lie among so many?

He remained motionless, his back to her, not confirming her statement, but not denying it, either. Again his silence hurt more than it should have.

"There's always been this chemistry between us," she continued. "Once I'm gone, we can both forget this ever happened. You can get on with your life. And I..." Her whole world felt ready to crumble around her. She *had* to tell him about Lyssa. Now. No matter what the consequences. He deserved to know. "Reece..."

He finally shifted to look at her.

Just then a car pulled up outside, and he moved to the window. "It looks like it might be Drew and Miss Adams."

Sarah closed her eyes and took a deep breath, not sure whether to be irritated or relieved at the interruption. Then she remembered what they'd been doing for the past hour, and her hands flew to her hair. "Do I look all right?"

Reece crossed the space between them and pulled a piece of straw from her braid. "You look like you got caught in the rain."

"Great." Sarah felt her hair for more straw. "Just so long as I don't look like I've been..." Her voice trailed off.

"Rolling in the hay?" he finished for her.

Embarrassed, she nodded. "Is it all gone?"

He glanced at the back of her head. "Yeah. It's all out."

"Okay, I'll go on up to the house."

"Fine. Tell Drew I'll be there in a minute."

Reece followed Sarah down the ladder and watched her walk away, her usually graceful gait stiff and uncertain. She'd talked a good game a few minutes ago, but their lovemaking had disturbed her as much as it had him.

And she was wrong.

He couldn't care less about her Indian blood. It had never mattered to him. In fact, he'd been proud of her, of her own pride in her heritage. When he'd brought her home as his wife thirteen years ago, his parents' reaction had shocked him. Oh, he'd expected them to be upset because of his age. What he hadn't anticipated was their horror at *who* he'd married. They hadn't taught him prejudice, and it had never occurred to him that they'd object to Sarah because of her Indian blood. Now he knew better. Prejudice still existed, though sometimes buried beneath the veneer of modern thinking. It might hurt his political goals to be married to Sarah—if he still wanted a political career—but he wouldn't let that influence him. Whether he continued with politics or dropped it altogether, Sarah's background made no difference to him.

If he loved her.

That was the real question. And he didn't have the answer. There was this crazy sexual thing between them, but he couldn't let that sway him. He'd spent so many years telling himself he hated her for leaving. Could he put that aside now? Forget it ever happened? Forgive her? And then, would he ever be able to trust her again?

These were the real questions that concerned him, the doubts that hovered in his mind. He needed time to sort through them, but Sarah would be leaving tomorrow. He considered asking her to stay, though he doubted she would. He'd have to let her go, and maybe it would be for the best. Once she was three hundred miles away, maybe he could think more clearly.

Then he thought of Michelle and felt his betrayal to the bottom of his soul. He hadn't considered her for a moment while making love to Sarah. Just like when they were kids, with Sarah in his arms, nothing else had mattered. Michelle deserved better. Even though their relationship was based on friendship and not love, it didn't excuse his lusting after another woman. No matter what he decided about Sarah, Michelle was entitled to know what had happened here today.

Leaving the barn, he realized the rain had stopped. Man, he thought, was he in bad shape. Something else he hadn't even noticed while caught up in his thoughts of Sarah. Shaking his head, he walked toward the house.

Halfway across the yard a twelve-year-old missile launched itself at him. "I passed!" Drew hollered, leaping into his father's arms. "I'm gonna be in seventh grade!"

Reece hugged his son, grateful for this one sure thing in his life. "I knew you could do it."

Drew wriggled free, grinning from ear to ear. "Miss Adams said I passed with flying colors."

"And did you tell her my little contribution to your success?" Reece teased. "After all, I was the one who insisted you take yesterday off."

"I told her."

"And what did she say?"

"She said you must be just as smart as me."

Reece ruffled his son's hair. "Well, let's go, and you can introduce me to this paragon of teaching wisdom."

Drew laughed, and they headed up to the house where they found Sarah, Millie and Rebecca Adams drinking coffee at the kitchen table.

"I found him," Drew called as he and Reece entered the room.

The prim Miss Adams was about what Reece expected, small and nondescript. Sitting next to Sarah, she seemed almost devoid of color, except for her light brown hair, which she wore short, and her eyes, which she hid behind wire-rimmed glasses.

"Miss Adams." He extended his hand. "Reece Colby."

"Please, Mr. Colby, call me Rebecca." She stood and tentatively took his hand, pulling away almost as soon as he'd touched her.

Odd, Reece thought. She was as nervous as a mishandled filly. But she wasn't his concern, he reminded himself, except when it came to Drew. "Rebecca," he said, acknowledging her request with a nod. "And you can call me Reece."

He made the mistake of glancing over at Sarah, who was looking over a set of Drew's papers on the table. She looked warm and beautiful and... Then he realized that Drew's teacher was still talking to him, and he jerked his attention back to her. "I'm sorry, Miss Adams. I mean, Rebecca. What were you saying?"

She smiled tightly. "All I said was that if I've learned one thing in the five months I've been teaching in Devils Corner, it's that no one here stands on formality."

"You've got that right." He gestured toward her chair. "Please, sit down. And tell me how Drew did."

While Rebecca did so, the thought came to him that he could no longer be around Sarah and function normally. Even sitting quietly across the table from him, she distracted him. She still had on the same clothes, dry now, but looking like she'd gotten caught in a downpour. It didn't diminish her beauty. Or his desire for her.

He thought about the panties he'd ripped off her and wondered if they were still in her skirt pocket. Just the thought of her sitting there without underwear made him hard, and he had to force his wayward thoughts back to explanations of sixth-grade-skills checklists.

Finally Miss Adams said her goodbyes, and Reece made his escape upstairs to get into dry clothes. He'd have thought that after their lovemaking in the barn, his desire for Sarah would have slackened somewhat. At least for a while. Long enough for her to head back home.

He'd been greatly mistaken.

SARAH DIDN'T KNOW how she made it through the next few hours without going crazy. Between Rebecca Adams's visit, Drew's exuberance over passing his test and her last dinner at the Crooked C, her emotions were in an uproar. She managed to talk and smile as though nothing was wrong, but she couldn't remember a word she'd said. She'd operated on automatic pilot, some deep survival instinct taking over, while the real Sarah Hanson watched from a distance.

It just hurt too much to be part of it all.

Finally everyone finished eating, and she retreated to the solitude of her room. Only then did she let herself feel the weight of how she and Reece had spent the afternoon and the sadness of her departure tomorrow.

After a while, Drew joined her, plopping himself down on the corner of her bed. "Do you have to leave?" he asked.

Forcing a smile, she pulled out her suitcase and set it beside him. "Afraid so."

"Won't you miss us?"

His simple question tore at her heart. "Yes. Of course." She opened the suitcase and crossed to the dresser to retrieve her clothes. "But it's time for me to get home."

A light knock on the door brought her around. Reece stood in the doorway, looking more handsome than any man had a right to be. Her world shifted out of focus again, but she fought for control. She probably wouldn't see Drew again for a long time, and she wasn't going to let her feelings for his father ruin these last few minutes with her son.

"Dad," Drew said, "help me talk Miss Hanson into staying for a couple of days. Now that I've passed my test, we can go out to the creek again."

"I'd like to," Sarah said, carrying her clothes over to the bed and placing them in her suitcase. "But school starts soon, and I haven't seen my daughter in five weeks."

"She can come here," Drew offered.

Sarah smiled at him. "I don't think so, Drew."

"You know you're welcome to stay a few days," Reece said.

Looking at him, she nodded tightly. "Thank you. But I need to get home." *I need to get away from you.* Then she returned to her packing.

"I understand," he said. And she suspected he did.

"Are we ever going to see you again?" Drew asked, voicing Sarah's biggest fear. Would she ever see her son again? Especially once she told his father about Lyssa?

Snapping her suitcase shut, she set it on the floor and sat on the bed next to Drew. She gave him a broad smile and forced a cheerful note into her voice. "You bet. In fact, I'm going to write to you. And I expect you to write back."

Drew scowled. "I don't like writing letters. Maybe I could come visit you, instead."

She smiled tightly, knowing Reece would never allow it. "That'll be up to your dad."

Drew turned toward him. "Can I, Dad?"

"We'll see." Reece moved into the room and urged Drew off the bed. "But you've had a big day today, and it's getting late. I think you need to call it a night, partner."

Drew yawned. "Okay." Standing, he headed for the door, but stopped before going out. "You won't leave before I get up tomorrow, will you?"

Sarah's heart contracted. "I'll be here for breakfast. I promise."

"Great."

"Good night, Drew."

"Night, son." Reece ruffled his son's hair as he passed.

Once Drew was in his own room, Reece turned back to Sarah. "Are you okay?"

She forced a smile. "Of course."

"Sarah, I'm—"

"Don't, Reece." Rising from the bed, she paced to the far side of the room and kept her back to him. She didn't want to talk anymore, didn't want to hear him explain away what had happened between them this afternoon. She wanted to forget it. She wanted *him* to forget it. "Don't apologize."

"I wasn't going to."

His statement surprised her into turning around. He'd moved into the middle of the room, his hands shoved into the back pockets of his jeans.

"You don't expect *me* to apologize, do you?" she said.

"No, of course not." Exasperation laced his voice. "It's just that . . ."

Sarah walked over to the rocking chair by the window and sat down. "Is this about Michelle?"

"No." She saw the guilt settle on his features. "I'll explain things to her."

An unexpected jolt of jealousy shot through her, yet Sarah knew she had no right to the emotion. Michelle was the one wronged here. "Reece, I'll be out of your lives tomorrow. There's no reason to tell Michelle what happened. You'll only hurt her."

"Michelle will understand."

Sarah doubted it, but it was obvious Reece had already decided how to handle things with his fiancée. "So, what is it then? What did you want to say?"

He hesitated and then walked over and shut the door before turning back to her. "Sarah, I didn't use any protection this afternoon."

How like a man, she thought, to remember after the fact. Then she realized she was being unfair. She hadn't thought of it, either. "It isn't the first time we've been careless."

"We were young then." He moved over and sat on the edge of the bed. "What's our excuse now?"

There was no excuse. "It shouldn't have happened, Reece. We both know that."

"Sarah, if you're—"

"I'm not," she insisted, though the possibility had occurred to her. "It's not the right time of the month."

He didn't look convinced. "That's hardly foolproof."

"You're right. But—"

"Sarah, if you're pregnant, I want to know." He leaned forward, resting his arms on his thighs and clasping his hands. "I want to be involved in my child's life."

Guilt washed over her, and she had all she could do to acknowledge his statement. "Okay."

What irony. Reece was ready to acknowledge a child who probably didn't even exist, while she'd kept the existence of another child from him.

"One other thing, Sarah," he said, the tone of his voice drawing her gaze to him. "You really ticked me off this afternoon." He stood and walked to the middle of the floor before turning back to her. "It never made a damn bit of difference to me who your ancestors were. Or that your family wasn't wealthy." He pointed a finger at her. "I resent your implying that it did."

With that, he stormed out of her room, leaving her confused and strangely pleased.

IT WASN'T UNTIL after she'd gone to bed that Sarah realized she'd missed yet another opportunity to tell Reece about Lyssa. She had no more excuses. Drew had passed his test and no longer needed her, and she was leaving in the morning.

She climbed out of bed and pulled the rocking chair closer to the window. Outside, the yard was dark and quiet. Maybe she should pull on a pair of jeans and go see if she could find Reece. She could still talk to him, still tell him the truth about Lyssa before she left.

Yet she held back.

She wasn't sure she wanted to be alone again with Reece, to meet him under the cover of darkness. Even here in her room, she felt the pull of him, her need to touch him and be touched. Yes, she wanted to go to him. But not to talk.

She couldn't risk it. Not and keep any part of her heart intact.

Besides, all the horses had already been moved into the barn for the night. Reece wasn't down there. He'd probably gone to bed hours ago.

REECE SAT outside in the shadows.

He saw her sitting in her chair by the window, a pale specter against the dark room. Rocking. As sleepless as he.

Sarah.

If he stepped out of the shadows, would she come to him? Would she let him make love to her again? He'd thought he wanted her before, but it was nothing compared to the desire he felt now. Now that she'd reawakened him. He could almost taste her mouth and feel the weight of her perfect breasts in his hands. A few feet into the light would be all it would take. She'd see him and come to him.

He couldn't do it. Not and let her go.

He needed time. And space. Away from her. Away from the lure of her. Tomorrow she'd leave, and he could begin to sort out the myriad feelings she aroused in him. Then he'd see.

CHAPTER ELEVEN

DREW STOPPED in front of the small wooden house, glanced at the crumpled paper where he'd written Sarah's address, and then looked back at the house. This was it. It wasn't what he'd expected, though there really wasn't anything wrong with it. It looked neat and well kept. It just seemed so small.

Hiking his backpack a little higher on his shoulders, he opened the gate and headed up the walk. On the porch, he hesitated. It had been a week since Miss Hanson had left the Crooked C, and he had no idea how she'd react to his showing up on her doorstep. He should have called first, he thought. But then, he'd been afraid she wouldn't let him come. Now that he was here, he knew she'd help him.

Taking a deep breath, he opened the screen and knocked on the door. Seconds later, he heard footsteps approaching, and he backed away, letting the screen snap shut.

A girl a couple of years younger than him opened the door. "Can I help you?"

"Hi," he said, suddenly nervous.

The girl scrunched up her features as if trying to figure out who he was. "Do I know you?"

"Uh, no. Does Sarah Hanson live here?" he asked.

"She's my mom."

"Oh, then you must be Lyssa." At least he'd gotten the right house.

"Yeah." The girl crossed her arms and frowned. "How'd you know my name?"

"Your mom told me." When she didn't respond, he hurried on. "I'm Drew Colby. She was my tutor this summer."

The girl stepped closer and studied him through the screen. "You're the boy from that big ranch up near Devils Tower?"

Drew nodded and slipped a hand under his backpack strap. "Yeah, that's me. Is your mom here?"

"She won't be back until later."

"Oh." Now what? It had taken him all night and half the day to get here. He'd never figured on Miss Hanson's not being home when he arrived. He was tired and hungry, and he'd spent most of his money and eaten the last of the crackers he'd bought in Buffalo this morning. He should have called first.

"Why are you here?" Lyssa asked.

"I, uh, just came to see your mom."

She seemed to consider that for a moment. "Well, she's not here. Are you going to wait?"

What choice did he have? "Yeah, I guess." He backed away and nodded toward the steps. "If it's okay with you, I'll just sit out here on the porch."

Lyssa hesitated a moment and then stepped forward and opened the screen door. "You can wait inside. If you want."

Drew thought about that for a moment. She really shouldn't let him in, but it was pretty hot out and he needed to eat something. Maybe she had some crackers or something. "Okay," he said, stepping into the house. "Thanks."

Lyssa started toward the back of the house, but Drew waited, not sure whether she expected him to follow.

"Come on," she said over her shoulder. "I was just fixing lunch. Are you hungry?"

Drew grinned. "Sure."

"It's just grilled cheese and leftover tomato soup from last night."

"Sounds good." They entered the kitchen, the warm cooking smells making his stomach growl.

"It's almost ready." She moved around the kitchen like she knew what she was doing, pulling out bread, butter and cheese from the refrigerator and setting a frying pan on the stove. "I'll just throw on another sandwich for you."

"Great." She seemed to have everything under control, and he had to give himself a shot before he ate. "Can I use your bathroom?"

She motioned in the direction they'd just come. "It's down the hall."

Drew started toward the bathroom.

"You can leave your pack out here," she said. "I won't look in it or anything."

Drew flushed. He needed his backpack, but he didn't want to explain his reasons to this kid. "Uh, that's okay. I'll take it with me."

Lyssa shrugged.

The small bathroom barely gave Drew room to maneuver. It was hardly the optimum environment to give himself a shot. But he'd manage. He washed up a bit, and then retrieved his insulin kit from the backpack. Setting it on the toilet seat, he pulled out his vials and a needle. Except for the cramped space, he may as well have been on automatic. He'd been doing this without help since he was nine. First, he rid the needle of air, then loaded it with a small amount of insulin from both vials, the regular and the long-lasting stuff. He pulled his shirt up, lowered the waistband of his jeans, and it was over in a matter of seconds.

When he returned to the kitchen, Lyssa was already sitting at the table, soup and sandwich in front of her. She'd set another place for him.

"I didn't know what you wanted to drink," she said. "There's tea, soda and milk in the fridge. Help yourself."

"Water's fine." He took the glass she'd set out for him to the sink and filled it.

For a few minutes neither of them spoke as they dug into their lunch. He didn't know kids her age could cook this well. The soup tasted homemade, richer and chunkier than any he'd had out of a can, and the sandwich was thick and gooey with cheese.

"This is good," he said.

"When I stay with my great-grandmother, I do all the cooking."

"My grandmother doesn't cook, either."

"Never?" She looked at him as if she'd never heard of such a thing.

Drew winced, a little embarrassed. He wished he hadn't brought up the subject. "We've got a live-in cook."

"Well, Grandmother cooks, when Mom or I aren't around to do it for her. Of course when Mom's there, Grandmother wants restaurant food."

"Restaurant food?"

She leaned toward him, as if revealing some big secret. "Kentucky Fried Chicken's her favorite." Shaking her head, Lyssa leaned back in her chair. "Mom says that Grandmother was born in the wrong generation. She's the only eighty-year-old Shoshone junk-food addict around."

Drew laughed. He had a hard time picturing Lyssa's great-grandmother. Especially since he couldn't have gotten his own grandmother within half a mile of a fast-food restaurant.

He went back to his lunch, but Lyssa wasn't done chattering. "So what was my mom teaching you?"

He wondered if she always talked this much. "Math and English."

"Are you going to get held back?"

"Nope. I passed my test."

"Well, that's good. I guess." She didn't seem impressed.

"What do you mean?"

She shrugged. "Well, you must be pretty dumb to need a tutor to begin with."

"I'm not dumb. Besides, what do you know about it?" She had the most irritatingly superior look on her face. "What are you? In third grade?"

"Going into sixth. And I'm in the gifted program, so I've started sixth-grade math already." She snapped her fingers in front of his face. "It's a cinch."

"Well, I thought it was boring."

She rolled her eyes, and Drew wondered how someone as nice as Miss Hanson managed to get such an obnoxious daughter. Even if she did make a mean grilled-cheese sandwich.

"Want another sandwich?" It was as if she'd read his mind.

"Sure."

"Figures." Lyssa grabbed his plate and headed for the stove. "Boys always eat a lot."

She was such a know-it-all. "I guess you've had a lot of experience with boys."

"As a matter of fact, I have." She buttered a piece of bread and, topping it with several slices of cheese, dropped it into the frying pan.

"Funny, I don't see any around here."

She turned away from the stove and set her hands on her hips. "For your information, I spent most of the summer at Joseph Bright Eagle's ranch. And he's got six grandsons."

Again Drew rolled his eyes without saying anything. She was too much. A ten-year-old brat who thought she knew everything. Then she returned to the table with his sandwich, and he felt a little guilty. After all, she'd let him wait in the house and she'd made him lunch. She wasn't all that bad.

"So," he said, determined to be nice, "is that where you stayed while your mom was at the Crooked C? At this Bright Eagle's place?"

"No. I was at Grandmother's. She lives real close to Joseph. I went over there every day, and then Mom came home and made me move back into town with her."

"You don't sound too happy about it."

Lyssa picked up her dishes and took them over to the sink. "I'm training for middle-school rodeo, and Joseph was helping me get ready."

"Really." Maybe she wasn't so bad, after all, if she liked rodeo. "My dad was a bronc rider."

"Yeah, well, my mom was one of the best barrel racers on the weekend rodeo circuit. She nearly made it to the finals one year."

Drew smiled. He had her on this one. "I know," he said, picking up his dishes and joining her at the sink. "Your mom told me all about it."

That seemed to shut her up, and for the next few minutes he had some peace while he helped her rinse the dishes and stick them in the dishwasher. She really wasn't a bad kid, he thought. For a girl.

"So, how come you're here to see my mom?" Lyssa asked when they were finished with the dishes.

"You sure ask a lot of questions."

She shrugged. "Mom says that's because I'm smart."

Drew shook his head. Too bad she didn't act like her mom.

"Well," she prompted, "are you going to tell me?"

"Tell you what?"

"Why you're here."

"Oh, well, I guess you'll know soon enough. I ran away."

Her eyes flew wide. "From home?"

"Of course from home. I thought you were supposed to be smart."

"Neat. So does your dad beat you or something?" she asked as if hoping to hear the gory details.

"No, he doesn't beat me."

"Oh." She seemed thoroughly disappointed. "So why did you run away then?"

"He's going to get married."

She stared at him blankly. "That's it?"

"What do you know about it?"

"Nothing. Only, I'd like it if my mom got married. It would be kind of neat to have a dad." Then she obviously thought better of the broad statement. "That is, if he was nice and all." Then her eyes lit up again.

"That's it. Your future stepmom hates you. Is she real ugly and mean?"

"Man, you watch too much TV." He shook his head and started out of the kitchen.

Lyssa followed. "Well, if she's not mean, I don't get it."

"I guess you're just not as smart as you think you are." He stopped in the living room and looked around. "Hey, have you got a Nintendo or Sega or something?"

"No. Nothing like that."

He turned toward her, frowning. "You've got to be kidding. Everyone's got one or the other."

"Not us." She looked embarrassed. "We can't afford one."

Drew instantly felt like a jerk. He didn't mean to hurt her feelings. Even if she was annoying.

"Hey," he said, "I'm sorry. I didn't mean ... Let's just watch TV while we're waiting for your mom."

EVERY YEAR it was the same thing.

Sarah had gone into school to start preparing for her September classes. And as usual, instead of the standard twenty-seven students per class, administration had given her thirty-five. Which wouldn't have been too bad in itself, but she only had twenty-eight textbooks and twenty-five desks. Now she'd have to spend the next couple of weeks scrambling, trying to lay her hands on more books and desks.

Of course, at this point she'd welcome anything that kept her mind off Reece Colby.

She'd been home a week, and her days and nights had been filled with thoughts of him. The oddest things brought back memories, fragments of their time together. Whenever it rained, she thought of their time in the loft, of the feel of his hands and the taste of his lips. When the sun shone, she remembered the day they'd roughhoused in the creek with Drew. She'd hear Reece's laughter, rich and full, mixed with Drew's boyish giggles. And when she sat with Lyssa eating a meal, she'd recall Reece at the dinner table at the Crooked C and wonder what he'd think of their daughter.

Then this morning her period had started, and she'd burst into tears. It had to have been the craziest reaction possible. With all the other things facing her, the last thing she needed was another baby. She and Reece had too much to work out between them as it was, without complicating it further. Still, she realized, she'd been secretly hoping she was again carrying his child.

Madness. Sheer madness.

And she still hadn't told him about Lyssa. She simply didn't know how. She'd considered writing him a letter but knew that was the coward's way out. A phone call was out of the question, as well. How could she tell him across three hundred miles of telephone cable that he had a daughter? Of course, in her moments of honesty, she admitted those were all just excuses. No matter how she told him, she knew he'd have the power to take Lyssa away. That was the real problem. Sarah needed her daughter and was afraid of losing her.

She hoped school starting would do the trick and let her have some peace. Maybe facing thirty-five rambunctious teenagers every day would exhaust her to the point where she could no longer think. No longer feel.

On the way home, Sarah stopped at the grocery store and picked up enough food to last for a few days. Juggling a full bag, her purse and keys, she let herself in the front door of the house. Then came to a sudden stop.

On the couch, with Lyssa sprawled out next to him, sat Drew. It took Sarah's breath away, seeing them like that. Both her children. Together. She wondered how anyone who ever saw them like this could not know they were sister and brother.

"Drew, what are you doing here?" she asked.

He jumped up from the couch. "Hi, Miss Hanson."

She set down the groceries on the hall table and zeroed in on her son. "Does your father know you're here?"

He shifted from one foot to the other, glanced at Lyssa, who was listening avidly, and shook his head. "No, ma'am."

"Lyssa," Sarah said to her daughter, "take these groceries into the kitchen."

"But, Mom—"

"Then go get the rest from the car."

"Mom—"

"Lyssa." Sarah kept her voice firm and her eyes on the boy in front of her. He looked ready to fall apart. She knew how he felt.

Lyssa grabbed the bag and, giving her mother a "not fair" look, trudged off toward the kitchen.

"Okay, Drew." Laying a hand on his shoulder, Sarah led him back into the living room. "Tell me what's going on." She sat on the couch and drew him down next to her.

"Promise you won't tell my dad I'm here?"

Sarah sighed and took his hand. "I'm not making any promises. Now, tell me what's going on."

Drew examined their joined hands for several moments and then said, "I ran away."

"Oh, my God, Drew." Sarah bit her bottom lip. "How did you get here?"

"It wasn't so hard."

"It's three hundred miles!"

"It was nothing. Being Saturday and all, I knew Tod would be going into town. So I hid in the back of his pickup. From there I hitched a ride with a trucker who was heading this way."

"A trucker picked you up?" She couldn't believe it.

"I gave him fifty bucks."

Sarah groaned and shook her head. "Okay. So you got here." She refused to think of all the things that *could* have happened to him on the way. "Why, Drew?"

"He's going to marry her."

His simple statement made her heart tighten. She had no doubt whom Drew referred to. And it hurt. Even though it shouldn't have, even though she'd known it would come to this. "You mean Miss Hawthorne?"

"Yeah. Her."

She couldn't let Drew see how this news affected her. "Well, Drew, your father and Miss Hawthorne have been engaged for months. Don't you think it's about time they got married?"

"No!" He pulled away from her and sprang from the couch. "I don't want him to marry her." He shoved his hands in the pockets of his jeans. "I mean, I was hoping...I don't know. I just don't like her."

"Does she treat you badly?" Sarah knew the answer. She'd seen Michelle with Drew. If anything she went out of her way to be nice to him.

Drew gave Sarah his standard shrug. "I guess not."

"Then what is it?"

"When she's around, Dad's always busy." He met Sarah's gaze, his eyes troubled and uncertain. "We never do anything together. Not like when you were there." His eyes glistened with unshed tears, but he held them back. "Now it's going to be just like it was before."

"Drew, you don't know that." She reached out and took his hand, pulling him back down onto the couch, all the while fighting the urge to put her arms around him. "You and your father have become such good friends."

"I heard them talking the other night. She wants him to run for another office."

Sarah sighed. "If that's what he wants, you have to respect that."

"Tod will take over again, and I'll never see Dad."

"Oh, Drew." She didn't know what to say to him. He was wrong. She knew that. Reece had discovered his son, and nothing would ever get in the way of that again.

"Please, let me stay here."

His request took her aback. Of course nothing would please her more. Still... "I don't know, Drew."

"Please." There was so much hope in his eyes. "Dad will never think to look for me here."

"Don't be so sure." Actually she was surprised Reece wasn't here already. Or at the very least, on the phone to her.

"I could help you around the house," Drew insisted. "I can't cook like Lyssa. But I'm good at fixing things."

"Slow down." Sarah again rested a hand on his shoulder. "First off, your dad needs to be told you're here. He's probably worried sick."

"He doesn't care."

Sarah squeezed his shoulder. "You know that's not true."

"Then why's he marrying her?"

Sarah sighed. How to explain adult relationships to a twelve-year-old? Especially when she didn't quite understand them herself. "Drew, you need to understand that your dad is human. He loves Michelle and wants to marry her. He's entitled to that. But it doesn't change his feelings for you."

Drew didn't look convinced, and she realized it was going to take more than a talk from her to bring him around. She changed her tactics. "What about your grandmother? Is she back yet? Maybe if you could—"

Drew shook his head, cutting her off. "She's not coming back. She called Dad a couple of nights ago. She's staying in Boston."

"For good?" It was the last thing Sarah expected.

"I don't know. For the winter at least."

Sarah hesitated a moment longer and then said, "Okay, I'll make you a deal." Even as she said it, she wondered if she was making a mistake. With Drew in her house, the truth would eventually come out about Lyssa. All Sarah's options would be taken away—that is, if she'd truly had any to begin with. But she couldn't turn her back on him. She'd done that once, eleven years ago. She couldn't do it again. No matter what it cost her. "If you agree to let me call and tell your father you're okay—"

"No."

"Hear me out, Drew." She used her stern-mother voice. "I'll try to convince him to let you stay here with Lyssa and me until school starts."

Drew looked at her, doubt in his eyes. "Do you think he'll let me?"

"He might. We'll continue with your schoolwork." She felt as if she was signing her own death warrant. "Don't frown. You may have passed the test to get promoted to seventh grade, but it's going to take more work to catch up with your classmates. So, what do you say?"

"Do I have a choice?"

"No." She smiled sympathetically at him. She understood his frustration. "Sometimes, we don't have a choice. One way or the other, I'm going to call your father and tell him you're here."

He looked defeated, and she felt like a traitor. "Okay," he mumbled.

"Promise me you're not going to run away again."

She saw his hesitation, but finally he nodded. "I promise."

"Did you bring your insulin?"

"Yeah. I took it before lunch."

"Good." Smiling, she rose from the couch. "Now, how about if you and Lyssa take a walk into town while I call and talk to your father?"

SARAH DIDN'T WANT to talk to Reece.

If every little day things brought back memories of him, she didn't want to think what the sound of his voice would do. But as she'd told Drew, sometimes you had no choice. She had to tell Reece that Drew was safe.

She dialed and Millie picked up on the third ring. "Crooked C."

"Millie, it's Sarah." She sat a little straighter, determined to go through with this. "I need to speak to Reece."

There was a heartbeat of silence. Then Millie said, "Lord knows I've been waiting to hear from you all week. But this isn't a good time, Sarah. Things aren't so good around here right now."

"I know. Drew's here."

"Sweet Mother Mary." Millie's relief was palpable, even through the phone line. "Is he okay?"

"He's fine. Please, let me talk to Reece."

"Sure. Sure. Of course." Millie set down the phone and a few minutes later, Reece picked it up.

"Sarah, Drew's there?"

"He's all right, Reece."

"Thank God." She could almost picture him running a hand through his thick blond hair. "We've been out all night searching."

Sarah closed her eyes. It was good to hear his voice. And so difficult. "I knew you'd be worried."

"Let me talk to him?"

"He's not here right now."

"Not there?"

"It's okay. I sent him into town with . . . my daughter." *Please, Lord. Get me through this.*

There was a pause on the other end of the line. "You didn't have anything to do with this, did you, Sarah?"

The question should have made her angry. Instead, it saddened her because she thought they'd gotten past this. "I think you know better."

"You're right." She heard his sigh. "I'm sorry. It's just that I've been worried sick. He ran off last night, and by the time I realized it, he was long gone."

"I know. He told me." She hesitated. "He also told me about your plans." Then, though it nearly tore her heart out, she added, "Congratulations. I wish you both the very best."

"Plans? What plans?"

She took a deep breath. He was going to make her say it. "Your wedding. That's why Drew ran away. He's afraid you won't have time for him once you and Michelle are married."

"Married? Where in the world...?" He sounded genuinely perplexed. "Oh, I know. Look, Sarah, he misunderstood me."

She opened her eyes. "You're not..."

"No. Not now. Look, why don't I fly down there? We can talk, and I'll explain everything. Then I can bring him home."

She reminded herself of the other reason for this call. Her promise to Drew. "Reece, give me a little time with him."

"Sarah—"

"No, it's not what you think." She leaned forward and took a deep breath. She was fighting for her son. "He's pretty upset right now. He needs some time."

"I told you. It's a misunderstanding."

"Fine. Then tell him that on the phone. I'll have him call when he and Lyssa get back."

"Sarah, we just spent the entire night searching—"

"I know, Reece. But he's just a boy. And he's very confused." She stood, taking the phone with her. "Let him stay here for a few days. Just until school starts. It's only two weeks away."

"I don't know." She could hear his resolve weakening.

"It'll be good for him. Lyssa is..." Sarah shook her head and laughed lightly. "Well, she'll be good for him. She's one of the most obnoxiously normal children you'll ever meet."

"I'd like to."

The statement threw her, and for a moment Sarah couldn't breathe. Then she assured herself he was just being polite. "Let him stay, Reece."

After a long pause, he said, "Okay, Sarah. But just for one week. Then I'll be down to get him."

REECE HUNG UP the phone and sank into his desk chair.

"Is he okay?" Michelle asked.

He looked up at her and nodded. "Fine."

"How did he get there?"

"I didn't ask."

"You didn't—"

Reece held up a hand to cut her off. "He's there. He's fine. I'll talk to him later."

Michelle looked a little put out that he'd cut her off, and he didn't blame her. Things had not been going well between them for the past week. He'd thought their relationship would get back to normal after Sarah left, but he'd been wrong. In fact, things had gotten worse.

Sitting here now, he realized why. Sarah. She may have left the Crooked C Ranch, but she hadn't left alone. She'd taken his heart with her. All the questions he still couldn't answer about their past hardly mattered. He loved her as surely as he had thirteen years ago.

He couldn't let this farce with Michelle continue.

"Drew ran away because he thought you and I had set a wedding date," he said.

"Where did he get that idea?"

"From me." She started to say something, but again he held up a hand to stop her. "He misunderstood. I asked him the other night if he missed having a mother. And how he'd feel about having one now." He paused. "Obviously he didn't like the idea."

She sat very still for a moment and then said, "Maybe he's smarter than we are."

"Maybe."

"It's not going to work, is it, Reece?"

He sighed, wishing there was some way to keep from hurting her. He could think of none. "No. It's not."

"Maybe we've been fooling ourselves all along."

"How so?"

"Thinking we could marry each other without being in love."

"It seemed like a good idea at the time."

"Yes." She stood and smiled sadly. "It did. But it seems things can fall apart even when you don't love someone."

He stood and, circling his desk, pulled her into his arms. "Take care, Michelle. I hope you find—"

She pressed a finger to his lips. "Don't. I can see how all this is tearing you apart. Don't wish it on me."

Smiling at her logic, he released her. "At least let me wish you happiness. And tell you that it's you who should be running for state representative."

Michelle paused while gathering her things. "Maybe I'll do that. And since we're handing out advice—" she nodded toward the phone "—Drew doesn't want a new mother because he's already found his real one. If you let that woman get away, you're a bigger fool than I thought."

CHAPTER TWELVE

FOR REECE, the next few days passed slowly.

More than once he questioned how he used to spend weeks at a time away from the ranch. Away from his son. Whenever he thought about it, he'd shake his head at how things had changed. He'd grown accustomed to having Drew around, to helping him with his chores or homework, or simply standing beside him watching Tod worked a new horse. With Drew in Oaksburg, everything was too quiet. Too empty.

Calling and talking to him only made things worse. He seemed to be having a great time and never once mentioned coming home. He spent his days with Sarah's daughter, working with horses out on some ranch on the reservation. Still, each night Reece made a point to call, and every night the conversation went about the same.

"Hey, Drew," Reece would start off, eager to hear his son's voice and hoping he'd be ready to come home, "how are things going?"

With his first few words, Drew would pop Reece's bubble. "Really great, Dad! Joseph helped me with my roping today. He said I could get real good if I practiced."

"I don't doubt it. Didn't I tell you that when we were working with the rope last week?"

"Yeah. But Joseph's been competing in rodeos for thirty years. He really knows."

"That long?" Reece was getting tired of hearing about the great Joseph Bright Eagle, but he wasn't about to let on to Drew.

"He also gave me some pointers on bronc riding."

Reece felt like an old-woman worrier, but the parent in him took over. "Drew, I don't think that's such a good—"

"Don't worry, Dad. He won't let me try it. He says that's something *you* need to teach me."

"Well, I agree with him on that at least."

Reece's comment seemed to sail straight over Drew's head. "Joseph was just pointing out some stuff while we were watching Adam."

"Adam?"

"One of Joseph's sons. The fourth I think."

Reece rested his elbow on the desk and leaned his head on his hand. "How many does he have?"

"Seven. There's—"

"That's okay, Drew. I won't remember all their names, anyway."

"Oh. Okay."

Reece felt like a heel. He hadn't meant to sound testy. Just because an old man had seven sons. "You're not getting in the way, are you, Drew?" he asked, changing the subject.

"Lyssa and I earn our keep. That's what Joseph says. We muck out the stalls and feed the horses. Then Joseph or one of his sons spends a couple of hours with each of us in the ring."

"Well . . . as long as you don't take advantage."

"Adam's riding in the rodeo over in Riverton this weekend. We're all going to go see him. Joseph says he's got a chance at the buckle..."

And so the conversation went every night. Drew's thoughts and words were filled with Joseph Bright Eagle and his sons. He knew it was ridiculous, but Reece couldn't help feeling a little jealous. He often found himself wondering what a man with seven sons and Lord only knew how many grandsons needed with Reece's son, anyway.

Then he got an idea.

It came to him on Wednesday, he nursed it through most of Thursday, and by Friday morning he'd thrown an overnight bag in the back of his truck and was heading southwest toward the Wind River Mountains. It wasn't until he was a hundred miles down the road that he admitted the truth to himself. He was going to Oaksburg to bring home his son.

And Sarah, as well.

SARAH CHECKED her watch as she set the casserole in the oven for dinner. The kids would be back in an hour. That would give her just enough time to shower, change and have a few peaceful minutes to herself before chaos ruled in her house again.

Not that she was complaining.

This week with both Drew and Lyssa around had been pure heaven. They'd taken to each other immediately, arguing one minute and sharing their deepest secrets the next. More than once she'd caught them huddled together, Drew's dark head and Lyssa's almost blond one, and wondered how anyone could not look at the two of them and see them for what they were. Her children.

Fortunately, if anyone had made the connection, they'd kept it to themselves. For now, anyway. But Sarah knew the secret couldn't be kept much longer. The kids deserved to know. As did their father. And soon, very soon, she would tell him. She just needed a little more time.

The doorbell rang, startling her.

She sighed and wiped her hands before heading for the front door. She didn't feel like chatting with any of her neighbors at the moment. She'd never get upstairs to shower and change. Then, stepping into the front hallway, she came to an abrupt stop.

Because of the heat, the front door stood open, a screen door keeping the insects outside. But even through the screen and with his back to her, she recognized him immediately. Broad shoulders and narrow hips. The way he stood, hands shoved into the back pockets of his jeans and one hip cocked higher than the other. A typical cowboy stance. But no one carried it off like Reece Colby.

It seemed time was running out faster than she'd thought.

"Reece," she said, and he turned to meet her gaze through the screen door. "What are you doing here?"

For a breathless moment he didn't answer. Then he took off his hat and asked, "May I come in?"

She hesitated and then nodded. "Yes, of course." She unlatched the door and held it open. He brushed past her, sending a sliver of recognition shimmying through her body.

Please, Lord, she silently begged. *Not again.*

She let the door snap shut on its own.

"You look good, Sarah."

She moved a hand to her hair to tuck away the fly-away strands that had escaped her braid. "I was just heading upstairs for—" She stopped. He didn't need to know that she was about to take a shower. Or had been, before he'd again shattered what little peace she'd found in her world.

"What are you doing here?" she repeated. "We weren't expecting you for a couple of days."

He studied his hat, working the brim in his hands. "I thought I'd come and see how Drew was doing." Then he raised his eyes to hers, and the warmth in them unnerved her.

"You could have warned us," she said.

"Yes. I suppose I could have."

She hadn't meant to sound so unwelcoming. But he disturbed her, standing here in her hall, dwarfing the small space with his size. And she'd thought she had a few more days. A little more time with her children before everything collapsed around her.

"I'm sorry," she said finally. "I didn't mean to be rude. You just . . . surprised me."

"I don't suppose Drew is home yet."

"No." She nodded toward the kitchen. "Come on. I'll get you something cool to drink."

Reece nodded and followed her to the back of the house.

"Did you drive?" she asked.

"Yes." He made himself at home, dropping his hat on the table and settling on one of her chairs.

How many times had she thought of him this way? In her home. In her kitchen. She'd fantasized about him for years after she'd left him. She'd dreamed of wild wonderful things, like his coming to claim her, demanding once again to make her his wife. And she'd imagined the mundane, like his sitting in her kitchen, just as he was now, while she cooked him a meal or got him something to drink.

But the only thing she'd ever received from Reece Colby in those years were divorce papers. He'd known where to find her, because they'd come to her grandmother's house.

"I don't have any beer," she said. "Is iced tea all right?"

"Great.

"So when do you expect Drew back?" he asked after she'd poured him some tea and sat down across from him at the table.

"Within the hour. They have an early day tomorrow." Then it struck her. "You're not planning on taking Drew back before the rodeo, are you?"

Reece smiled and she thought her heart would melt. "And risk having him hate me forever? Not on your life."

"Good." Sarah breathed a sigh of relief. "They're both looking forward to it."

"Actually I thought I'd come along. That is, if you don't mind."

Sarah didn't know what to say. She couldn't very well deny him, but spending time with him was hard on her. Didn't he realize that? Of course, all she had to do was tell him about Lyssa, and he'd go away for good. Not yet, she reminded herself. The kids had been looking forward to this weekend. She wouldn't ruin it on them. Just a couple more days, until after the camping trip....

"Oh, I forgot," she said. "There's a camping trip Sunday night. Did Drew tell you?"

"No." Reece shook his head. "I was planning on taking him home Sunday."

"You can't. I mean, I guess he was going to tell you about it when you called tonight. A couple of the coaches from school are taking a group of kids on an overnight trip up into the mountains Sunday night. They're not going far, and it's only for one night. But Lyssa's been looking forward to it all summer, and they've invited Drew to go along."

Reece studied his glass for a moment and then looked up and smiled. "Well, I suppose I'll just have to stay until Monday then."

"Reece . . ." She didn't want him to stay. Couldn't he understand that? How was she supposed to forget him when every time she turned around he was there? But she wouldn't ask him to leave. She'd let her children have their weekend. Then she'd tell Reece the truth about Lyssa. And she'd have the rest of her life to get over him.

"Could you excuse me for a few minutes?" she asked. She told herself she wasn't running, just getting a little breathing space. "I've been working in the yard all afternoon, and I was just heading for the shower when you arrived. I'd like to get it over with before the kids get back."

"Sure."

She rose from the table. "Make yourself at home. There's more tea in the refrigerator and a television in the living room if you get bored."

After Sarah left, Reece picked up his tea and wandered around the house. Sarah's house. It looked like her, smelled like her, from the mismatch of no-nonsense furniture and handmade quilts and afghans, to the profusion of plants lining the window seat in the living room. Mixed in with the greenery was a progression of childhood pictures, a little girl, starting when she was an infant and going till she was about eight or nine years old.

Reece picked up one of the later photographs of the child he assumed was Sarah's daughter, Lyssa. She was a beauty. Like her mother. Only different. Sarah possessed a dark earthy allure, which men responded to. Lyssa's looks were more exotic. Her coloring alone set her apart. She had eyes a rich shade of caramel, hair a mixture of hues from pale blond to light brown—as if she'd been permanently kissed by a tropical sun—and skin a shade lighter, but still blessed with the warmth of her ancestors. Yes, indeed, when she was a little older, Sarah's Lyssa would turn heads.

He wondered about her father, and a knot of jealousy formed in his gut. The man obviously wasn't Shoshone, but fair haired and skinned. So where the hell was he?

Then another, more recent picture caught his attention. One Sarah hadn't gotten around to framing yet. It was a photo of Drew and Lyssa standing arm in arm. The resemblance was startling, despite Drew's darker coloring.

Just then the front door whipped open, and two whirlwinds blew into the front hall. Drew, and a smaller bundle of flying dark blond ponytails and flashing caramel eyes.

Lyssa.

"He did so!" she said, planting her fists on her hips and glaring at Drew. The beauty was a hellion, as well, and Reece smiled.

"What do you know about it?" Drew demanded, and then he spotted Reece and surprise replaced indignation. "Dad!"

"Hey, son." Reece's smile broadened. "Sounds like the two of you are having one heck of a disagreement."

Drew snapped his mouth shut, and wariness crept into his eyes. "Uh, it's nothing."

"Do I get a hug?" Reece asked, holding out his arms.

Drew shrugged and moved forward on wooden legs. "Sure, I guess."

Reece held him as long as Drew allowed and then turned to the girl. "You must be Lyssa."

"Lyssa Laughing Water," she said formally. "And you must be Drew's father. Mr. Colby."

Reece chuckled. "That I am. Only you can call me Reece."

Drew rolled his eyes. "That's not her real name. She made it up."

"I did not."

"You did too." Drew crossed his arms. "You're always making stuff up."

"Hey, what's going on here?" Sarah asked from the staircase. "Are you kids still arguing?"

Reece turned, and the sight of Sarah nearly took his breath away. She'd left her hair unbraided. Tied to one side with a bright blue ribbon, it hung like a curtain of black silk almost to her waist.

Shaking her head at the battling children, she finished descending the steps. "Sorry, Reece. I see you've been properly inducted into the chaotic world of a household with more than one child."

She'd put on one of those long floral skirts and simple buttoned shirts again. Ah, those buttons, he thought. She colored visibly, and he realized he'd been staring. No doubt she, too, remembered the last time she'd worn a shirt like this around him.

"So how come you're here, Dad?" Drew's question brought Reece back to the present. And the two children standing beside him.

"Aren't you glad to see me?" Reece tousled Drew's hair.

"Yeah, but..."

"I thought you might be a little homesick by now."

"He can't leave yet," Lyssa insisted. "We're going to the rodeo tomorrow to see Adam win a silver buckle. And then we're going camping in the mountains on Sunday night."

"So your mom said." Reece glanced at Sarah, who gave him an I-told-you-so smile. Only he wasn't sure if it was because she'd told him about their plans or warned him about her daughter. "I thought I might come with you guys. To the rodeo, that is. And then I can keep your mom company Sunday while the two of you are off camping."

"All right!" Drew said. "That'll be neat."

"Is that okay with you, Lyssa?" Reece asked.

"Sure," she answered, glancing from Reece to her mother and then back again. "But where are you going to sleep?"

"Well," Reece replied, a little taken aback by her question, "I spotted a motel on the outskirts of town. I thought I'd stay there."

"You can have my room," she said, as if hers was the final say in the matter. "I can sleep with Mom."

"Oh, I don't think—"

"Yeah, Dad, come on. It'll be great."

"Really, kids..." Reece glanced at Sarah for help, but she looked shell-shocked. He could hardly blame her. He hadn't planned on moving in with her for the weekend. "I think it's best if I stay at the motel."

"Come on, Dad!" Drew turned to Sarah. "Miss Hanson, tell him it's okay."

Sarah suddenly snapped out of it. "Well, I guess there's no reason why not."

He knew she didn't want him to stay. But though he hadn't planned on it, staying at her house might work out. He'd come here to talk to her, to get some answers to old questions. The kids' camping trip was going to give him the perfect opportunity, and it would be a lot easier if he and Sarah were under the same roof.

"Well," he said, "if you're sure it won't be any bother."

He saw the surprise in her eyes. She'd thought he'd turn her down. "No," she said. "Lyssa's right. She can move in with me for the weekend, and you can have her room."

"All right!" Drew said. "Come on, Lyssa, let's go get my dad's bag."

The two of them scrambled out the door, leaving their parents alone in the hall.

"This isn't a good idea, Reece."

He smiled. "We can't disappoint them."

"Yes, we can."

"Come on, Sarah." He took a step toward her. "I'll be on my best behavior."

"That's what I'm afraid of."

SARAH COULDN'T BELIEVE she'd agreed to this. Reece staying in her house. It spelled disaster in so many ways she couldn't even begin to list them. What had come over her? What had come over Lyssa? Offering to give up her room like that? Although Sarah shouldn't have been surprised by her daughter. Lyssa had a way of taking charge of things, running everything and everyone.

Except Drew.

Sarah had to smile. Drew fought his little sister every step of the way. Bossing her as much as she bossed him. And it had won him Lyssa's eternal devotion—though she wouldn't have admitted it to save her life.

Of course, none of that had anything to do with Reece's staying in their house. She supposed tonight and tomorrow wouldn't be too bad. They'd have two kids as chaperons. But what was she going to do with Reece on Sunday, once Lyssa and Drew went off camping? Just the thought of spending a night alone with him sent shivers of anticipation through her system, while at the same time scaring her half to death.

"YOU KNOW," Reece said the next day as the four of them climbed out of Sarah's car near the Freemont County fairground, "I can't remember the last time I was at a rodeo."

"Mom and I go all the time," Lyssa said.

Sarah looked at him and shrugged. "We both enjoy it."

Drew and Lyssa ran ahead, and Reece took Sarah's hand. She instantly tensed and then relaxed, evidently deciding as he had that for today, at least, they were together.

"I think the last time I went to one of these was before Drew was born," he said. "Back when you and I were still competing in them."

"Haven't you missed it?"

"Missed it?" Reece let out a short laugh. "I've never thought about it. I've been too busy. First I was in school for four years, and then when Dad died, I came home to run the ranch."

Turning her head to look at him, she rested her free hand on his arm for a moment. "Reece, I never told you how sorry I was to hear about your father."

"That's okay. It's been eight years. But thanks, anyway." He squeezed her hand. He didn't want to think about his father today. Or anything else unpleasant. "Anyway, after I got a handle on running the ranch, there was, of course, my political ambitions. So, rodeos wound up at the bottom of my priority list."

She threw him another sideways glance, only this time she grinned. "You know what they say about all work and no play."

"Yeah, well, that's why I'm here." He laughed lightly. They'd taught him that this summer, she and Drew. How to relax and enjoy himself with people he cared about.

They reached the edge of the rodeo grounds, and a rush of nostalgia hit him: the grandstands already filling with people, the loud bark of the announcer, the smells of horses and cattle, and the rush of contestants getting ready for their events.

"Brings back memories, doesn't it?" Sarah said.

He stopped walking and pulled her around to face him. Lord, she looked good today, young, fresh, almost like the seventeen-year-old girl he'd fallen in love with so long ago. "Yeah," he said, taking her other hand. "It reminds me of an Indian princess I once knew. She was the prettiest cowgirl who ever ran a barrel race."

She laughed nervously. "Sounds like a line to me."

He let his gaze drift lower, to the bright red shirt covering her full breasts and the jeans hugging her nicely rounded hips and bottom. Nope. This wasn't the same girl. This woman was a whole lot better. Stepping a little closer, he said, "It ain't no line, lady."

She blushed. "I think we should find the kids," she said, but the breathless quality of her voice betrayed her. He affected her as strongly as she did him.

"Think so?" He bent to kiss her, just one light touch of his lips, but she backed away.

"Yeah, cowboy," she said, and pulled her hands from his. "I think we definitely need to find Lyssa and Drew."

SARAH NEEDED SPACE. Away from Reece Colby. Fat chance, she thought, shaking her head. He was here for another forty-eight hours, and he seemed intent on sticking close. Too close. The man definitely had a warped sense of behaving himself. Of course, that was one of the things she'd always loved about him.

She fought with the best weapon in her arsenal. "Aren't you supposed to be engaged?"

He hesitated a moment and then said, "We called it off."

Surprised, she stopped and swung around. "I know you said that Drew had misunderstood about the wedding, but I didn't realize you'd canceled your engagement entirely."

"It was a mutual decision."

She didn't say anything for a moment, reluctant to ask the question uppermost in her mind. But she had to know. "Was it because of what happened between us?"

"Only indirectly." He took her hand again and started walking. "You see, Michelle and I had an arrangement."

"An arrangement?"

"We both had political ambitions, although Michelle's were always stronger than mine. So we decided to combine our families' names and influence to try and make something of it."

She shook her head. He couldn't mean what he was saying. "I don't think I understand."

"It was going to be a marriage of convenience." He shrugged as if that kind of thing was commonplace. "She's a friend. Nothing else. It never went further than that."

Sarah could hardly believe it. Did people really do that? Marry for convenience? "You mean you never..."

"Never." He chuckled. "Actually I don't think it ever occurred to Michelle."

"What about you?" The question slipped out before she could stop it.

He looked at her and grinned. "It would've been like making love to my sister."

The whole thing appalled her. The idea of living with someone you didn't love was unfathomable. "Were you planning on children?"

He chuckled again, and this time Sarah detected embarrassment in the sound. "Of course. What's a political career without children?"

"But if you didn't love each other and there was no attraction..." Lord, she was making a mess of this. She should just leave it alone. "How were you going to..."

"Actually," he answered, though she'd never completed the question, "the thought did occur to me that things were going to be a bit awkward."

They continued in silence, while Sarah thought about the eighteen months when she'd been married to Reece. It hadn't been easy. Not even in the beginning when they'd been wildly in love and thought nothing could ever touch them. They'd both had to adjust to sharing their space with another person. She couldn't imagine going through that without all the times that were pure heaven, without loving the other person above all else.

Reece broke the silence. "So, I owe you."

"Owe me?"

"If you hadn't shown up at the Crooked C, I probably would've gone through with it." He released her hand and slipped his arm around her waist. "You made me realize that Michelle and I were cheating each other."

Sarah didn't know what to say to that. Nor how to respond to the feel of his arm on her waist. Some rational part of her mind told her to step away. The rest of her very much liked the closeness. Finally she spotted Lyssa and Drew. "There are the kids," she said to Reece. "Over there near the horse trailers with Joseph and Adam."

Reece groaned silently, and Sarah suppressed her smile.

At dinner last night, Lyssa and Drew had regaled Reece with stories of their adventures over the past

week. Sarah felt sure Reece had learned more about
Joseph, his ranch and family than he'd ever wanted to
know. She'd considered stepping in and rescuing him
once or twice, but thought better of it. He'd wanted to
stay. So let him deal with the ramifications.

Now he got to meet the children's hero.

"Come on," she said, stepping away from his arm.
"Joseph really *is* a nice man."

"No doubt," he said dryly.

Meeting Joseph and his son turned out to be less
painful than Reece had expected. The big friendly man
pumped Reece's hand and told him what a wonderful
son he had. Reece couldn't argue with that. Then Joseph's own son needed help getting ready for the first
event, and Joseph hurried off.

"Nice guy," Reece said, wondering why he'd been
dreading this meeting. Joseph obviously thought the
world of Drew.

Sarah laughed. "Yes, he is."

Reece glanced at her, waiting for the "I told you
so." It didn't come. It didn't have to. Her warm eyes
danced with amusement. Which was just as bad.

"Well," he said, "looks like they're ready to begin. You kids think it's about time we found a seat?"

They headed for the grandstand, both kids scam-
pering around them, talking a mile a minute, trying to
outdo each other explaining everything they saw.

"One thing's for sure," Reece said quietly to Sarah.
"This is going to be different."

"How so?"

"I've almost never been into spectator sports," he
answered. "This is the first time since I was a kid that
I was at a rodeo and not competing."

"You get used to it."

"I wonder."

"Hey, Dad," Drew interrupted. "Can I have some money? Lyssa and I want some popcorn and Coke."

Reece pulled out a few dollars. "Need help?"

"Nah." Drew shoved the bills into his back pocket. "We can get it."

"Are you sure?"

Drew gave him an are-you-kidding look and turned to Lyssa. "Come on."

Sarah smiled and nudged Reece with her elbow. "Feeling a little useless, Dad?"

"Hell, no." He shoved his hat to the back of his head. "I supplied the money." Still, he moved up alongside the concession stand where he could help carry the stuff if the kids needed him.

Sarah joined him, and they waited as Drew and Lyssa worked their way to the front of the line. Finally it was their turn, and the man working the stand rested his elbows on the counter to bring himself closer to their level.

"What can I get you kids?"

"Two bags of popcorn, one Coke and one Diet Coke," Drew said.

Nodding, the man filled their order. "Here you go, partner," he said a few minutes later. As Drew pulled out the money, the man handed one of the bags of popcorn to Lyssa and asked, "Is the regular Coke yours, honey, or your brother's?"

Drew scowled as he plopped the money on the counter. "She's not my sister."

"Sorry, son." The man looked surprised. "I thought you were related."

Reece felt the statement slice through him. Of course Drew and Lyssa looked alike. They both resembled their mother. He glanced at Sarah, who stood rigidly still, her usually warm complexion ashen.

"What's wrong?" he asked.

She didn't answer, but stared at her children as the man behind the concession stand gave Drew his change. Then she turned to meet Reece's gaze, her eyes wide and frightened.

"It's okay, Sarah," he said. He rested his hand on her arms. "It's no big deal."

"Reece..." She glanced furtively back at Lyssa and Drew, who'd moved away from the crowd around the concession stand.

"I know."

"Come on, Dad!" Drew called. "It's gonna start."

"Just a minute," he answered, and then turned back to Sarah. "I know how upset you are."

"Do you know how dangerous this is?"

He sighed and rubbed her arms. "Yes, and it's time we put an end to it. We need to tell them the truth. Drew should know that you are his mother and that Lyssa is his sister."

She gasped and pulled away from him. Without a word, she spun on her heel and made her way to Drew and Lyssa. She put a hand on each of their shoulders and led them toward the grandstand.

Reece watched them go, wondering what he'd said wrong.

He understood why the concession worker's comment had upset her. Neither one of them wanted the kids to figure out their relationship on their own. The knowledge that Reece and Sarah had once been married and that Sarah was Drew's mother needed to be broken gently. But he'd thought Sarah would be pleased, relieved even, that he planned to tell Drew the truth. He'd thought that was what she'd wanted all along. Either she'd changed her mind, or there was something else here that he didn't understand.

THE REST OF THE DAY was lost on Sarah.

Beside her, Drew, Lyssa and Reece immersed themselves in the rodeo events, picking their favorite contestants and cheering them on. Sarah participated on the surface, while underneath she steeled herself against the approaching pain by deadening her senses to everything around her. Even when Adam won the silver buckle for getting the highest points of the day, her smile, which should have come easily and spontaneously, was forced.

She couldn't allow herself to think, to feel. Not now. Or else she'd never do what needed doing.

The time had come.

No more excuses. Tomorrow, as soon as the kids left on their camping trip, she would tell Reece the truth.

CHAPTER THIRTEEN

SARAH PULLED into the school parking lot a little before noon on Sunday. Already, a dozen kids waited impatiently to get started, chasing each other around the lot and generally wreaking havoc. She wondered how many more children were expected. It was the end of summer, and this was the kids' final fling before returning to school. She didn't envy the chaperons.

After parking her car, she helped Drew and Lyssa unload their camping gear and then headed to where several adults were loading equipment into the trucks.

"You can go now, Mom," Lyssa said, obviously eager for her mother to leave. "Drew and I will be okay."

"Don't be in such a rush to get rid of me, young lady." Sarah tugged playfully at her daughter's braid. "I'm going to go talk to Coach Davis for a minute. If that's okay with you."

Lyssa looked at her feet. "Do I have a choice?"

"No."

Sighing heavily, Lyssa said to Drew, "Come on." Then she led him over to the other kids.

Sarah watched them go, shaking her head.

Lyssa was right. She should just head home. Lyssa and Drew would be fine, and Reece was waiting for her back at the house. Of course, that was exactly why she wasn't in any hurry to get home. She wasn't ready to face him.

Walking up to one of the men stowing gear in the back of his truck, she said, "Hey, Bill, anything I can do to help?"

"Not unless you want to come along, Sarah."

She shook her head and smiled. "No, thanks."

He chuckled. "Well, in that case, I think we can handle it."

"Oh." She'd really been hoping they would need an extra set of hands. "Okay. Well, maybe I can just keep an eye on the kids for you."

He looked at her. "We really do have everything under control."

"I just thought I'd wait until all the other kids show up."

He gave her a knowing smile. "Sarah. Go home. Lyssa and Drew will be fine."

Heat tinged her cheeks. "Okay, so I'm being a slightly overprotective mother."

"You're entitled," he said, grinning. "Now get out of here before one of those poisoned looks Lyssa's sending this way finds a target."

Sarah had been dismissed. Whether she liked it or not, it was time to head back to the house. To Reece.

She took the long way home, readily admitting to being nervous. Reece had told her not to make any plans for the day. He had something special in mind. But so had she. Today nothing would keep her from telling him about Lyssa.

Pulling into the driveway of her house, she sat for a moment before going inside. She'd vacillated all summer about whether to tell Reece about his daughter, knowing she should but afraid she'd lose Lyssa in

the process. Then Reece had dropped that bomb yesterday at the rodeo about telling Drew the truth, and
Sarah couldn't stall any longer.

Gathering her courage, she climbed out of the car
and headed up the walk. Reece deserved to know the
whole truth. And so did Lyssa and Drew.

No more secrets.

After today, Reece would probably despise her.
Then tomorrow, when she told their children, they
might hate her, as well. She didn't know how she was
going to live with that. But she knew she could no
longer go on living a lie.

"Ah, just in time," Reece said, greeting her as she
closed the door. Then before she could speak, he
slipped his arm around her waist and pulled her close,
kissing her hard on the mouth.

For a moment she was too stunned to react, then she
pushed him away. "Reece, what's this all about?"

"Come on." Grinning like a schoolboy and not
looking the least bit repentant, he grabbed her hand
and led her into the living room. In the middle of her
coffee table sat two glasses and a bottle of wine nestled in a bucket of ice.

"Sit down," he said, motioning toward the couch.
"You've been waiting on the three of us all weekend.
Now it's my turn."

She considered pointing out that they'd spent yesterday at the rodeo, and he'd insisted on paying for
everything from admission to dinner afterward.
"Reece, this is crazy. I can't drink wine in the middle
of the day." She started to stand.

"Uh-uh," he said, pressing her back down on the
couch. "No arguments. And why not wine in the afternoon? This is our day alone without the kids. I

think we should make the best of it. We're going to kick back and relax.''

She sighed. He wasn't going to make this easy. But then, he never did. "Reece, we need to talk."

"Exactly what I had in mind." He sat down next to her and retrieved the glasses from the table. "That..." he planted a quick kiss on her forehead "...and other things."

"Reece—"

"I've got a couple of thick sirloins marinating in the kitchen for later."

"This isn't a good idea," she said as he poured the wine and handed her a glass.

Reece smiled devilishly, making her heart skip a beat. "So kick me out."

It was a thought, but they both knew she wouldn't do it. "Why are you here, Reece? Why are you doing this?"

"What am I doing?" He feigned confusion.

"The wine. The food."

"I thought we'd have a relaxing afternoon and then a quiet dinner together. Just the two of us." He grinned. "Now that the little monsters are gone."

Sarah sighed. "It doesn't make sense."

"That I want to spend the day with you?"

She set her glass down on the table. "I thought we put this to rest before I left the Crooked C."

He took a sip of his wine without taking his eyes off her. "I know we raised a lot of questions before you left the ranch. But I don't remember anything being resolved."

"Please, Reece." She scooted forward to sit on the edge of the couch. "I can't do this again. You can't just come pushing your way back into my life. I don't know what you want from me."

"Tell me why you left, Sarah."

His question, coming from nowhere, threw her. "Why I left?"

"When Drew was a baby."

Her heart skipped a beat, and she swallowed hard. "I . . ." She started to stand, needing to put some distance between them, but he grabbed her arm.

"Please," he said, pulling her back down beside him. "I was young and stupid back then. I believed everything you told me. Now I want to know the truth."

She studied his face for a moment, his wonderful blue eyes and his mouth. God, how she'd always loved his mouth . . . No. She couldn't let her thoughts stray in that direction. Not now. "What makes you think you don't already know the truth?" she asked.

He smiled sadly, and she felt something catch inside her. "Because over the last few weeks, I've gotten to know you, Sarah. Better than I ever knew you when we were married. I've watched you with Drew and Lyssa. The woman I see would never have walked out on one of her children without a very good reason."

"Oh." She took a deep breath, realizing that Reece, too, had decided that today was the time for truth. Only, he had no idea what he was asking for.

"There wasn't another man, was there," he said, sounding very sure of himself. "Not then, at least."

She shook her head. "No, not then." *Not ever*.

"Tell me the rest."

Sarah sighed and closed her eyes. This wasn't how she'd envisioned telling him. She hadn't planned on rehashing why she'd left him. She just wanted to tell him about Lyssa. But she couldn't resist the chance to explain, to at least tell him why she'd done the things she had.

"We were drowning," she said, "the three of us. You. Me. Drew. But you couldn't see it."

"I know we were broke, but—"

"We were more than broke." She opened her eyes and looked at him. "You didn't understand. Probably because you'd never known what it meant to be really poor."

He took her hand. "Sarah, I'm sorry."

"For what? It wasn't your fault."

"It was my job to provide for you, to take care of you."

Sarah sighed. "You were only a boy." She sat straighter and leaned forward to emphasize her point. "How do you think you could have done that?"

Rising from the couch, he started to pace. "I don't know. I could have sold the car or gotten a second job at night. Maybe if I'd—"

"Stop it, Reece."

He froze midstride and turned to look at her. He was the most handsome man she'd ever known, and she loved him deeply. This was so hard, talking to him about their unhappy past, when all she wanted to do was throw herself in his arms and beg him to make love to her.

But she couldn't forget the past any more than he could.

"Listen to yourself," she said. "Do you hear what you're saying? You're thinking like that boy again. You're a man now, and you know better. We were too young."

For a moment he remained silent, and she could see the battle waging behind his eyes. He wanted to believe they could have made it, that he could have done something. She knew the moment he acknowledged the truth. He sighed heavily, acceptance blanketing him like a cloak.

"Okay." He returned to the couch and sat next to her. "You're right. So, is that why you left? Because we were broke?"

"Yes. No. I mean, if it had been just the two of us, or if Drew hadn't been sick, it wouldn't have mattered. I'd have gone to work. We'd have gotten by somehow."

She took a deep breath, wishing she didn't have to relive those difficult days. "But Drew *was* sick. He needed expensive medicine and full-time care. We didn't have the money for the medicine, and I couldn't work to help pay for it because I provided the care."

"And I was never around."

Surprised, she looked up at him and met his gaze. So he remembered. "Yes. You were very unhappy."

"I loved you."

"I know. Maybe that's why you were so miserable." She stared at her hands. "It was more than either of us could handle. And it frustrated you that you couldn't do anything about it." After a moment's hesitation, she added, "Then your mother showed up."

"Damn!"

"She did what she thought was best for you and Drew."

"You mean she was trying to control me. Control my life. Just as she always has."

"She offered us a solution." Sarah took a deep breath. "She offered *me* a solution."

"How kind of her." Again he deserted the couch, this time his anger almost tangible. "She convinces my father to disown me, and then when I fall on my face, she buys off my wife."

"She promised me that if I left you, she'd take care of Drew and make sure he had everything he needed. She kept that promise."

"How could my own mother..."

"I was angry with her for a long time, too."

"And now, Sarah? How can you *not* be angry with her?" He made a sweeping gesture with his hand. "Your own son doesn't even know you."

His statement stung, stirring her old resentment as he'd doubtless meant to do. Both she and Elizabeth had been wrong. Terribly wrong. But Sarah had learned long ago that anger was a useless emotion.

"I could have said no," she said simply.

Her statement stopped him. Looking into his eyes, she could see the turmoil within him. Then he said, "You did it for us."

"Yes. For you and Drew." *Now the whole truth*, a voice inside her screamed. *Tell him...*

He moved back to the couch and, sitting down, took her hand. "And the money?"

Sarah's face heated. That was the worst part—she'd taken money to leave them. "I didn't want to take it at first. But..." *There was Lyssa*. "I had nothing. No job. No skills. And hardly enough gas to get back to my grandmother's. It gave me the means to go back to school and make something of myself." *For Lyssa*.

Reece wrapped an arm around her shoulders and pulled her head against his chest. Sarah resisted for a moment and then gave in, to his strength, to the comfort he offered. She'd carried this burden alone for so long, struggling with it, rationalizing it, trying to make sense of the choices she'd made. It felt so good to be held, to unburden herself to this man she loved.

"I was wrong, Reece." The first of her tears slipped from her eyes. "I'm so sorry."

"Hush, baby." He stroked her head as one tear followed another, like streaks of fire down her cheeks. "It's over now. It was a long time ago."

"No, it's not over." It was far from over. "There's more."

"Enough. For now." He shifted sideways and covered her mouth with his, silencing her.

Just one kiss, she told herself, one sweet kiss. But he didn't stop at one. Instead, he cradled her face with his hands and plunged his tongue into her mouth again and again, until she lost the ability to think of anything beyond the feel of his lips and the taste of his tongue.

When he finally released her, she swayed against him, resting her forehead against his chest. He stroked her cheek with his knuckles and then pulled back and lifted her chin so that she had to look at him.

"Sarah," he said, "I love you."

It was too much. The irony of it, the absolute tragedy of his saying this to her now. His words tore at her heart, and she knew her time had run out.

"Reece, don't. You can't love me."

"No." He pressed a finger to her lips. "I know this is sudden." He grinned. "So don't say anything more." He lowered his head to her throat, stroking the sensitive skin with his tongue. "Let me make love to you. Let me show you."

Sarah sighed and let her head fall against the back of the couch. She should stop him, put an end to this before it started. Instead, she buried her fingers in his hair, pulling him closer. One more time. She wanted him just one more time.

Then she'd tell him the truth and watch him walk away.

"Yes," she murmured. "Please."

Reece's chest tightened at Sarah's words. He'd fought this for so long. Telling himself for years that he no longer cared, that his love for her had died when she'd left him. Then when she'd shown up at the Crooked C, he'd convinced himself that it was nothing but lust.

He'd been lying to himself.

He loved her. He'd never stopped. Now his feelings for her nearly overwhelmed him. The sacrifices she'd made humbled him. No one else had ever loved him that much, nor made him feel the way she did. No one else ever would.

He sought her mouth gently, trying to convey without words how much she meant to him. She kissed him back, lightly at first and then deeper, until it wasn't enough. He wanted to be inside her. Pulling away, he stood and offered her his hand. "Let's go upstairs."

She smiled that bewitching smile of hers. "And waste a perfectly good couch?"

"The couch will be here for another time." Reaching down, he took her hand and brought her to her feet. "This afternoon, I want to make love to you properly. Slowly. And in a bed."

He drew her to him, wrapping her arms around his neck and kissing her until he felt the sweet length of her melt against him—her soft breasts pressed against his chest, while the apex of her thighs rubbed tantalizingly against his erection. He moved his hands to her bottom, bringing her closer.

She pulled away from his mouth, laughed seductively and tossed her head back, giving him access to the pulse at the base of her neck. "You really think we're going to make it upstairs?"

Reece met her challenge, nipping at her throat and then shifting quickly to lift her in his arms and head for the stairs. "Yeah. We're going to make it."

She wrapped her arms more tightly around his neck and laughed, a low throaty sound that sent a fresh surge of desire to his groin. "Reece, you've got to stop doing this."

"What?" He'd reached the bottom step. "Making love to you?"

"Carrying me around."

"If I put you down, will you promise to head straight up to your room without acting up?"

She smiled slowly and lifted a finger to run lazy circles around his ear. "Well, that depends," she said in her soft sorceress voice. "On what you mean by acting up."

With a low growl he started up the stairs, Sarah still in his arms.

It amazed him that they actually made it to her room. Because by the time he set her back on her feet, he could think of nothing else but burying himself inside her.

"Well," she said, backing away teasingly. "Looks like you were right. We're here."

He grinned and took hold of her braid, drawing her closer. Then he deftly removed the covered elastic band that held her hair in place.

"What now?" she asked.

"You'll see." Carefully he worked the dark silken strands free of their weaving and spread her hair, letting it fall free over her shoulders. "I've wanted to see you like this since that first day you walked into my office. Every time I closed my eyes, I'd remember how it used to look spread across our pillows."

Sarah heard the love in his voice and lost yet another piece of her heart. It was so good to be with him. As if they'd never been parted. Loving. Laughing. They meshed perfectly, bodies, souls and hearts. Two parts of one whole. As if they'd been together forever, from one lifetime to the next.

She pulled her blouse free of her skirt and lifted it over her head.

"I like the buttons better," he teased.

Smiling, she reached out and started undoing his shirt. "Me, too." He started to help her but stopped when she shook her head. "Let me." She shoved the fabric off his shoulders and ran her hands over his chest, relishing the feel of his strength beneath her fingers, the rise and fall of his muscles, the tightness of his skin.

Reece groaned and found the front clasp of her bra, released it and tossed it aside. Then his hands caressed her, and her breath caught in her throat.

"Ah, Sarah, you feel so good."

"You, too." She stepped back and undid her skirt without taking her eyes off him. He worked at the zipper of his jeans, and within minutes, they stood facing each other with nothing between them.

Sarah smiled and held out her arms. "Love me."

SOMETHING TICKLED her cheek, and Sarah batted it away. Then again, and this time her hand connected with something solid, bringing her more fully awake. Reluctantly she opened her eyes. Reece lay sprawled beside her on the bed, teasing her with a piece of her hair.

"Hi," she said.

"Hi, yourself."

Yawning, she shifted on her side to face him. "I didn't mean to fall asleep."

He kissed her gently on the lips. "Guess I wore you out."

"Fishing for compliments?"

"Always."

She slipped one hand around his waist. "Well, on a scale of one to ten I'd say you're a . . . an eight."

"An eight!" Laughing, he had her pinned beneath him in a heartbeat. With one knee, he spread her legs and pressed himself against her. "Is that all?"

Between her giggles and the feel of him once again hard and ready, Sarah could barely speak. "What's wrong with an eight? It's better than average."

"Better than average!" He rubbed a little harder, and she moaned.

"Much better than average."

He lowered his head and nipped at her mouth. "How much better?"

"Oh, Reece." She wound her arms around his neck and pulled him closer. "How do I know? There's never been anyone else."

He grinned, started to kiss her again and then froze.

That was all it took for Sarah to realize what she'd said. The truth was out at last. "Reece . . ." she whispered.

He rolled off her and stood, staring at her like some kind of insect he couldn't be rid of fast enough. Then he looked at the top of her dresser, where she kept Lyssa's baby picture.

Sitting up, Sarah pulled a blanket around her. "I was going to tell you."

He looked at her, but she couldn't read his expression. His face seemed carved of granite. Then he backed away, never taking his eyes off her, and grabbed his jeans, yanking them on and heading for the door.

Sarah let out a cry of dismay and snatched up her own clothes, pulling them on as quickly as possible and following him down the stairs. She found him in her living room, the picture of Drew and Lyssa in his hand.

"Lyssa," he said. "She's mine."

Sarah straightened, wrapping her arms around her waist. "Yes."

He put the picture down and turned away, but not before she saw the agony rip across his features. He ran his hand through his hair. And then again. "I should have known."

"No. You couldn't have known."

"The man yesterday at the rodeo... God, they look so much alike. And Lyssa's coloring." Then he turned and pinned her with his eyes, dark with anger. "You were pregnant when you left." It was an accusation, a sharp bitter accusation.

Sarah bit her lip. "Yes."

The rage on his face seared a hole straight to her soul. "Did you know?" When she didn't answer, he closed the distance between them and grabbed her arms. "Answer me, Sarah. Did you know when you left us that you were pregnant?"

Sarah nodded, and he thrust her from him.

"How could you do that?" He paced the floor, an injured animal seeking some kind of relief. "How could you keep her from me? Didn't you think I had a right to know?"

"I was going to tell you..." She stumbled over to the couch and sat down.

He turned on her. "When?"

"Today. This afternoon. Then we... I would have told you tonight."

"That's a pretty convenient story. What about all the other times we've been together?" He took a couple of steps toward her. "What about when you first came to the ranch? Or any time after that?"

"Would you have been any less angry if I'd told you then? Any less hurt?"

"Hell, no!" He moved away from her. "You should have told me eleven years ago. She's my daughter. I had a right—"

Suddenly Reece went perfectly still, his attention riveted on something behind her. Fear coiled in her stomach, and Sarah turned to see what he was looking at.

Drew and Lyssa stood in the doorway.

CHAPTER FOURTEEN

THEY SEEMED in shock.

Lyssa, her bright eyes wide and already filling with tears. And Drew, stepping in front of her as if to shield her, his expression hurt and angry. "Is it true? Is *she* my mother?" He nodded toward Sarah, though he never took his eyes off his father.

"Yes." Reece felt his son's pain more sharply than if it were his own. "Sarah is your mother."

"And Lyssa?" Drew continued, his voice charged with outrage. "She's my sister?"

Reece looked from one to the other, his *two* children, and wondered how he and Sarah could have done this to them. "Yes."

Lyssa let out a startled cry and bolted for the front door. Drew just stood there, his accusing eyes locked on his father. "You lied to us." He turned to glower at Sarah. "You *both* lied to us." Then he, too, fled out the front door.

Stunned, Reece stood rooted to the floor. *What had they done?* Instead of protecting their children, he and Sarah had hurt them terribly.

Sarah's voice snapped him out of it. "Reece, go after him!" she said frantically, abandoning the couch. "He's going to run away."

Her words mobilized him, and Reece dashed for the front door. "Drew! Wait!"

The silence outside unnerved him.

"Lyssa!" Sarah called as she came out behind him onto the porch and then scrambled down the steps into the front yard. "Drew! Lyssa! Where are you?"

She ran around the house toward the backyard, and Reece circled the other way. Nothing. No sign of either child. Back in front, he called to Sarah while motioning toward one end of the street. "You go that way. I'll go the other."

Nodding, Sarah set off at a near run, calling to Lyssa and Drew as she went. Reece went in the opposite direction, telling himself not to panic. Drew and Lyssa were justifiably upset, but they wouldn't go far. He or Sarah would find them any minute.

An hour later he returned to the house, hoping Sarah'd had better luck than he had. He found her on the phone.

"If you see them, Bill, please hold on to them and give me a call." She paused. "Okay. I'll try." Another pause. "Thank you."

"Who was that?" Reece asked as she hung up the phone.

"Bill Davis. He's one of the coaches who was chaperoning the camping trip. He hasn't seen them, but he's putting together a group to search his end of town." She hesitated, and he sensed her fear, barely held in check. He had the urge to take her in his arms and tell her it would be okay. They'd find Drew and Lyssa. But he couldn't. Not after what she'd done.

"I've tried every friend of Lyssa's I can think of," she said. "No one has seen them. And I called the sheriff's office." Her voice caught, but after a moment she regained control. "Half the town is out looking for them."

"We'll find them, Sarah." She looked up at him, and he saw the agony in her eyes. He softened his voice, unable to deny her at least this small measure of comfort. "I promise."

"This isn't like Lyssa. She's never run away before."

"This is the first time she's found out that her mother deceived her." The words slipped out before he could stop them, and Sarah flinched as if struck. He could have kicked himself. She didn't need him pointing a finger now. The important thing was to find Drew and Lyssa. There would be time later for him and Sarah to settle their differences.

"Look..." he began, running a hand through his hair, but then cut off his apology. His own anger at her hovered too close to the surface. "What happened to the camping trip?" he asked, instead. "What were they doing back here?"

"Bill said there's an early snowstorm closing in on the mountains. The group got up there and decided they better come back before they got stuck."

Reece cursed under his breath. Leave it to the Wyoming weather to throw everyone a curve. What were the chances that Drew and Lyssa would walk in just when they did? An hour later, he and Sarah would have already hashed out this mess and could have broken it to the kids gently. An hour earlier... No, he didn't want to think about what they'd have walked in on if they'd arrived home earlier.

"What do we do now?" Sarah asked, obviously at a loss.

"We get in our cars and start looking."

She nodded, pressing her lips together, and he wondered how long before she fell apart.

"Are you okay?" he asked.

"Yes." She straightened her shoulders and pulled her hair to one side, then quickly began to braid it. "Let's go."

"Just a minute." He had an idea. "What about Joseph?"

Sarah's fingers stilled with her braid half-finished. "You don't think they'd go all the way out there, do you?"

"I don't know what to think. But Drew's proved how resourceful he can be at running away." Again he ran a hand through his hair, guilt settling inside him right alongside the fear. "I never should've let him off the hook when he ran off before and came here. Now he thinks he can get away with this sort of thing."

"It's not your fault, Reece. He's had a shock. They both have."

He almost smiled. In the midst of all this craziness, she was attempting to comfort him. But he didn't want comfort from her. He didn't want anything from her ever again. "Call Joseph."

He saw his rebuke reflected in her eyes. Then, nodding, she quickly finished with her hair and picked up the phone.

While Sarah called Joseph, Reece went back outside. He circled the house again and checked with the neighbors. He didn't expect to find out anything new, but he had to be sure he hadn't overlooked something obvious.

A few minutes later Sarah joined him. "Joseph hasn't seen them. But he agrees with you that they might head out that way. He said he'll watch for them. He's also going to run over to my grandmother's and see if they're there."

"Okay. Let's start looking." Reece started for his truck. "I think we should go separately, use both vehicles. We can cover more ground."

Sarah held back. "Reece, one of us should stay here. In case the kids return or someone spots them."

"Fine. You stay."

"But I know the town better."

She was right, but... "It will be dark in an hour, and I can't sit around here waiting for someone else to find my kids." He pulled his keys from his pocket and nodded toward the house. "If you think someone needs to wait by the phone, then do it. I'm going out to look for Lyssa and Drew."

Sarah watched him climb into his truck and drive away.

She couldn't fall apart, she told herself. She needed to get through this, find Lyssa and Drew and then face them all. Drew. Lyssa. And Reece. Until then, she had to hold herself together.

Reece had only been gone a few minutes when the sheriff stopped by. Sarah's heart leapt when she saw him pull into her driveway, and then it instantly plummeted when he climbed out of the car alone.

"I've come for a picture," he said as she opened the door for him. "If you've got a recent one."

"I took one just last week." Walking into the living room, she grabbed the photograph she'd taken of Lyssa and Drew together. Her hands shook as she handed it to him. "Here."

"Sarah, don't worry. Kids do this sort of thing all the time," he said, trying to reassure her. "They get mad at their folks and decide to run off. Then they show up tired and hungry a few hours later. That's why in a bigger town the cops wouldn't even start looking for them for another twenty-four hours."

"I hope you're right," she said, fervently wishing that, in their case, it had been just a normal parent-child disagreement. She hadn't gone into particulars when she'd explained to the sheriff over the phone why Drew and Lyssa had run away.

An hour and a half later it was nearly dark, and there was still no word. Sarah paced the floor, fighting the panic that every few minutes threatened to reduce her to a useless puddle of tears. For the hundredth time, she reminded herself that she couldn't fall apart. Her children might need her.

Suddenly the phone rang, and Sarah jumped. "Hello."

"Sarah." It was Joseph. "They've been here."

"Been there? But they're not now?"

"No. They must have snuck in while I was over at Tuwa's. But two horses are missing. You need to get out here right away. The weather's getting bad. I'll start looking for tracks, but there's no one else here. The family's all still over in Riverton."

Sarah wrapped the phone cord around her finger. "Are you sure it was Lyssa and Drew who took the horses?"

"As sure as I can be without seeing them myself. I found one of Lyssa's barrettes in the stall."

"Okay." Sarah's mind raced. She needed to notify the sheriff and find Reece. "I'll be there within the hour."

"Okay. I'm going out to see if I can pick up their trail."

"I'll look for you out by the stables," she said, hanging up the phone.

She left a note for Reece in case she couldn't find him and then called the sheriff's office. She conveyed Joseph's information to the dispatcher and then hurried out to her car. She would make one sweep of the surrounding few blocks looking for Reece. If she didn't find him immediately, she'd head out to Joseph's and let the sheriff find Reece and send him after her.

Fortunately she spotted Reece's truck three blocks from her house near one of the town parks. She pulled her car up next to it and climbed out.

"Reece!" she called, walking toward the woods. "Reece!"

A moment later he appeared from under the trees, jogging toward her. "Did you find them?"

"No. But you were right. They went out to Joseph's. They took two of his horses."

"Let's go." He darted for his truck, and Sarah climbed in on the passenger side. "How far?" he asked as he pulled out of the parking lot.

"Thirty minutes under the best conditions."

Reece made it in twenty.

Yet the silent drive seemed longer than any time she'd driven this road in the past. Fear and guilt battled for dominance within her. This whole mess was her fault. If she'd told Reece from the beginning about Lyssa... If she'd told Drew the truth about who she was... If she and Reece hadn't made love earlier... If... An endless list of things she could have, should have, done differently. And overshadowing it all was fear. A heart-pounding brain-numbing certainty that her children were up in the mountains alone with a snowstorm closing in.

They found Joseph checking the ground by a creek west of his barn. "They left pretty clear tracks," he said, pointing to the two sets of hoofprints in the mud. "They're headed toward the mountains."

Sarah's heart sank. "What are they thinking? They know it's starting to snow up there."

"They're *not* thinking," Reece stated. "They're reacting."

"I agree," Joseph said. "Drew's angry and he wants to be as far from both of you as possible right now. Lyssa is just going along."

"But how...?" Sarah stared at him. She hadn't told anyone why Drew and Lyssa had left.

Joseph shrugged. "It's obvious he just found out that Lyssa is his sister."

"You knew?" Reece demanded, bringing his angry eyes to rest on Sarah. "Am I the only one who *didn't* know?"

"She did not tell me," Joseph said. "You have only to look at the two of them to see it."

Reece turned back to glare at Joseph and then visibly took a deep breath. "Okay. So where would they go?"

Sarah searched her mind for a place Drew might have run to. The problem was, he didn't know this area very well. This was Lyssa's domain.

"Joseph," she said, "did Drew and Lyssa go riding in the hills alone at any time?"

He shook his head. "No. I wouldn't allow it."

"Then it's Lyssa who's decided where they're going," she said. "Drew doesn't know these mountains."

"What about the old hunting cabin up on the ridge overlooking the lake?" Joseph suggested.

"That's it," Sarah said. "It's one of Lyssa's favorite spots. We usually ride up there once or twice a summer and spend the weekend. It's isolated. And you can only get up there on foot or horseback."

"Could she find it on her own?" Reece asked.

Sarah considered that. "In daylight and good weather, she could."

"But it's neither now," Reece said. "Could she find her way there tonight?"

"I don't know, Reece. I just don't know."

"I'll take you up there," Joseph said.

"No, Joseph." She wasn't about to drag the old man out in the kind of conditions they might find in the mountains. "Reece and I will go. I could find the cabin with my eyes closed. Stay here and send help after us when it arrives."

"Come on then," Reece said. "Let's get moving."

Fifteen minutes later, they had two horses saddled and ready to go. Joseph had outfitted them with big heavy jackets, gloves and thick wool ponchos for the rain and snow. He'd also packed extra blankets, hot coffee in a thermos and food.

"I'll call the sheriff and get some more men up there," Joseph said once Sarah and Reece mounted their horses.

"Okay," Reece said. "If the weather's too bad, we'll bed down in the cabin for the night."

"Good luck," Joseph said, and Sarah and Reece set off.

AT FIRST the going was easy. But as they neared the mountains and began the steady climb upward, the temperature dropped rapidly. They both pulled on the heavy jackets and ponchos. Sarah led, following a path she'd taken every summer since Joseph had first brought her here on her tenth birthday. Neither of them spoke.

Soon the rain started, a light irritating drizzle. But it wasn't long before it began to fall in earnest and turned icy, stinging their faces as the wind picked up. Sarah silently thanked Joseph for the protective clothing while making a mental checklist of the clothes Lyssa and Drew had with them when they headed out for their camping trip. They'd both packed for the mountains, with warm woolen jackets and bright yellow rain slickers, but they hadn't counted on a snowstorm. Still, as long as they stayed dry and didn't get lost on their way to the cabin, they'd be okay.

She was hardly aware that the rain turned to snow until her horse slowed his pace. She reined the animal to a halt, letting Reece ride up beside her. They scanned the horizon. Nothing. And Sarah wondered if they'd even be able to tell if Lyssa and Drew had passed this way recently. The falling snow would have covered their tracks within twenty minutes. And the children were at least an hour ahead of her and Reece.

"Do you know where you are?" Reece asked.

"Yes. The cabin is still several miles to the west. Over those hills." She motioned in the direction they'd been traveling. "Do you think they could have made it this far?"

"I don't know. It'd be easy to get lost in this weather."

They rode on for another fifteen minutes, while fear grew inside her. What if they got to the cabin and Lyssa and Drew weren't there? No! She couldn't think like that. She and Reece would find their son and daughter alive and unharmed. Then Sarah would face the consequences of her lie. Gladly. No matter what happened. No matter what retribution Reece exacted. Even if Lyssa went to live with him, Sarah would let her go. *Just, please, Lord,* she prayed, *let them be alive.*

"Sarah!" Reece's voice cut into her thoughts.

Pulling up short, she shifted in her saddle to look at him. "What is it?"

He came up alongside her. "Down there." He pointed to the ravine on their left. "I thought I saw movement. In that group of trees." Turning his horse, he retraced his steps several yards, scanning the small narrow canyon. Sarah followed him.

"There," Reece said, pointing again. "Horses. Come on, boy." He headed down the steep slope, with Sarah right behind him, her heart beating wildly.

Please, Lord. Let them be all right.

They came upon the two animals, huddled together near a copse of trees along a small creek bed. But there was no sign of the children. Then Sarah spotted a splash of yellow, and her heart skipped a beat.

"Reece, over there," she called, sliding off her horse and pointing toward the side of the hill. "It looks like one of the kids' slickers."

His heart pounding, Reece leapt to the ground and raced toward the snow-covered plastic. He was almost on top of it before he realized that the coat blanketed a small mound. The sight sent a fresh shock of fear straight to his gut.

"Oh, my God," Sarah whispered behind him. "No!"

"Drew! Lyssa!" Reece dropped to his knees and brushed the snow away from the coat and then pulled it aside, uncovering a sleeping bag underneath.

Sarah joined him, digging at the snow around the bag. An eternity passed or possibly a few seconds—he couldn't say which—before a faint voice came from inside the bag. "Dad? Is that you?"

"Yes! Drew!" Relief washed over him as Reece unzipped the bag a few inches, and Drew's head appeared over the top.

"You found us!" Drew scooted upright, revealing Lyssa's blond head beside him. "You really found us!"

Drew threw his arms around his father's neck, and Reece grabbed him. He started to haul him out of the sleeping bag and then realized his son didn't have on a shirt. "Drew, are you okay? Where are your clothes? Your jacket?"

"Mom." Lyssa's voice sounded small. "I'm so cold."

Sarah quickly shifted to her daughter's side. "Oh, my God, Reece. She's hypothermic."

"She fell in the creek," Drew said, words laced with fear tumbling out of him. "I tried to keep her warm. I dug a hole in the snow for the sleeping bags. I made her get out of her wet clothes and put on dry ones. I got in the bag with her. I did everything you taught me. But it didn't do any good."

"Lyssa." Sarah bent urgently over Lyssa. "Sweetie, can you hear me?"

Lyssa nodded, shivering uncontrollably.

"Come on, Drew." Reece pulled off his poncho and draped it over his son. "Grab your clothes and put them on. We need to take care of Lyssa."

Drew pulled his shirt and coat from inside the bag and scrambled out of the way.

"We need to do something," Sarah said. "Fast."

"Here, let me look at her." Reece scooted over to where Sarah pressed the sleeping bag around Lyssa.

What he saw scared him to death. "Sarah, grab that coffee," he said, unfastening his heavy coat. "We need to get her warm."

Sarah hurried toward the horses, and Reece unbuttoned his shirt. "Does she still have on her jeans and shoes?" he asked Drew.

Drew nodded.

"I'm going to need that poncho as soon as you get your own shirt and jacket back on."

Drew pulled off the poncho, and Reece asked, "Are you okay? Not too cold?"

"I'm fine, but is Lyssa going to be all right?"

"I hope so, son. I sure hope so." With that, he pulled Lyssa out of the sleeping bag and into his arms, her bare back against his chest. Closing his shirt around her as far as it would go, he buttoned the huge jacket around them both. "Okay, Drew, put that poncho over us."

Sarah returned with the thermos of coffee and, squatting next to Reece and Lyssa, poured the warm liquid into the plastic lid. "Come on, sweetheart," she said to Lyssa, holding it up to the child's mouth. "Drink some of this. It'll warm you up."

As Lyssa sipped at the coffee, Reece asked Sarah, "How far is the cabin?"

"Maybe thirty, forty minutes in this weather."

He cursed silently. Lyssa was in bad shape. Even wrapped tightly against his warm body and drinking the coffee, she still shivered.

"We're going to have to try for it," he said. He saw the fear in Sarah's eyes and understood. All too well. But fear wouldn't get Lyssa out of this alive. "I'm going to carry Lyssa like this. Son—" he looked over at Drew "—are you okay to ride?"

"Yes, sir."

"Good. First, I want you to drink some of this coffee, too."

Lyssa had drained the cup, but Sarah refilled it and handed it to Drew. "When did you give yourself your last insulin shot?" she asked.

"Before dinner, like I was supposed to."

Reece's mind raced, sorting through all the possibilities, trying to plan for further complications. "You probably need something to eat," he said to Drew. "But you should check your blood sugar first to make sure. Do you have your kit with you? And a candy bar or something?"

"I'm okay, Dad."

"We need your help, Drew," Reece said. "We can't afford for you to get sick."

Drew straightened his shoulders and nodded. "Okay. My kit's still in my saddlebag."

"Go take care of it then."

While Drew was gone, Reece turned to Sarah, who was giving Lyssa more of the coffee. "You sure you can find this place?" he asked.

"I'm sure." She nodded toward Lyssa. "Can you get up on your horse holding her like that?"

It was going to be tough. "I'm going to hand you the poncho, but I'm not taking her out of this jacket."

Reece could see the fear in Sarah's eyes, but she held it in check. He had to admire her courage. And it suddenly struck him that there was no one else he'd rather have by his side in this situation. Sarah would do anything for her children. Including keeping a clear head and steady hand despite the sheer terror she must be feeling.

A moment later, Drew returned with a candy bar.

"Are you all right?" Sarah asked, taking the once again empty lid and returning it to the thermos.

Drew nodded. "Are we going to the cabin?"

"If you're ready, we're going to leave in a couple of minutes," Reece answered. "Now help Sarah roll up those sleeping bags and tie them onto Lyssa's horse. We're going to need them when we get there."

A few minutes later everything was loaded onto the horses, and Sarah returned to where Reece still held Lyssa, trying to warm her with his body. Grabbing her under her legs and across her waist, he stood and carried her toward his horse.

"Okay, sweetheart," he whispered to Lyssa. "I'm going to need your help. We're going to have to do this together."

Lyssa nodded against his chest.

"I'm going to hand the poncho to your mom for a moment. Then when I put my foot in the stirrup, you're going to rest your left leg on mine. Then I'm going to grab your right leg under the knee, and you need to help me swing it over the saddle when we mount. Can you do that?"

Again she nodded.

To Drew he said, "I'm going to do this quickly, son, so hold the horse steady."

Reece pulled the poncho off and handed it to Sarah.

"Everyone ready," he said. He gripped the saddle horn with his left hand and stuck his foot in the stirrup. "Hold steady, fella."

"Let's do it." In one fluid motion, Reece swung up, the muscles in his left arm and leg straining as he used all his strength and skill to pull his and Lyssa's weight into the saddle.

"There," he said to Lyssa. "Now that wasn't too bad, was it?" Sarah handed him the poncho, and he draped it once again over Lyssa and himself. "Okay. Let's find that cabin."

Sarah and Drew mounted their own horses and followed Reece back up the hill to the trail above. Then Sarah took the lead, with Drew in the middle, and Reece and Lyssa bringing up the rear. All the way he talked to her, telling her silly stories about his days in the rodeo, trying to make her laugh, trying to keep her awake as they trudged through the still-falling snow.

For Sarah it was the longest ride of her life. And she had her moments of doubt. It was one thing to find the cabin on a bright summer day. Quite another to find it under the current conditions: during a snowstorm in the dead of night. What if she couldn't find it? What if she got lost? The four of them would be no better off caught in this freak storm than Drew and Lyssa alone.

No! She couldn't let herself think like that.

She knew the way to the cabin. Hadn't she told Joseph she could find it with her eyes closed? And it wasn't as if they were caught in a blizzard. Even though it was dark and snowing, she could still see, and she knew this mountain well.

Just then, the cabin rose out of the snow like a beacon of hope, and she breathed a sigh of relief.

"We're here," she called behind her, and quickly dismounted. Wrapping the reins around the wooden railing in front of the cabin, she hurried over to Reece and Lyssa.

"Okay," he was saying to Lyssa. "This is going to be just like falling off a horse."

Lyssa giggled softly, and Sarah's heart contracted. He was so good with the kids. Reece threw his and Lyssa's legs over the saddle horn and slid to the ground.

"Get the sleeping bags," he said to Sarah. "You need to climb in one with her while Drew and I get a fire going and take care of the horses."

Grabbing the sleeping bags from Lyssa's horse, Sarah followed them inside. Within minutes she and Lyssa were zipped up tightly in one of the bags. She wrapped her arms around her daughter and held her close.

Reece got a fire going and then warmed some soup he'd found in one of the cabinets. Slowly Lyssa's shivering stopped, warmed by her mother's body, the warm liquid and the fire.

Then Sarah let Lyssa sleep.

She herself must have dozed off, because the next thing she knew, Reece was squatting next to her, gently shaking her awake. She opened her eyes but remained still, not wanting to wake Lyssa.

"The mountain-rescue team is here," he said. "They've radioed down for a helicopter to take Lyssa out."

"What about the snow?"

"It stopped." He shook his head. "It'll probably be all gone by noon." Nodding toward Lyssa, he asked, "How is she?"

"She's going to be fine."

"No point in taking any chances. The helicopter will be here in about thirty minutes, and they'll take you and Drew out, as well. I'll ride back with the rangers."

"Is Drew okay?"

Reece nodded, and Sarah could see his pride in his son. "Yeah. He did real good. Probably saved his sister's life."

Sarah closed her eyes and said a prayer of thanks. For both of her children. When she opened them again, she met Reece's gaze and knew, if nothing else, they shared this. Their children were alive.

"I need to get dressed before that helicopter gets here," she said.

"Yeah." He reached over to where she'd left her clothes and laid them on top of the sleeping bag. "Here. I'll give you a little privacy." Then he turned and went back outside, leaving her to get dressed in the empty cabin.

CHAPTER FIFTEEN

LYSSA WAS KEPT in the hospital overnight for observation.

Sarah wanted to stay with her until she awoke, but the nurses shooed her out a couple of hours before dawn. Lyssa was sleeping soundly, and there was nothing her mother could do for her. Sarah thought of her own bed at home but knew she wouldn't be able to sleep.

Still, she'd go home and try.

As she walked past the waiting room, she spotted Reece scrunched up on one of the couches sound asleep. She hadn't realized that he was here, or that he'd gotten back down the mountain already.

She thought about letting him sleep. Then thought better of it. He was going to ache in the morning if he stayed on the small couch much longer.

Walking over to him, she said, "Reece, wake up."

He stirred but didn't open his eyes.

"Reece." She reached down and touched him on the shoulder.

He came awake with a start and sat bolt upright. "What's wrong?"

"Nothing." Sarah smiled sadly. Actually there was a great deal wrong, but not in the way he meant. "Lyssa's asleep. The doctors say we can take her home in the afternoon."

Reece yawned and ran both hands through his hair. He looked about the way Sarah felt. Exhausted. "And Drew?"

"He went home with the sheriff for the night," she answered. "He's got two boys close to Drew's age."

"So what are you doing?"

She sat in the chair next to the couch. "One of the nurses just kicked me out of Lyssa's room. She told me to go home and get some sleep. Maybe you should do the same thing."

He seemed to consider that for a moment and then turned his tired eyes on her. "We need to talk."

She sighed. "I know, but we're both beat. How about tomorrow?"

"Tomorrow we'll have to deal with Drew and Lyssa. There are things you and I need to discuss alone. And besides, do you really think you can sleep before we get this settled?"

"Probably not." Nodding reluctantly, she stood up. "All right. Let's go back to the house, and I'll make some coffee."

"I think someplace neutral would be better. Somewhere public."

Sarah felt herself blush. Did he think if they went to her house, she'd try to seduce him or something? After everything they'd been through in the past twenty-four hours? But then, she decided, it wasn't worth arguing about, and she was in no position to make demands. She just wanted this over.

"There's an all-night diner across the street," she said. "We can go there."

A few minutes later they were settled in a booth that reminded Reece of the night he'd gone to Devils Corner to offer Sarah a job. The chipped Formica tables, cracked vinyl seats and fluorescent lighting could have come straight out of that other restaurant. Thankfully, though, the coffee was strong, and they had the place pretty much to themselves.

"Well," he said once the waitress had filled their cups and left them alone, "what do we do now?"

Sarah straightened, obviously bracing herself. "You tell me."

He sighed and looked out the window. Yesterday afternoon, before Lyssa and Drew had run off, he'd wanted to strike out at Sarah, to hurt her like she'd hurt him. But not anymore. She'd been through enough. They both had. "Drew and I will be leaving for the Crooked C tomorrow. I want to take Lyssa with us."

"Yes." He heard the resignation in her voice, and it twisted inside him. "I thought you might."

He turned back to look at her. Despite everything she'd done, it still disturbed him to see her in pain. He realized that would probably never change. "I want to be part of Lyssa's life," he said. "But I won't make this a legal battle if you don't. And I won't try and force her. I'm going to make the offer and leave it up to her."

Surprise registered on Sarah's face. And gratitude. "I won't fight you, Reece. Legally or otherwise. Lyssa is your daughter. You have as much right to her as I do."

Reece let the silence linger a few moments as he sipped his coffee. There was still so much between them, their past, their children. And she was everything he'd ever wanted in a woman. Strong. Loving. Passionate. Even now, he couldn't deny how he felt for her. How she made him feel. They could have had a good life together, if only . . .

"You shouldn't have kept her from me, Sarah."

She closed her eyes and nodded. "I know."

"Why?" he asked gently, knowing that no matter how she answered, he could never trust her again.

She opened her eyes, and again he saw surprise on her face.

"Tell me why you did it," he prompted when she didn't speak.

She took a deep breath. "I'd already lost Drew. I was afraid of losing Lyssa, as well."

He sighed and ran his hand through his hair. It was what he'd thought. "I never would have taken her from you."

"I didn't know."

They lapsed into silence again. He couldn't let her take all the blame for this. She'd kept Lyssa from him, but he'd played his part. Maybe if he'd done things differently, she would have, too. Finally he said, "I should have let you tell Drew the truth."

"I should have insisted."

"Damn it, Sarah. You can't put all the blame on yourself."

Tilting her head, she gave him an odd look. "Is that what I'm doing? Funny, I thought I was finally taking responsibility for my actions."

SARAH COULDN'T LET Reece take the blame.

This whole crazy mess was her fault. She'd started it eleven years ago when she'd walked out on him, knowing that she was carrying his second child. Over the years she'd paid for that mistake. But not enough.

Not nearly enough. Her son had grown up without a mother, her daughter without a father.

She suspected she deserved to pay for the rest of her life.

She picked up Lyssa from the hospital early in the afternoon. The doctors said she was fine. She just needed to take it easy for a couple of days to rebuild her strength. But all the way home Lyssa was unusually quiet. Once or twice Sarah thought to say something, to try to draw her daughter out and gauge how she felt about her new knowledge of her parents. Then Sarah would change her mind, leaving Lyssa to her silence. In a short while, there would be more than enough words between them.

When they arrived at the house, Drew and Reece were waiting outside. Sarah took a deep breath and climbed out of her car.

It was time to face her lies.

As SHE'D EXPECTED, explaining things to her children was one of the hardest things she'd ever done. She told them the truth. All of it. She explained how young and foolish she'd been, how she'd been unable to provide the care Drew needed, and how she'd panicked when she'd found out she was pregnant with Lyssa. She also told them she'd left knowing that Reece's family would take care of Drew. The only piece she left out was Elizabeth's part. There was no use blaming Reece's mother when in the end it had been her own decision. Her own mistake.

Drew sat listening stoically the entire time, his eyes boring holes into her. She could feel his anger, his sense of betrayal. She prayed she hadn't done him irreparable harm, and that Reece would still be able to

get through to him. Lyssa, on the other hand, sat off
to the side, her hands folded neatly in her lap, never
once looking at either of her parents. It was so unlike
her bossy precocious daughter that Sarah felt totally
unnerved. She didn't know which of her two children's reactions was worse.

"Well," she said, gripping her hands tightly together to still their trembling, "that's the whole story.
Now you know it all." She'd managed to hold back
her tears, but her voice broke as she added, "Except
that I love you both very much. And I never meant to
hurt either of you."

For a few minutes, neither child spoke, and Sarah
felt the silence like a weight on her heart. There was
nothing more she could say, nothing else she could do
to make them understand.

Then Drew turned to his father and said, "Can we
go now?"

His words twisted inside her, and even Reece looked
a bit shaken. "In just a moment, son. There's something I want to add." Reece met her gaze and held it,
and it was like a lifeline to her. "What your mother
isn't telling you is that this was as much my fault as
hers." His words surprised her, and she shook her
head, willing him to stop.

"When we were married," he went on, ignoring her
silent plea, "I made things difficult for her. I'd started
drinking and staying out late with my friends. I wasn't
there when she needed me." He paused, smiling sadly
with his eyes still locked on Sarah. "I drove her away."

Tears slipped from her eyes. She couldn't stop them.
Pulling her gaze away from him, she grabbed a handful of tissues. All these years she'd blamed herself for
what had happened. After all, she'd been the one

who'd made the decision. Now she realized that Reece was right. He'd played a part in her leaving, even if neither of them had acknowledged it until now.

Now, when it was too late.

Looking back at him, she said, "Thank you."

He nodded and turned toward Lyssa. "There's one other thing, Lyssa."

For the first time since they'd started talking, Lyssa lifted her head.

"I want you to come back to the Crooked C with Drew and me today." He got up and squatted down in front of her. "Just to see if you like it."

"You want me to live with you?"

"Yes." He took her small hands in his. "You're my daughter, and I love you."

"What about my mom?"

"You could still see your mother." Reece threw a glance over his shoulder at Sarah. "You could come back here on holidays and during the summer." When Lyssa didn't say anything, he added, "You don't have to make a decision now. Just come stay for a couple of weeks. See what you think."

Sarah held her breath, though she tried to keep her expression impassive. This had to be Lyssa's choice.

"No, thank you," Lyssa said. She got up and moved to sit next to her mother on the couch. "I'll stay here."

Sarah felt a rush of joy, but she couldn't have her daughter making sacrifices for her. "Lyssa." She reached over and took her hand. "It would be just two weeks. You should go and get to know your father and brother."

Lyssa's topaz eyes widened. "Do you want me to leave?" Her voice trembled slightly.

"Of course not." Sarah pulled her daughter into her arms and held her tight. "I want you here." Then she pulled away to look again into Lyssa's eyes. "But only if it makes you happy."

"I'm happy here."

Sarah met Reece's gaze over Lyssa's shoulder. He looked disappointed but nodded his acceptance. "That's fine, Lyssa," he said. "Drew and I are going to leave now. But you're always welcome at the Crooked C."

He and his son started toward the door.

"Wait," Sarah said. She released Lyssa and crossed the room. "I have something for you, Drew."

"I don't want anything."

"I think you'll want this." Reaching into her pocket, she pulled out a slim silver buckle depicting a bronc rider. "It's your father's. He won it the year before you were born."

Drew's gaze locked on the buckle, but he didn't make a move to touch it. Sarah looked up at Reece. There was so much emotion in his eyes. Surprise. Gratitude. And something else. Something softer that she was afraid to name.

"Go ahead," she said to Drew, never moving her gaze from Reece. "Take it."

"I don't want it."

She looked back at Drew and could see the lie on his face. He wanted the buckle. He just wasn't going to admit it. It nearly broke the last of her control, but she held on, fighting back the tears. There would be time for them later.

"Maybe you'll change your mind." She glanced back at Reece. "Your father can keep it for you."

Reece hesitated for a moment and then took it, only to have Drew turn and run out the door.

Closing her eyes for a moment, she took a deep steadying breath. "I'm sorry, Reece. Hopefully he'll want it someday."

"He'll come around."

Sarah nodded, though she wasn't so sure. She walked back to Lyssa and sat down. Then watched the only man she'd ever loved take their son and walk out of her life.

AS SUMMER GAVE WAY to fall, Reece admitted he'd never been more miserable in his life.

It was even worse than when Sarah had left him eleven years ago. Although he couldn't have said why exactly, except maybe that this time, he'd been the one to walk away. But who could blame him? he'd remind himself. She'd kept his daughter from him for ten years.

How did you love someone you couldn't trust?

Still, day and night she occupied his thoughts, until he thought he'd go crazy thinking about her. He'd thrown himself into the running of the ranch and spending time with Drew. The work helped. It left him too exhausted to think of much else. But spending time with Drew only succeeded in reminding him of everything he'd thrown away when he'd left Oaksburg.

Sarah and Lyssa.

Despite everything, he wanted them both here. His ex-wife and his daughter. And he wasn't happy about it.

Drew was another story.

Since they'd returned, the boy hadn't once mentioned Sarah. Reece had tried to bring up the subject, to get a better feel for how Drew was dealing with knowing his mother was alive. But Drew refused to talk about it.

Finally Reece decided to invite Lyssa up for the weekend. The girl had a way about her, and she and Drew had formed a special bond. He'd seen it over that one short weekend they'd all spent together. Maybe she could break through the wall of anger Drew had built against his mother.

SARAH SAT on her back-porch swing, enjoying the weather. The crisp fall air was a welcome relief after the hot summer months. The trees were in full regalia, and she thought of the cottonwoods beside the creek where Drew had taken her on the Crooked C. They would be beautiful this time of year.

The weeks since Reece and Drew had returned to the Crooked C had passed slowly. School had gotten under way, but it didn't feel the same as it had in the past. The rush of adrenaline she usually experienced every September was missing. Teaching had become a job. Someplace to be every day while her thoughts were three hundred miles away, with her son and his father. She missed them both terribly, and she wondered if she'd ever stop.

"Mom?"

Sarah turned and smiled at Lyssa. "Hey, sweetie." She patted the seat on the swing next to her. "Come on out."

Lyssa stepped out onto the porch and came over to sit next to her mother. They sat silently for a few minutes, with Lyssa pushing at the floor with her feet, rocking them unevenly back and forth.

Lyssa had become a lot like her old self again, but the changes were there—if you looked closely. The night in the mountains and finding out she had a brother and a father had left their mark on her. Every now and then, Sarah caught her just sitting, staring off into the distance. When Sarah asked what she was thinking, Lyssa just smiled and said, "Oh, nothing." She, too, missed Drew and Reece, Sarah guessed. And sooner or later she'd have to send Lyssa to the Crooked C. It was only a matter of time.

"Mom," she said finally, "can I ask you a favor?"

"Sure, honey. What is it?"

Lyssa turned sideways on the swing and crossed her legs. "Promise you won't get mad or anything."

"I'm not going to get mad at you for asking. Whatever it is."

"Promise."

Sarah shook her head. "Lyssa, what is it?"

"Dad just called."

Fear coiled in her stomach, but Sarah pushed it down. Reece called Lyssa often—several times a week—and nothing ever came of it. "So, what did he have to say?" she asked.

"It's not a big deal," Lyssa said. "And if you don't want me to, I understand . . ."

"What, Lyssa?"

"He wants me to come up for Halloween weekend."

Sarah couldn't answer. Not at first. Of course she had to let Lyssa go. She should get to know her father and Drew. They were part of her life now.

"Can I, Mom?" Lyssa prompted. "It's just for a weekend, and it's going to be really neat. They're having a big party with hayrides and costumes."

"Of course you can go." *Just for a weekend.* Sarah forced some enthusiasm into her voice. "I think it'll be great."

"Really? Gee, thanks." Lyssa threw her arms around her mother's neck and hugged her. "You're the best." Then Lyssa jumped from the swing. "I'm going to go call him right now and tell him."

"Sounds like a good idea to me." Sarah smiled, though her heart was breaking, and Lyssa ran off to make her call.

DREW DIDN'T KNOW how he felt about Lyssa's coming to spend the weekend at the Crooked C. She'd been okay and all when he'd stayed at her mom's. She rode real good and wasn't afraid of much like some of the girls he knew. Still, that had all been before he'd found out the truth about Miss Hanson.

Every time he thought about her, he got mad.

She'd pretended to be his friend, letting him think he could trust her. While all the time she'd been lying to him. Maybe all that stuff she'd said had been true—about being young and making a mistake and all—but why did she have to pretend to be someone else all summer long?

He didn't think he could ever forgive her for that.

"Hey, Drew," Tod said. "You gonna ride that stallion or let him ride you?"

"Oh, sorry." Drew shifted his weight and brought the Appaloosa back alongside Tod's horse. He knew better than to let his mind wander while riding the Ap.

Tod shot him a grin. "I think that ol' son is beginning to think you belong to him."

"Nah, he just tolerates me." Drew tried not to show how much the compliment pleased him, even though he knew Tod was right. The Appaloosa *was* beginning to respond to him. Some things had changed for the better since he and his father had returned to the Crooked C. His father and Tod had started taking him with them when they went out to mend a fence or work with the herd. And usually he rode the Ap. Sometime over the summer, when he hadn't been paying attention, Drew had learned to handle the big stallion.

"Your dad's real proud of you, you know," Tod said.

"Think so?" This time Drew grinned despite himself.

Making his dad proud was about the best thing he could imagine. Because his dad hadn't been happy about much lately. There was stuff bothering him. Drew figured it had to do with Lyssa being his daughter and not living with them and all. He knew his dad was glad she'd decided to come up for the Halloween weekend. So maybe that made her visit okay. Maybe she'd cheer him up.

As long as she didn't want to talk about her mom.

SARAH FORCED HERSELF to smile as she took Lyssa to the airport late Friday afternoon. And it just about killed her as Lyssa hurried toward the waiting plane.

But why shouldn't Lyssa be excited?

She'd recently discovered she had a father and brother. It was only natural for her to want to spend time with them. It was, after all, just for a weekend.

Sarah had repeated the litany over and over for the last week.

It didn't make her feel any better.

Now she had almost three full days to herself, and she hadn't the faintest idea what to do. She started to drive home and then changed her mind. Instead, she stopped at Kentucky Fried Chicken and then headed for the reservation. She'd surprise Tuwa with dinner and spend a day or two with her.

It was infinitely better than going back to an empty house.

When she pulled into the yard, Tuwa stepped out onto the porch to greet her. "Sarah, you're two days early."

Smiling, she climbed out of her car. "Can't I come see you on a day other than Sunday, Grandmother?" She gave the old woman a warm hug. "Besides, Lyssa's gone for the weekend, and I thought we could spend some time together."

"I would like that."

"Me, too. And..." Sarah stepped back to her car and pulled the bucket of chicken from the back seat. "I brought dinner."

Tuwa broke into a huge grin. "Now you really are welcome." She led the way into the house. "Where did Lyssa go?"

Sarah kept her voice neutral. "She went to spend the weekend with Reece. They're having some kind of Halloween party or something."

"That's good." Tuwa grabbed a couple of plates from her cabinet and set them on the table. "Why didn't you go, too?"

Sarah's hands stilled and she looked at her grandmother. "Why would I?"

"You are their mother. Lyssa's and Drew's." Tuwa shrugged as if the answer were obvious. "And you are his wife."

"Ex-wife."

"Hah!" Tuwa sat herself at the table.

"What's that supposed to mean?"

"You still love him."

As always, her grandmother saw too much. Sarah sat down and kept her hands and eyes busy divvying up the food. "That doesn't have anything to do with it," she said. "Reece will never forgive me for not telling him about Lyssa."

"Are you sure?"

She couldn't help it. She looked back at Tuwa, who wore a knowing smile. Suddenly Sarah knew where Lyssa got her know-it-all attitude. She'd inherited it from her great-grandmother.

"He can't forgive you, Sarah," Tuwa said, "until you forgive yourself."

LATER, TUWA'S WORDS came back to Sarah again and again. She heard them in her mind while she built a fire and they sat and talked of other things. And she felt them in her heart, as she lay awake in the bed she'd used as a child.

Until you forgive yourself.

Eleven years ago she'd deserted her husband and son, taking the secret of her unborn child with her. How could she forgive herself for that?

The answer came to her in the dead of the night, whispering in the wind that brushed against her window.

You were a child yourself.

She'd been seventeen when she married Reece, eighteen when she'd left him. Eighteen and broke, with an infant who needed constant care and expensive medicines. Eighteen and married to a man-child, a boy who refused to face the severity of their situation. For the first time, she remembered how she'd felt then. Really remembered. Her desperation. Her loneliness. And her love. She'd loved Drew and Reece more than her own life. And she'd loved her unborn child. Her daughter. Lyssa. She would have done anything for them.

Then Elizabeth had shown up on her doorstep.

At the time, Sarah thought she'd had no other option. Give her son and husband over to her mother-in-law or watch her marriage crumble and die, while her children paid the price. She'd chosen life for all of them. Or so she'd thought.

Looking back as an adult, she realized there had been other options. She could have forced Reece to face their situation, begged him to go to his father and ask for help for their son. He would have done it. If she'd pushed hard enough. And if that hadn't worked, there were government agencies that would have helped them. Or they could have returned to the reservation. Her grandmother would have helped—if only to watch Drew while Sarah and Reece worked. And there was Elizabeth herself. Sarah knew now that the woman loved her grandson. She never would have let him suffer to rid herself of an unwanted daughter-in-law. Sarah should have called her bluff.

Hindsight. It seemed so clear.

All the would-have's and could-have's didn't amount to much. She'd made a mistake, but she'd done it out of love. That was what really mattered.

Reece had seen that. The last night they'd made love, he'd understood better than Sarah herself how she'd talked herself into walking away from him.

And what about Lyssa?

That, too, had been a mistake. She should have told him. The fact was, however, she hadn't. But that, too, was in the past. All the secrets were out in the open now. Yet they continued to pay. All four of them. Sarah. Reece. Drew. Lyssa.

It wasn't right.

They belonged together. They were a family who loved each other. And when you loved someone, you forgave their mistakes.

On Saturday, Sarah stayed and helped her grandmother prepare her house for winter. Feeling better than she had in years, Sarah could hardly wait to get back home. Tomorrow, her life would begin again.

After dinner, she kissed her grandmother goodbye. "Thank you, Grandmother. For everything."

Tuwa studied her for a moment and then nodded. "I think everything's going to be fine now. Am I right?"

Sarah smiled. "Yes. You are. I'm going to be gone for a few days. But I'll come see you when I return."

"You've decided to go to them?"

A warmth filled Sarah at the thought. "I'm leaving first thing in the morning."

Tuwa nodded. "I've always had faith in you, child."

"I know." Tears welled in Sarah's eyes. "You were right. I'm his wife. It's about time we both remembered it."

BRINGING LYSSA UP for the weekend had been a brilliant idea, Reece admitted. She added a spark of life and vitality to everything, jumping smack into the middle of the party preparations the minute she'd arrived at the Crooked C. Millie had instantly fallen in love with her, and even Drew had seemed more like his old self.

Reece had called his mother in Boston, not sure yet whether he was willing to forgive her, but needing to let her know about Lyssa. He introduced them over the phone. The ten-year-old chatted nonstop, as if she'd known her grandmother all her life. He doubted Elizabeth even got a word in edgewise. But when he took the phone back, his mother sounded absolutely charmed, telling him she couldn't wait to come back for a visit to meet her newest grandchild.

Yes, indeed, Reece thought as he headed down to ready the wagon for the hayride that night. Pure genius.

As he approached the barn, he heard voices.

"So, what do you think about having a sister?" Lyssa asked. "And a mom?"

Reece stopped just outside the door, eager to hear his son's response.

"Not much." Reece could visualize Drew's shrug.

"What does that mean?" she asked.

"You may be my sister," Drew answered, "but I don't have a mom." His words hit Reece hard, sparking his anger, and he started to step out and face his son. He needed to set Drew straight on a few things.

"Well, that's dumb," Lyssa said, stopping Reece with her words before he showed himself. "You can't just decide you don't have a mom."

Reece shook his head. She was something else. Her big brother didn't scare her one bit. Though it was obvious she adored him.

"You can think what you want," Drew said. "I haven't ever had a mom, and I don't need one now. Especially one that lies."

"Dad lied, too."

The truth hurt, but Reece kept his silence.

"Yeah, well, that was different," Drew said.

"Oh, yeah? How?" It was the same question Reece himself would have asked, and he realized he'd been as unfair to Sarah as Drew had. Probably more so. After all, he was supposedly the adult.

When Drew didn't answer right away, Lyssa picked up the slack. "Besides, you're only hurting yourself."

"You don't know what you're talking about."

"Don't I? Well, one thing's for sure, Drew Colby. I was right about you from the very beginning." Her voice faded, and Reece could picture her stomping off. "You're not too bright."

Reece backed away from the barn door, circling toward the corrals. The wisdom of children. She could have been talking to him, instead of Drew. All this time, he'd been telling himself he couldn't trust Sarah and that was why they could never have a life together. What a crock! She'd proved herself more than worthy of his trust. Hadn't she worked all summer with Drew without telling him who she was—even though it must have nearly killed her to do so? And that night on the mountain. Hell, he'd put all of their lives into her hands.

No, the truth was he'd been punishing her for lying to him. Just like Drew. And where did that leave him?

Where did that leave any of them? They were all suffering because of his damnable pride, because he wouldn't admit he'd been as wrong as she was. And forgive her.

He loved Sarah. He always had and always would. With her, he could have the family he'd always wanted. All he had to do was put the past aside and forgive her.

SARAH HAD ANOTHER sleepless night.

Unlike the night before, however, it was anticipation that kept her awake. Tomorrow she planned to storm the Crooked C and Reece Colby—if that was what it took. She'd lay it on the line for him and dare him to turn his back on her. He loved her. She knew it in the deepest part of her soul. They had two beautiful children who needed them both *and* each other. She wasn't going to leave unless he could look her in the eye and tell her he didn't want the same things she wanted. A family. Their family.

She finally fell asleep just before dawn.

THE SOUND of her front doorbell woke her.

Moaning, she rolled over and looked at the clock. It was after ten. How could she have slept so late? She'd wanted to be on the road by nine.

The doorbell rang again, and she climbed out of bed. Grabbing her robe, she wondered who could be at her door on a Sunday morning. She cinched her robe and headed downstairs. When she opened the door, she came fully awake.

Reece stood on the other side of the screen.

She thought first of her children. "What's wrong? One of the kids—"

Reece held up a hand, cutting her off. "They're fine. In fact, they're probably driving your grandmother nuts about now."

"My grandmother?"

"Drew hasn't seen her since we returned to the ranch, and it was the first place he wanted to go. Although I'm willing to bet they end up at Joseph's before noon."

"Reece, what are you talking about?" He was obviously much more awake than she was. "What are you doing here?"

He grinned, and her heart skipped a beat. "Can I come in? Or do you want me to stand on your front porch all morning?"

She moved away from the door. Removing his hat, Reece stepped inside and closed the door behind him.

"There," he said. "That's better."

"So." She crossed her arms. She was just beginning to realize that this might be a good thing. His showing up on her doorstep. It would save her a very long drive. "What *are* you doing here?"

He laughed lightly and ran his hand through his hair. "It seems to me you've asked me that before."

"You do have a tendency to show up unannounced."

"Touché."

Lord, he looked good. Tall, broad, and smelling of the crisp autumn air. She had all she could do to keep her hands to herself. Then she smiled. If he wouldn't listen to what she had to say, she could always seduce him.

"Funny you're here," she said. "I was planning on driving up to the Crooked C today."

"Really? What for?"

"Nope. You go first."

He took a moment to answer, his eyes drifting up and down the length of her. "I came for you."

"Oh." She tried to keep her voice calm, despite her heart's sudden acceleration. "Why's that?"

"I think you know."

"You can't keep your mind off my body."

"There is that," he said, grinning.

Sarah felt the heat of his gaze, but she couldn't give in to it yet. "What about Lyssa and Drew? Do they know about this?"

"It was practically Lyssa's idea." Again, that devastating grin. "She's quite the boss lady."

Sarah had to smile. "Give her a few years. She'll be running the Crooked C for you."

Reece shook his head in amusement. "No doubt."

"And Drew?"

"He has a little too much of his father in him." Reece dropped his gaze to his hand, to the hat he still held. "He's stubborn. Proud."

Sarah nodded. "Ready to cut off his nose to spite his face."

"A cliché." He looked up at her and smiled. "Though in this case, very appropriate. But he's coming around. When given the option of staying at the ranch or coming with us . . . well, he's here."

"Don't tell me—Lyssa gave him the option."

"Well, she was the one who more or less rubbed it in."

Sarah laughed.

"Your turn," he said. "Why were you heading up to the ranch?"

She let her gaze run over him as he'd done to her. "Same reason as yours."

"Couldn't keep your mind off my body."

"Something like that."

He took a step forward and slipped his hands around her waist. "So, what are we going to do about it?"

"Well, this is a start." She wrapped her arms around his neck. "Then I think it's time we forget the past."

Bending, he nipped at her neck, at the one spot he always found. The spot that drove her crazy. "And what then?" he whispered against her neck.

She sighed and melted against him. "You get your wife back."

EPILOGUE

SARAH WANTED sunshine for her wedding.

It wasn't a lot to wish for, except in late December. Standing at her bedroom window, she looked out at the yard of the Crooked C. Winter had settled in, stripping the trees of their leaves while covering the ground with a layer of snow and shielding the sun with a blanket of clouds.

Sarah shivered. A cold day. When it should have been warm.

"Well, don't you look pretty!" Millie said from behind her.

Sarah turned away from the window. "Is the dress okay?" She moved to the full-length mirror to check her appearance for the dozenth time. "Do you think he'll like it?"

She'd chosen a simple two-piece silk dress in off-white. She'd liked the clean lines and the way the delicate fabric felt against her skin. Now she wondered if she'd made the right choice. Maybe she should have picked something with a little more style.

"He'll love it," Millie said, walking over and adjusting one of the blue silk flowers she'd earlier helped weave into Sarah's braid. "Of course, if you'd waited until June, like normal folk, these flowers would be real."

Sarah smiled, remembering why she and Reece hadn't wanted to wait. Earlier in the month, the fall term had ended, and Sarah had resigned her position at Oaksburg High. Then she and Lyssa moved across the state to the Crooked C. Living three hundred miles from Reece had been hard. Living in the same house, without the benefit of marriage, had been harder still.

"We have two preteens in the house," she said. "Remember?"

Millie laughed abruptly. "Don't remind me." She took a step back, appraising her work. "It'll have to do." After a moment's pause, she asked, "Are you all right? You look a little peaked."

"Just a mild case of prewedding jitters," Sarah said, trying to make it sound like nothing.

Millie assessed her for a moment. "It's Drew, isn't it?"

Sarah laughed nervously. It had been nearly two months since she and Reece had decided to remarry, and Drew still had not fully accepted her. "You're as bad as my grandmother."

"Why? Because I can tell when something's bothering you?" Millie took Sarah's hand and patted it reassuringly. "Don't worry. I know that boy. He'll come around. Either that or his sister will have his hide."

Sarah grinned. "She does tend to be a little domineering."

"She's a wonder, all right."

Sarah leaned forward and kissed the other woman on the cheek. "Thanks."

Millie flushed. "For what?"

"For being a friend." For once, Millie seemed at a loss for words, and Sarah laughed again, feeling bet-

ter now. "Go on," she said. "You need to get yourself ready."

"You sure you'll be okay?"

"I'm fine." Sarah moved back to the mirror, pretending to fuss with her makeup. "Will you send Lyssa
in when she's ready?"

Millie hesitated a moment longer and then moved
toward the door. "Sure. I'll send her in."

Once Millie left, Sarah deserted the mirror and
wandered back to the window. Millie was probably
right. Drew would come around. Already things were
better between them—at least he talked to her now.
When he had to.

"May I come in?"

Sarah spun around. "Elizabeth! I didn't expect...I mean, we didn't think you'd..."

"You didn't think I'd come?" Elizabeth stepped
into the room. "Well, to be honest, I didn't plan to."

For a moment, Sarah was at a loss for words.

At first, Reece hadn't wanted to invite his mother to
the wedding, and Sarah had to admit she'd had mixed
feelings herself. Eventually he'd changed his mind,
however, and admitted he'd hoped to talk things out
with Elizabeth. But when they hadn't heard from her,
they'd assumed the worst—that, as she'd done thirteen years ago, she was going to refuse to acknowledge her son's marriage.

Finally Sarah said, "I'm glad you're here." And she
meant it. "It will mean a lot to Reece."

"Yes. I expect it will."

Again Sarah didn't know what to say. She would
have liked to make peace with her husband's mother,
but she didn't know how. "I really love him, you
know." It wasn't what she'd planned on saying, but it

was the truth. And the only thing she could offer Elizabeth.

"I know. I knew eleven years ago."

"Then why?" Although, as a mother herself, Sarah thought she understood Elizabeth better than she ever had before.

"You were both so young. How was I to know it would last?"

"And now?"

"You still wouldn't be my first choice. But..." She shrugged.

"But?"

"You're the woman my son has chosen and the mother of his children." She hesitated a moment and then went on, "So I imagine we'll just have to learn to deal with each other."

Sarah smiled. It wasn't much. But it was a start. "I imagine we will."

"Mom, how do I look?"

Both Sarah and Elizabeth turned to see Lyssa, who stood in the doorway, a young lady in a calf-length dress the color of the clear Wyoming sky. Millie had pulled Lyssa's golden hair away from her face and pinned flowers at the crown of her head. The rest hung in long curls down her back and over her shoulders.

"And who is this pretty little miss?" Elizabeth asked.

"This," Sarah answered, feeling a little taken aback at how mature her daughter, her baby, looked, "is Lyssa. Lyssa, come in and meet your grandmother Colby."

Lyssa entered the room, her charmer smile firmly in place, and gave Elizabeth a hug. "I'm so glad you came, Grandmother."

"Oh, dear, you mustn't be so formal. Call me Grandma." She held Lyssa at arm's length to get a better look at her. "You're lovely."

"Absolutely gorgeous," Sarah agreed.

"Come on now," Elizabeth said, without releasing Lyssa's hand. "There are guests waiting downstairs, and we need to let your mother finish getting ready." She started to lead Lyssa out the door but stopped on the threshold. "By the way," she said to Sarah, "that dress is lovely."

Sarah's heart softened toward her mother-in-law. Maybe there was hope they'd more than just "deal" with each other.

"We'll send someone up for you when they're ready downstairs," Lyssa called as she and Elizabeth disappeared down the hall.

The wait wasn't long, but the last person Sarah expected to come for her was Drew. He appeared in the doorway, fidgeting uncomfortably in his new blue suit.

"You look very handsome," she said.

Then she spotted the buckle, Reece's silver buckle, and her heart skipped a beat. It was far too big for his twelve-year-old body. But it looked wonderful.

Following her gaze to his waist, Drew said, "Tod attached it to my belt for me." He shifted from one foot to the other and then looked back at her. "I hope it's okay if I wear it."

Sarah's eyes filled with tears, only this time they were tears of joy. Millie was right. Everything was going to be all right. "It's perfect."

"Uh, well, if you're ready then, I can walk you down."

"I'd be honored." She crossed the room to her son and slipped her arm through his.

He looked up at her then, and she saw the caution in his eyes. But there was a warmth, as well, and maybe the beginnings of renewed trust. Suddenly he looked behind her and broke into a huge smile. "Hey, Mom, look. The sun's out."

It was a moment before Sarah could move. Drew had called her Mom.

She turned toward the window to see a sliver of sunshine dance its way across the floor. It was beautiful, but nothing compared to the light she felt in her heart. Nothing compared to her son's acceptance of her as his mother.

A few moments later, Drew walked her downstairs. The living room had been set up like a chapel, with rows of chairs and a long white runner leading to a wooden arch covered with silk flowers.

They were all there. The people she loved.

Her grandmother, nodding and grinning. Joseph Bright Eagle, sitting next to her, looking too large for the rented metal chairs. Millie, in her best Sunday dress, a handkerchief clutched in her fist. Tod, sporting clean jeans and a brand-new shirt. Lyssa, her hand still firmly anchored in Elizabeth's, and Drew, who'd walked over to sit on the other side of his grandmother.

Then Reece moved up beside her, and she forgot everyone else in the room. She saw only him, his warm blue eyes shining with love and a smile that promised more than he could say aloud in a room filled with people.

"Are you ready, Sarah?" he whispered. "To become my wife?"

She smiled up at him, feeling his love wash over her. "In my heart, I've always been your wife."

UNLOCK THE DOOR TO GREAT ROMANCE
AT BRIDE'S BAY RESORT

Join Harlequin's new across-the-lines series, set in an exclusive hotel on an island off the coast of South Carolina.

Seven of your favorite authors will bring you exciting stories about fascinating heroes and heroines discovering love at Bride's Bay Resort.

Look for these fabulous stories coming to a store near you beginning in January 1996.

Harlequin American Romance #613 in January
Matchmaking Baby by Cathy Gillen Thacker

Harlequin Presents #1794 in February
Indiscretions by Robyn Donald

Harlequin Intrigue #362 in March
Love and Lies by Dawn Stewardson

Harlequin Romance #3404 in April
Make Believe Engagement by Day Leclaire

Harlequin Temptation #588 in May
Stranger in the Night by Roseanne Williams

Harlequin Superromance #695 in June
Married to a Stranger by Connie Bennett

Harlequin Historicals #324 in July
Dulcie's Gift by Ruth Langan

Visit Bride's Bay Resort each month wherever Harlequin books are sold.

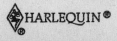

BBAYG

HARLEQUIN SUPERROMANCE®

That Old Devil Moon
by Anne Logan

The New Orleans cops are calling Madeline Johnson's brother's death a suicide. But Maddie knows Michael would never take his own life. All she needs to do is convince Detective Alex Batiste to keep an open mind. Unfortunately, she's up against some stiff opposition. Alex is due for a vacation and his teenage daughter is demanding he spend time with her. His colleague—and best friend—wants the case closed immediately.

Can Maddie get Alex to trust her—and the feelings they're beginning to share?

Watch for *That Old Devil Moon* by Anne Logan.

Available in April 1996
wherever Harlequin Superromance books are sold.

Yo amo novelas con corazón!

Starting this March, Harlequin opens up to a whole new world of readers with two new romance lines in SPANISH!

Harlequin Deseo
* passionate, sensual and exciting stories

Harlequin Bianca
* romances that are fun, fresh and very contemporary

With four titles a month, each line will offer the same wonderfully romantic stories that you've come to love—now available in Spanish.

Look for them at selected retail outlets.

 HARLEQUIN ®

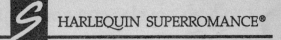

HARLEQUIN SUPERROMANCE®

Welcome to Westbank Ranch, Wyoming

Fraser McKenna owns this ranch in cattle country, but what
he's ranching these days is *sheep*. Doing well at it, too. What
he's not doing *quite* as well at is being a father to two little
girls. So Fraser figures he needs someone to care for the
children—temporarily. He advertises for a "lady companion."

And that brings **Martha Thomas** into his life. Into *their* lives.
Martha's an ex-newspaper woman at loose ends. She likes
kids; she thinks this sounds like a good way to spend a couple
of months.

Living together—living as a makeshift family— Fraser and
Martha find that their situation isn't as simple as it first
seemed....

Watch for
The Man from Blue River by Judith Bowen
Available in April,
wherever Harlequin books are sold.

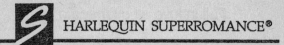

HARLEQUIN SUPERROMANCE®

From the bestselling author of
THE TAGGARTS OF TEXAS!
comes

Cupid, Colorado...

This is ranch country, cowboy country—a land of high mountains and swift, cold rivers, of deer, elk and bear. The land is important here—family and neighbors are, too. 'Course, you have the chance to really get to know your neighbors in Cupid. Take the Camerons, for instance. The first Cameron came to Cupid more than a hundred years ago, and Camerons have owned and worked the Straight Arrow Ranch—the largest spread in these parts—ever since.

For kids and kisses, tears and laughter, wild horses and wilder men— come to the Straight Arrow Ranch, near Cupid, Colorado. Come meet the Camerons.

THE CAMERONS OF COLORADO
by Ruth Jean Dale

Kids, Critters and Cupid (Superromance#678)
available in February 1996

The Cupid Conspiracy (Temptation #579)
available in March 1996

The Cupid Chronicles (Superromance #687)
available in April 1996

Fall in love all over again with

This Time... MARRIAGE

In this collection of original short stories, three brides get a unique chance for a return engagement!

- Being kidnapped from your bridal shower by a one-time love can really put a crimp in your wedding plans! *The Borrowed Bride*— by **Susan Wiggs**, *Romantic Times* Career Achievement Award-winning author.

- After fifteen years a couple reunites for the sake of their child—this time will it end in marriage? *The Forgotten Bride*—by **Janice Kaiser**.

- It's tough to make a good divorce stick—especially when you're thrown together with your ex in a magazine wedding shoot! *The Bygone Bride*— by **Muriel Jensen**.

Don't miss THIS TIME...MARRIAGE, available in April wherever Harlequin books are sold.

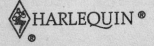

HARLEQUIN ®

BRIDE96